Unresolved Issues

Wanda B. Campbell

www.urbanchristianonline.com

Urban Books, LLC
78 East Industry Court
Deer Park, NY 11729

ISBN 13: 978-1-60162-724-7
ISBN 10: 1-60162-724-6

First Printing August 2012
Printed in the United States of America

10 9 8 7 6 5 4 3 2 1

This is a work of fiction. Any references or similarities to actual events, real people, living, or dead, or to real locales are intended to give the novel a sense of reality. Any similarity in other names, characters, places, and incidents is entirely coincidental.

Distributed by Kensington Corp.
Submit Wholesale Orders to:
Kensington Publishing Corp.
C/O Penguin Group (USA) Inc.
Attention: Order Processing
405 Murray Hill Parkway
East Rutherford, NJ 07073-2316
Phone: 1-800-526-0275
Fax: 1-800-227-9604

Unresolved Issues

Unresolved Issues

Wanda B. Campbell

Dedication

For my brothers and sisters in the kingdom who are struggling or who have struggled with low self-esteem. Know that your true validation comes from our Heavenly Father.

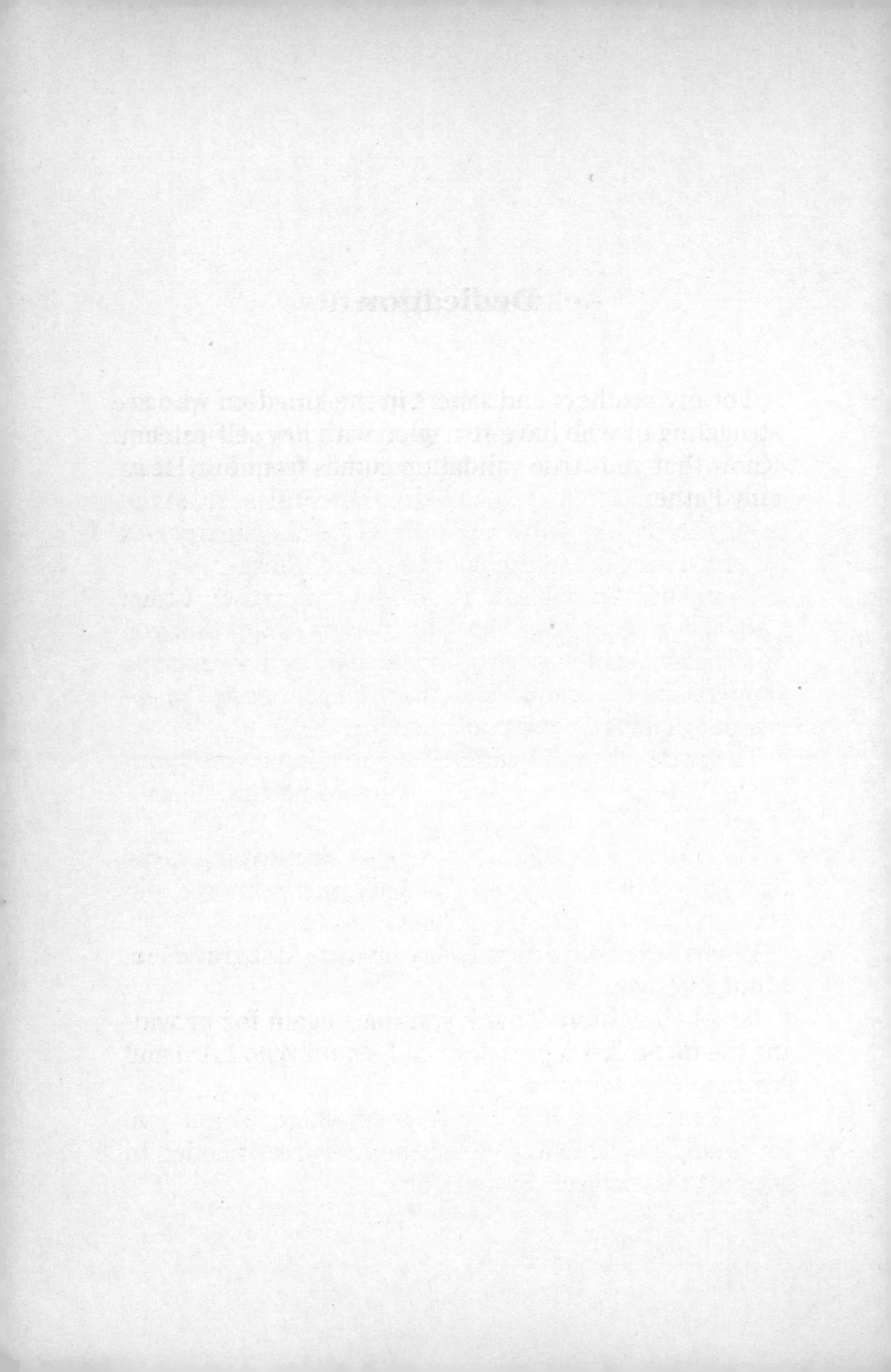

Acknowledgments

Once again, I am humbled by the grace God has extended to me with the gift to pen this work of ministry. *Unresolved Issues* is my fourth published novel in as many years. I am truly amazed and breathless from the exhilarating ride. Father, thank you for the journey and for entrusting me to minister to your children.

To my best friend, soul mate, and life partner, Craig: I am able to do all that I do only because of all that you do. Thank you for twenty-three years of unwavering support and devotion. Celine Dion sings it best: *I'm everything I am because you loved me.*

To my daughter, Chantel: Keep pressing toward your goals. You have the power in you to accomplish *anything*.

To Jonathan & Craig Jr.: You give new meaning to the term, *mama's boy*. Thanks for looking out for me, but you can drop the "clothes police" routine.

Dinari: You will always be my favorite first grandson. Mimi loves you.

Israel Houghton: Thank you once again for providing the fuel to keep pressing on. *I Know Who I Am* and *Nothing Else Matters*.

To Readers and Book Clubs everywhere: Thank you for taking the time and using the resources needed to support this project. Enjoy!

Acknowledgments

For I know the thoughts that I think toward you, saith the LORD, thoughts of peace, and not evil, to give you an expected end.

Jeremiah 29:11

Prologue

Countless thoughts bombarded Staci's mind as she stared out the window. The gray clouds peeking through her bedroom window reminded her of the rain forecast from the previous night's news weather report. She turned her head to the left, trying to decide which pair of leather boots she'd wear and where she'd last seen her umbrella. The outcome of the basketball game between the Golden State Warriors and Sacramento Kings the night before, as well as what to get her father for his birthday, puzzled her.

She closed her eyes and remembered she needed to pick up her dry cleaning before her wardrobe dwindled down to jeans and sweatshirts. Then, thoughts of her brother/boss nagging her for the quarterly report forced her eyes open once again. She placed her hands behind her head, then rolled her eyes toward the ceiling, where a large spiderweb caught her attention. She made a mental note to spend Saturday morning deep cleaning her bedroom.

Staci shifted her body and began counting. Ten, nine, eight . . . It was just a matter of time before the killer bear would roar. *What did I ever do to deserve all this?* Staci wondered. Five, four, it was almost over. Three, two, finally, the killer bear roared, then collapsed on top of her.

Staci quickly pushed her husband off of her and went into the bathroom and started the shower. If she hurried, she could stop at Starbucks before going into the office.

Chapter 1

After securing her seat belt, Stacelyn Garrison checked her rearview mirror before backing her silver Mercedes out of her three-car garage and on to Tunnel Road. As she slowly drove away, the massive image of her house filled the rearview mirror and Staci wondered how two people could live in a house as beautiful as hers and not be happy.

The Garrisons lived in the Oakland-Berkeley hills overlooking both Oakland and Berkeley and the Caldecott Tunnel. From her hilltop home, she enjoyed great views of both the Oakland and San Francisco skylines. The two-story, six-bedroom, Mediterranean-style home was a wedding present from her parents nearly one year ago. "It's only been a year," she stated out loud while driving down the winding narrow road that would lead her to Highway 13. It felt more like a decade.

Her husband, Derrick, had opened his dental practice just one year ago and had already established a steady flow of patients. Staci served as chief operating officer of MS Computers, a company founded by her brother, Marcus. Lack of money was not an issue for the Garrisons. Their stock portfolio looked good. Real estate investments showed marginal profits thanks to the real estate boom in California before the current slump. The couple could drive the best and wear the best. If they so desired, they could eat at five-star restaurants every night. So why weren't they happy? Staci had been asking herself that question quite often lately.

The two met in her sophomore year at Humboldt State where she was a business major. Derrick was a senior and a biology major. Staci remembered the day Derrick walked into her life as if it were yesterday.

After three days of pestering, Staci allowed her roommate, Crystal, to talk her into going to a football game against Fresno State. Crystal dated one of the wide receivers on Humboldt's team and wanted to match Staci up with one of the linebackers.

"What's wrong with him?" Staci had asked for the umpteenth time.

"Nothing is wrong with Derrick," Crystal answered.

Staci wasn't convinced. "Then why are you trying so hard to fix him up? I'm sure there are plenty of females on campus ready and willing to date a jock. Especially, if he's as great as you claim he is."

"Derrick plays football, but he's not a jock, at least not in the way you may think. He keeps to himself and is very polite." Crystal fell to the floor and looked underneath the bed for her brown, fur-cuffed boots. "He's different, like you," she said once she found the boots.

Staci was really concerned now. She folded her arms. "What do you mean he's different like me?"

"You know, he's a church boy."

Staci leaned against the closed door and exhaled. "You assume I'll like him just because he attends church?"

Crystal slipped on her boots, then turned to face Staci. "Look, girl, you're always talking about how you want to find a saved man to have a godly relationship with. I don't think you'll find anyone more saved than Derrick Garrison. He's so saved, he car-

ries his Bible with him everywhere he goes. When he's asked how he's doing, Derrick replies by saying, 'Blessed and highly favored.'" Crystal laughed.

With that comment, both their eyes fell on Staci's bed, where her Bible lay open. "I'm telling you, the two of you will be good together."

Staci's resolve waivered. "What does he look like?"

Crystal stretched to reach the photo album from the top shelf of her closet. The picture she had of the Lumberjacks didn't offer a good image of Derrick Garrison. But from what Staci could make out, he didn't look like a serial killer. He appeared tall and well built with curly hair. "He might be okay," Staci conceded.

Reluctantly, Staci agreed to meet number seventy-two because she hadn't yet met anyone suitable to her spiritual and physical taste, and mainly because she didn't want to stay in her dorm all weekend. After the football game, the team was meeting at the team's dormitory for what they hoped would be a victory celebration. A party might be just what she needed.

"Just this once," Staci said and went to her small closet to find something to wear.

Staci watched sports with her two brothers and many uncles and was familiar with the game of football. During the game at the Redwood Bowl, Staci followed along with such intensity that Crystal had to tell her to stop yelling in her ear. Staci observed number seventy-two for the Lumberjacks tackle runners with little effort and sack the quarterback three times. After each play, number seventy-two always offered a hand of assistance to his victims. Staci thought the gesture nice. Maybe he really was a Christian. She was well aware of brothers using the "Jesus card" to get the sisters underneath the sheets, and then leaving them to face judgment alone. Several guys had tried the exact thing with her, but she stood her ground vowing to remain sexually pure until marriage.

While waiting for the team after the game, Staci's nerves got the best of her and she changed her mind about meeting Derrick, but it was too late. Rodney, Crystal's boyfriend, approached with what Staci considered a giant. Up close, Derrick Garrison was huge! Six feet five and Staci guessed, over 250 pounds. Like in the photo, his black hair was thick and curly. On his bright-complexioned face rested a thick mustache. She thought he resembled Tom Selleck with a tan on the vintage show Magnum PI. *As for his torso, former California Governor Arnold Schwarzenegger in his youth never looked as good as Derrick Garrison did at that moment. As he got closer, she noticed the Bible tucked underneath his arm.*

"Staci, I'd like for you meet the Preacher Man," Rodney chuckled, then turned to Derrick. "This is Missionary Evangelist Stacelyn Simone."

After rolling her eyes at Rodney, Staci smiled at Derrick.

Derrick didn't respond to Rodney's mocking. Staci assumed he was accustomed to it. Crystal had mentioned his teammates referred to him as Preacher Man or Church Boy.

"Hello, Ms. Simone. My name is Derrick Garrison." He extended his enormous hand to her, and she slowly, almost timidly, shook it.

"Hello, Derrick, it's nice to meet you. Please, call me Staci." The temperature outside was less than fifty degrees, but Staci suddenly felt a heat wave.

"Sure," Derrick said. "Although I think Stacelyn is more beautiful."

Staci wasn't sure of what to say next. Derrick appeared not to know either. They stood there in silence smiling at each other.

"We'll see you guys at the party, providing the two of you remember how to walk and talk before midnight," Crystal teased. Then she and Rodney sprinted away before either Derrick or Staci could protest.

Staci and Derrick never made it to the party that night. After the awkwardness passed, they went back to Staci's dorm. Barely anyone hung around the dorms on Saturday nights. They had the lounge area to themselves. That first night, they sat on the couch eating Chinese takeout and discussing the Bible for over two hours. When Derrick finally left, the only things Staci knew about Derrick Garrison, outside of his love for God, were that he had also grown up in the Bay Area and planned to attend the University of San Francisco's School of Dentistry.

For the first two months, they met on the weekends and discussed the Bible. If their schedules permitted, they would attend Sunday services together at a local church. The services weren't as lively as the Bay Area services, but it was enough to get them prepared for the week ahead. After service, they would grab a bite at Porter's, the favorite local BBQ spot, and just talk. They weren't dating, just spending time together and getting to know each other.

Over time, Staci learned that Derrick was from a single-parent home. He was the product of an interracial, extramarital affair; his mother, an African American nurse, and his father, a white cardiac surgeon. It would be years later before Staci learned how much growing up without a father had damaged Derrick. He had a younger teenage sister and considered himself to be the man of the family.

When Staci told Derrick she was from a wealthy family, he didn't seem to mind and didn't treat her any differently. She appreciated him for that.

As time went on, Staci found herself growing fonder of Derrick. From day one she was physically attracted to him. Secretly, Staci nicknamed him teddy bear, because when he hugged her good night, he felt like a big teddy bear. She looked forward to his compliments and his nightly phone calls almost as much as she did going to class. It was during one of those eleven-fifty-nine phone calls about six months into their friendship that he invited her to dinner in his dorm kitchen.

That night after she finished the dinner he'd prepared for her, Derrick asked her in his special way to be his girl. While taking away her dirty dishes from the table in the dorm lounge, he handed her a folded note that read, Will you go with me? *Staci thought it was cute and immediately checked the yes box.*

Suddenly, the words on the green and white billboard caught Staci's attention. She was so caught up in her trip down memory lane, she almost missed her exit. She quickly darted over into the far right lane amid honking horns and offensive hand gestures. Staci apologetically waved to the drivers behind her and exited the freeway.

She pulled into her reserved stall at the Emery Bay parking garage, but still couldn't take her mind off of her marriage. Since their honeymoon almost a year ago, Derrick seemed to have lost interest in her. Lately, he was always too busy to spend time with her except when he wanted to have sex. That was only once or twice a month, on the days he thought she was ovulating. At first, Staci overlooked his behavior because she knew how much Derrick wanted a baby. She figured she would have conceived quickly since they didn't use any form of birth control, but that didn't happen.

At first, Staci didn't mind, but now his lack of interest was slowly depleting her self-esteem. She was beginning to think the only reason Derrick married her was so he could have a baby to replace the one she aborted. The encounter this morning was evidence of that. Derrick had pounced on her the second the alarm sounded. Her soft teddy bear transformed into a killer bear seeking its prey. He didn't even say good morning.

Staci reached into the backseat for her briefcase and tried to remember the last time Derrick told her he loved her, and couldn't. She couldn't remember the last time they had a romantic evening alone. Or the last time he held her just because. Or the last time he called her his beautiful Stacelyn. The last time they took a shower or bubble bath together felt like a lifetime ago. She could, however, remember the last time she had a satisfying sexual experience. That was three months ago.

"God, help me find ways to please my husband," she whispered as she stepped from the car and entered the building. "Show me what to do to renew his interest in me." She voiced the frustrated prayer before stepping into the elevator.

Chapter 2

Derrick walked into his dental office wearing a big smile. "Good morning, Phyllis," he greeted his office manager on his way to his office.

"Good morning, Doctor. What are you so happy about this morning?"

He looked over his shoulder and answered, "Life."

Today, life was good for Derrick Garrison, DDS. He'd been tracking Staci's menstrual cycle for months, and he was sure he had the right day. If anything was going to happen, it was going to be today. To ensure the connection was made, he had denied himself the entire month to make sure he had a plenteous supply for this day. Yes, today was the day. He was sure he'd impregnated Staci this morning.

He knew Staci hadn't enjoyed their encounter this morning, but that was a minor detail. Once she was pregnant, he would take more care and more time to satisfy her needs.

You said the same thing last month and the month before that and before that, his conscience reminded him, but he quickly shook that thought away. Surely Staci understood how much he wanted to have a baby after what happened before. They would have the rest of their lives to enjoy their lovemaking. He wanted a baby right now, especially since his boys, Marcus and Brian, were expecting.

True, Derrick hadn't been able to hold a conversation with his wife without it turning into an argument, and, yes, he spent more time than needed at the office, but his office had only been open a year and he needed to work hard to survive, he rationalized. Derrick completely ignored the fact that his first year had been so successful, he had to hire another dentist and a hygienist to assist with the patient load. He attributed his phenomenal success to the favor of God. Now, if God would favor him with a baby, he'd be happy.

"Maybe I should bring her some flowers or cook her favorite meal for dinner," he mumbled from his guilty conscience. He considered the notion, but then decided against it, not wanting to leave the office early.

Derrick sat at his desk and studied his schedule for the day. Three root canals, six fillings, and a crown. *Not bad,* he thought. His eyes roamed his office. Staci had done a wonderful job of decorating it for him. The doctor's private office resembled the office of a business executive. He loved the oversized oak desk and matching custom cabinet and bookshelf. The blue window treatments matched perfectly with the blue specks in the plush gray carpet. One wall was reserved for his degrees, the other three were covered with framed African American art. On his desk, a fourteen carat gold-trimmed name plate read: Derrick Garrison, DDS.

"You always know how to take care of me," he said in reference to his wife after he opened the minirefrigerator Staci kept stocked with his favorite snacks for the times when he wouldn't be able to take a lunch break.

In his opinion, Staci was the perfect wife. She even bought his clothes because, as Staci put it, he didn't have a clue when it came to color coordination. On their first official date, he wore blue jeans, an orange- and green-striped shirt, tan jacket, and black shoes.

After opening the cabinet that encased his minisound system and hitting the PLAY button, Derrick picked up the picture of him and Staci on their wedding day while enjoying the jazz sounds of Tim Bowman. There was no one on earth more beautiful than his Staci; maybe his mother, but in a different way. He loved Staci's smooth, light brown skin and shoulder-length, naturally curly hair. Staci was his heart, his love, the only woman he'd been intimate with, and the only one he wanted. No one knew him like Staci, and that's the way he liked it.

They went through a very rocky time after breaking their vows to God and practicing fornication and ended up with an unplanned pregnancy. It took awhile, but Derrick was able to forgive Staci for having an abortion, and then married her. Derrick never doubted Staci loved him no matter what and would always be there for him. She showed him every day, even on days like today when he'd shown little regard for her feelings. He knew no matter what time he strolled into the house, dinner would be waiting for him in the microwave and his pajamas lying on the chaise. If he needed anything, Staci would stop whatever she was doing and be right by his side.

Why can't you show her the same consideration? Why can't you show her how much you love her?

"Staci knows how much I love her," he said out loud to his conscience.

I don't know how; you haven't told her in a while.

Derrick didn't have time to battle with his mind. He quickly changed into his work smock and went to see his first patient.

Chapter 3

"Good morning, Chloe," Staci greeted her secretary as she retrieved her messages.

"Mr. Simone would like to see you when you get a minute."

"Thanks, Chloe, tell him I'm here."

Staci set her briefcase on her desk and stared out the window. The San Francisco skyline was obstructed by a thick blanket of fog hovering over the Bay. The sight reminded her of the fog that had settled over her marriage. She knew it was there, but she couldn't see it clearly; just an outline of what was supposed to be. Her first-year wedding anniversary was only a few weeks away. She had to do something to chase the dark clouds away from her marriage, but what? Staci prayed every day and read every scripture she knew about marriage. Now it was time to be innovative. She had to figure how to get her husband interested in her again before her marriage fell apart.

"A wise woman builds her house," she mumbled. That's what she'd heard all her life at church and at home. Being the only daughter allotted her plenty of one-on-one time with her mother. Having been married for almost thirty-five years, Alaina Simone was a good role model. As far as Staci's memory could take her, her parents have always been in love and didn't care who knew it. Many times she and her brothers would catch them kissing or playing games with each other, but they didn't care. Carey and Alaina felt it was important for their children to see healthy and loving interaction in the home.

Alaina respected Carey as a king. Carey practically worshipped the ground Alaina walked on. From observing her mother, Staci knew how to make a man feel like the king of his castle. She knew how to balance working outside the home and at the same time not neglect her man. Alaina had successfully run an advertising agency and raised three children.

From her father, Staci learned how a woman should be honored and cherished. As a little girl, her father opened doors for her and pulled out chairs. He brought her flowers on her birthday and candy on Valentine's Day. When she was sick, he prayed for her, and he always kissed her good night. For her sixteenth birthday, her father took her on her first date to dinner at a revolving restaurant overlooking San Francisco, and then to see *Phantom of the Opera*. In her eyes, Carey Simone was the ultimate man. That's what attracted her to Derrick.

In the beginning, Derrick gave her the same love and respect her father had. When she was with him, Derrick made her feel like she was the most important person in the world. When they were together, she never had to worry about anything. She felt secure and loved. That was then; now, most of the time, she felt open and vulnerable.

Spiritually, she knew Derrick was falling too. She hadn't seen him reading his Bible lately, and his morning-prayer and meditation hour had dwindled to a quick recital of rehearsed words.

Staci sat at her desk and turned on her computer. She was smiling at her wedding picture screen saver when Marcus stepped into her office.

"Good morning, I have an idea I want to run by you." Marcus walked around her desk and stood next to her and spread the blueprints out on the desk.

Staci loved her big brother beyond measure. Marcus was more than her brother; he was her friend. Marcus trusted Staci with his life and more important, with his money, and allowed her to run MS Computers while he pursued his music career. On paper, Marcus was the CEO and Staci the COO. In actuality, they were more like partners. Marcus never made a final decision without Staci's input. And as long as the bottom line showed a profit, Marcus gave Staci the liberty to run the company as she saw fit.

"What's on your mind?" Staci asked.

"These are the floor plans for our fourth store."

"I didn't know you wanted to go ahead with this so soon," she replied with a raised eyebrow. "Do you really think Corte Madera has the right market?"

"Based on the research I've done, I think it's perfect."

Marcus was probably right. She hadn't had a chance to look over the research yet.

"I want to get this out of the way while Shannon's pregnant. After the twins are born, I'm taking some time off from music and the business. You know, to do the father thing."

"I wish it was me taking time off to do the mother thing." Staci hoped her desperation didn't sound in her voice.

"Give it some time. You haven't been married a year yet."

She rolled her eyes. "That's easy for you to say. Shannon got pregnant on your honeymoon."

"What can I say? I've got some powerful stuff," Marcus chuckled. "Give my boy some time. He'll catch on."

"How is Shannon?" Staci had to redirect the conversation before she said something she'd regret. Marcus didn't know she and Derrick had premarital sex so she couldn't tell him Derrick had plenty of practice and when he wanted to be, was a very skillful lover.

"My baby is wonderful. She's starting to show more, and she is too cute carrying my babies."

Marcus beamed and Staci felt a tug of jealousy. Not because her sister-in-law was expecting, but because she wanted Derrick's face to light up like Marcus's when he talked about her. Marcus loved Shannon, and he made sure she and everyone else knew it.

"We're getting together this weekend with Brain and Lashay. Are you and Derrick hanging with us?" Marcus asked.

Staci didn't have any idea what her husband's plans were for the weekend. Before his inversion, it was a given he'd be hanging out with his boys on the weekends. But now, Staci didn't know what Derrick's plans were from day to day. She didn't even know if he was coming home for dinner.

"I'll have him call you." Staci turned her attention back to the prints. "Let's get back to business."

Derrick walked into his bedroom after eleven o'clock and found Staci asleep with her opened Bible pressed against her chest. He leaned over her and brushed a curl from her face. He appreciated her naturally curly hair; he would never have to wake up to the horrific sight of rollers and a hair scarf. Carefully, he removed the Bible and placed it on the oak nightstand, then kissed her. She didn't move. When he returned from the shower, she was still lying there on her back. He pulled back the down comforter and was welcomed by the soft fragrance she used on the sheets. He crawled into their king-sized bed and with his fingertips, outlined her face.

"You are so beautiful," he whispered, before kissing her lips. That's when her eyelids fluttered, and she gazed groggily at him.

"How was your day?" she whispered and offered him a half smile. Still half-asleep, she turned unto her side.

"Better now that I'm with you." Derrick pulled her into his arms and to his chest. Her soft warm body brought back the morning's attack.

"Baby, I'm sorry about this morning. I'll make it up to you next time." He really meant those words, hoping Staci was pregnant. She didn't respond to his apology, probably because she'd heard it before, he reasoned.

"It's late. Where have you been?"

"I went to visit my mother."

Staci raised her head and looked at him almost accusingly. "When I talked to her this afternoon she didn't mention that she was expecting you."

"She wasn't," he answered, then pressed her body closer to his. "I decided to stop by at the last minute."

Staci pulled away from him and made direct eye contact again. "Derrick, when are you going to decide to spend time with your wife?"

"Staci, you know I've been busy at the office," he answered and brought her back to him. It was easier talking to her without having to look into her sad eyes.

Staci rested against his chest and wrapped her arms around him. "Honey, I know you're busy. I'm busy too, but I always make time for you. Why can't you make the same effort for me?"

Derrick kissed her forehead. "I will, baby."

Staci was too sleepy to remind him that he'd been saying those same words to her for at least three months.

Chapter 4

"If I have to pull over for one more bathroom break, we're stopping at Walgreens for a pack of Depends." Staci and her girls were trying to make it to the annual lingerie show at Union Square in San Francisco, but at the rate her cousin Lashay and her sister-in-law Shannon were going, the show would be over by the time they arrived. They had already stopped twice prior to this stop.

"You try carrying twins and see how well you control your bladder," Shannon said, after adjusting her seat belt.

"Girl, if you try to hand me a Depends, I will cut your hand off." From the backseat, Lashay rolled her eyes at Staci.

Staci pulled back into traffic for the third time, then glanced at her girls. That's when the thought came to her. Shannon was twelve weeks pregnant with twins and Lashay, sixteen weeks pregnant.

"Why are we going to a lingerie show? Don't you think it's a little late for lingerie? You guys are already knocked up," Staci asked.

"Pregnant or not, I can still look sexy," Shannon answered. "I'm still a newlywed, you know."

"I won't be pregnant forever," Lashay responded. "Plus, my anniversary and Brian's birthday is coming up, and this year, I'm going to make him give me his birthright."

"Girl, you are crazy," Staci said, once she stopped laughing.

"I know what you mean," Shannon jumped in. "All I have to do is show Marcus red lace, and he's as humble as a little baby. He will even suck his thumb."

Staci released the steering wheel long enough to grab Shannon's hand. "I've got to shake the hand of the woman that broke my conceited brother down to a helpless invalid."

"In all fairness, Marcus has a right to be conceited. He can back up everything he says," Shannon said, after the handshake. "Can't you tell? I'm just as messed up as your brother."

"We know!" Lashay and Staci said in unison, causing Shannon to blush.

"Girl, don't be embarrassed. Brian messed me up so bad on my wedding night, it took me three days to remember my name."

"Lashay, you are so crazy." Staci was near tears.

"That's all?" Shannon asked, jokingly. "I don't think all my thinking faculties returned until the end of that first week."

"You guys are too much." Staci wiped her eyes. She hadn't laughed this hard in a long time.

"And you're not? I know Dr. Garrison has shown you some new . . . *procedures,"* Lashay baited.

"And some new technology," Shannon added.

"He's certainly shown me something new," Staci answered, not wanting to dampen the playfulness with her problems. She couldn't tell her girls that in less than a year her husband had become bored with her.

"And tonight, you're going to show *him* something new," Lashay assumed. "Follow my lead. I'm not buying anything that has more than half a yard of material. And half of that must be see-through."

Shannon turned around. "That's why you're going to spend the next ten years pregnant."

Staci laughed along with her girls but ached inside. There was no chance of Derrick touching her tonight. Her cycle had started the day before, much to Derrick's disappointment. He even had the nerve to ask her if she was secretly taking birth control pills. Lashay's suggestion did give Staci an idea for her anniversary celebration, though.

The traffic approaching the toll booth leading to the Bay Bridge was more congested this Saturday than on regular commute days.

"This is why I hate going into the city," Staci complained and hit the steering wheel. "Why can't people stay home?"

Lashay and Shannon ignored Staci's frustration and continued reveling in marital bliss.

"I can't take it anymore," Shannon exclaimed, then dug into her purse for her cell phone. "All this talk about my baby is making me miss him."

"Me too," Lashay pouted, but before she opened her cell phone, Brian's ringtone sounded.

Staci fixed her eyes on traffic to avoid seeing the joy radiating from her sister-in-law's and cousin's faces. Nor did she want to hear the enduring sentiments being conveyed from Shannon to Marcus or Lashay's giggling from the backseat. Staci willed her ears to only hear the light jazz sounds coming from the radio. However, there was nothing Staci could do to soothe the ache she felt in her heart.

After four hours of shopping with her girls and endless trips to the bathroom, Staci was armed with enough ammunition to rekindle the flame in her marriage; at least she hoped it would. She was too excited to go home to an empty house after dropping Lashay and Shannon off at the parking garage, so she decided to stop by and visit with Miss Cora. She hadn't seen her mother-in-law in over a month and had been thinking about her all day.

Miss Cora was dying from cancer. What originally started as breast cancer had metastasized to her lungs. That was one reason Staci tolerated Derrick's recent, inconsiderate behavior. He was very close to his mother, she being the only parent he knew. After his mother dies, Derrick wouldn't have any connection to his roots and at times that was unbearable for him. During those times, he would be even more distant than he normally was.

Derrick had never seen his white father, but his mother didn't keep the details surrounding his conception a secret. Not that Miss Cora was proud, but she felt Derrick deserved to know the truth. It was common knowledge in the Garrison household that Dr. John Archer didn't want a scandal to interfere with his marriage or with his plans to advance his career. Therefore, he paid Miss Cora good money to keep Derrick out of sight and out of mind. Miss Cora made sure Derrick's education, including dental school, was all taken care of by the good doctor. The only thing Derrick lacked was his father's presence and love.

Staci used her key to let herself into Miss Cora's house. "Miss Cora," she called, stepping into the living room.

"Staci, is that you?"

"Yes," Staci answered cheerfully, happy that Miss Cora's voice was strong. Some days she could only speak above a whisper.

"I'm back here on the patio."

Staci nearly skipped through the house. If Miss Cora was on the patio, then she was having a good day.

"Hi, Miss Cora." Staci bent down and kissed her mother-in-law on the cheek, then sat on one of the patio chairs opposite her. "How are you feeling today?"

"I am wonderful today; not in any pain at all," Miss Cora answered with a smile.

Staci studied her face to see if she was telling the truth. There had been many days when Miss Cora would deny the pain she was in just to keep people from making a fuss over her.

"Is my son with you?"

A stranger would have never guessed Miss Cora was talking about Derrick. He didn't resemble his mother at all. Even with her head bald and blotchy skin, Staci could tell Cora Ann Garrison was once a beautiful woman. When she met her seven years ago, Staci thought she resembled Diahann Carroll.

"No, Miss Cora. I don't know where Derrick is." Staci quickly looked away, hoping Miss Cora missed the loneliness in her eyes. Miss Cora didn't miss anything; she just waited until now to voice her concern.

"Staci, I owe you an apology."

"For what, Miss Cora?" Staci moved closer, giving her undivided attention.

Before Miss Cora rested back in the chair, she took a sip of water. "I've been thinking a lot lately. I messed Derrick up. I should have insisted that John included some quality time with his son along with his monthly check."

Staci narrowed her eyes and tried to follow Miss Cora's train of thought.

"I have been in denial about Derrick most of his life. He needed a father more than I realized. His uncle did what he could, but my brother couldn't fill Derrick's need for a father. For years, I thought Derrick was just trying to overachieve because he wanted to make me proud. He had to be the best student, the best football player, the best Christian, and now, the best dentist."

Staci would rather he work hard at being the best husband.

"I've since realized he wasn't trying to please me at all. Derrick was trying to make his father accept him. Derrick was trying to be this perfect person in hopes of gaining his father's acceptance."

Staci didn't quite understand what Derrick and his father had to do with her. "Miss Cora, you don't have to apologize to me for that."

"Huh?" Miss Cora appeared momentarily confused, and then recovered. "Yes, I do. You're absorbing the blows that are intended for me and John Archer." Miss Cora used her elbows to lean closer to Staci. "I've been watching how Derrick doesn't know how to relay his real feelings to you. That boy spends more time away from home than he does at home. Like the other night, I had to make him go home."

"You're right about that," Staci snickered.

"I know I'm right. Derrick is introverted and insecure. But the sad part is he doesn't know or at least he won't admit to it." Miss Cora shook her head. "Baby, I tell you that boy is half crazy."

"Oh," was the only response Staci had. Staci had been in denial herself about Derrick. She really thought she could change him.

"On the other hand, my son is a good man. He just doesn't know it yet. Unfortunately, you're going to have to suffer until he recognizes the awesome person he is. But, when his light comes on, trust me, it's going to shine bright. I probably won't be around to see it, but I know he's going to shine and be a good husband to you eventually."

Staci wanted to scream: *how long?* "Is there anything I can do to help him?" she asked instead.

"Pray for him. Can't nobody but God help my baby."

Chapter 5

"Good morning, Dr. Garrison," Staci greeted her husband with a welcoming smile when he walked into the kitchen.

"Good morning." Derrick looked puzzled, as if attempting to figure out what special occasion had Staci up so early this morning.

"Have a seat," she said, then directed his attention to the formal dining room. "Breakfast will be served shortly."

Before walking back to the stove, Staci removed her robe. Derrick looked perplexed as if he was trying to recall if he'd seen the black lingerie before. However, he didn't ponder too long before offering his smile of approval before she strolled away.

Inside the formal dining room, he found a table fit for a king. Staci had set the table elegantly with fine china and gold-trimmed stemware.

"What did I do to deserve all of this?" he asked when she returned with his favorite morning meal: a Denver omelet with home-style potatoes and fresh squeezed orange juice.

"Nothing." She sat on his right side, making sure he had a nice view of her assets.

Derrick found it difficult to enjoy his breakfast. His eyes kept wandering to his wife's voluptuous body. Twice he missed his mouth and dropped potatoes on his shirt.

"I hope you come home early tonight. I have something special planned for you." Staci gently ran her finger along his massive forearm.

He took a sip of his orange juice before asking, "What's the occasion?"

Derrick was too busy watching Staci's cleavage to notice that her smile had disappeared and her finger had stopped stroking him.

It wasn't a surprise to Staci that he'd forgotten today was their first wedding anniversary. He never remembered any of their special days. Still, she felt like a half-naked fool. She swallowed hard and gripped the seat of her chair to keep from running upstairs and locking herself in the bathroom.

"It's our anniversary. Our first anniversary." Chill bumps suddenly covered her bare arms.

"Oh, Staci! Baby, I'm sorry. I forgot." Derrick redirected his eyes upward to her face.

She pasted on a smile. "I know you did. It's early, and you still have time to do something about it." Staci hoped her voice carried more optimism than she felt. "Now eat your breakfast before it gets cold."

When she stood to leave, he stood also and took her into his arms. "I like this," he said and slowly ran his hands over the black lace. "And I am sorry. I'll make it up to you. I promise."

When he kissed her hungrily and subsequently set her on the mahogany table, Staci's hopes soared at the thought of some early-morning fun. They were quickly squashed when he suddenly backed away from her. She still held her smile.

"Make sure you eat all of your breakfast. You're going to need a lot of energy later," she said after replacing the black straps on her shoulder.

"I'm in trouble," she heard him mumble as she sashayed away from him.

***

"Happy Anniversary, Dr. Garrison," Phyllis greeted him excitedly.

Derrick was too embarrassed to tell his office manager he'd forgotten his own first-wedding anniversary. He simply nodded his thanks, then continued on to his office. Derrick still couldn't understand how he had forgotten the special day. His younger sister had even called from out of state before he left the house to mark the occasion, but he had forgotten. It wasn't like the day was unimportant; it just slipped his mind.

"This will not happen again," he said to himself as he admired the wedding picture on his desk.

Derrick spent his lunch break trying to find something for Staci. He'd looked on the Internet and learned the first anniversary was celebrated with paper. At first he started to just write her a check, but Staci didn't need money and would find that impersonal. Then he thought, since paper comes from trees, he'd pick up a tree from the nursery and plant it in their backyard, but that wasn't romantic enough for him. Then he remembered. A local art gallery carried an original oil painting by one of Staci's favorite artists. Next year he vowed to be more prepared. Staci deserved that. She deserved much more.

Hours later and ready to make retribution, Derrick stepped from his SUV and after removing the painting, started for the front door. He stopped short of using his key when he spotted what appeared to be a formal invitation affixed to the etched glass on the oak door. He nearly dropped the painting when he read that there was a private lingerie showing being held with him as the honored guest. He entered his home with excitement and at the same time wondered if he had enough willpower to stick to his agenda.

Inside the sunken living room, his favorite scented candles were arranged around the room, accompanied by the glowing fireplace. The bearskin rug in front of the fireplace was sprinkled with freshly cut rose petals. Sounds of their favorite love songs permeated through the sound system. Staci had set the mood.

"Happy Anniversary," Staci purred from behind, taking the painting from him and positioning it against the coat closet.

"Happy Anniversary," he responded, wondering what she had on under that robe. His hands decided to explore.

"Not yet," she whispered, catching his hands in hers and bringing them to her lips. She kissed them. She then led him over to the center of the room where she'd placed a chair. Before he sat down, Derrick brought her to him and kissed her passionately. Reluctantly, she pulled away from him again.

"Ready for your private show?" Once he was seated, she removed her robe.

Derrick's eyes nearly protruded from his head, and his complexion turned a shade of red. Staci was beautiful and delectable in red and black lace and spiked heels. He sat there speechless and thoughtless, watching Staci model lingerie he'd never seen before. She modeled five little outfits. Derrick enjoyed his present. The hunger in his eyes and the way his mouth consistently hung wide open served as confirmation.

After modeling the last piece, Staci treated him to a dance. That proved too much for him. In no time, his hands and lips were all over her. In a matter of mere minutes, clothes were strewn over the floor and the two lovers were on the rug with the rose petals. Staci closed her eyes. Then it happened. Derrick pulled away from her.

Staci leaned up on her elbows. "What's wrong?"

Derrick sat against the marble on the fireplace after reaching for his underwear. "Baby, we can't do this today." His chest expanded rapidly, and his jaw muscles flexed.

Staci rubbed her finger against her ear as if she needed to have her hearing checked. "What did you say?"

"You don't ovulate for another two days. We have to wait until then."

Staci's confusion turned into hot anger. "So you're refusing to have sex with me because I'm not ovulating? It's our anniversary, stupid!"

Derrick watched her collect her clothing. "Baby, you know if we have sex today, my sperm count may not be high enough for when you ovulate."

"That's a good thing!" she yelled between blowing out candles. "You don't deserve to reproduce!"

Derrick walked over to her and tried to reason with her. "Two days, baby, that's all. I promise I'll make it memorable." He tried to kiss her, but she pushed him away.

"It will be memorable, because in two days you can satisfy yourself!"

She stomped up the stairs and slammed the bedroom door. Her anger was so strong, it didn't allow her to feel the hurt of having Derrick reject her after all the effort she'd put into making their anniversary special.

"Are you gay?" she charged when he entered the bedroom.

"Staci, you know me better than that."

"Are you sleeping around with someone else?"

He shook his head. "No!"

"Then *what* is wrong with you?" she screamed. "There is no reason for a man, a married man at that, to walk away from his naked wife whom he hasn't touched in weeks!"

"Staci, you know how much I want a baby."

"Derrick, do you know how much I want a husband? You want a baby." She pointed at herself. "I want a husband. Did it ever occur to you that, if you would be a husband to me, you would have a baby?"

"Staci, what are you talking about?"

"Figure it out, Einstein!" She slammed the door again on her way back downstairs.

An hour later, hurt replaced her anger. Every candle Staci put away and every rose petal she threw into the trash brought down a new tear. She didn't bother to hang her new lingerie. She left it in a pile on the bed in the downstairs guest bedroom.

Going into the kitchen didn't make her feel any better. She looked inside the refrigerator at the chocolate-dipped strawberries she'd made for a halftime snack and cried some more. Then she turned on the oven. She was going to have her lobster tail with or without her stupid husband. She'd just stood from bending down to retrieve a cookie sheet for the garlic bread when she felt Derrick's arms around her waist.

"I'm sorry, baby," he whispered in her ear.

Staci shook her head. "No, you're not. You always say that, but you don't really mean it."

"Yes, I do mean it, and you're right. I am stupid," he admitted and turned her around, then kissed her lips.

At first, Staci didn't receive his kiss, but he knew how to handle her. By the time he carried her into the living room and laid her back down on the rug. She was responding to more than his kisses.

"I don't want to anymore," she pouted as he untied the belt on her robe.

"Yes, you do."

"This will not solve anything." Staci tried to maintain her focus, but his skillful touch made it impossible. She stopped trying, for now.

"Derrick, I'm sorry I called you stupid, but we have some serious problems," Staci said after feeding him a chocolate-covered strawberry. His head lay in her lap.

"I know," Derrick agreed. "And I am at the root of those problems. Give me a little more time. I'm working on something that's going to make me a better man."

"Why can't you tell me what it is?"

"I have to do this on my own."

"Honey, why do you always shut me out?" She played with his curls.

"Baby, I don't mean to."

Staci thought about what his mother had said. Derrick was an introvert. But Staci loved him, and she'd have to work with what he gave her. She kissed him and gave him a look that said she understood, but she really didn't.

"I loved my present." He licked a drop of chocolate from the corner of her mouth.

"Where's mine?"

Staci watched Derrick's bare body walk to the foyer. When he returned, she couldn't decipher which she liked better, the painting or him.

"I love it." Staci was used to reassuring him, so she added, "It's beautiful."

The smile on his face communicated to her that he was convinced.

"Where are you going to put it?" he asked.

"In my office. Every time I look at it, I'll think of you." She kissed him. "I love you."

"Will you ever stop?"

Staci heard his insecurity in the musing. "Derrick, I'll never stop loving you."

"Even when I act stupid, like I did tonight?"

"If you do that again, I'll cut you."

Chapter 6

Staci sat at her desk examining her anniversary present. It really was a beautiful painting. She just wished the lovemaking between her and Derrick last night had been as beautiful. It was enjoyable, but it wasn't what she expected for her first anniversary, especially after all the effort she'd put into it. Physically, they responded to each other, but emotionally, something was missing. At least it was for her. Derrick appeared to be totally content. This morning, he fed her breakfast in bed, something he hadn't done in a long time. Secretly, Staci wondered what it was he was working on that, as he put it, would make him a better man. Whatever it was, she hoped it would be completed soon.

The rejection she felt last night almost broke her spirit. Leaving her on the floor open and vulnerable like that served a severe blow to her self-esteem. She'd never been self-conscious of her body until now. But this morning after showering, Staci studied her natural form in the full-length mirror. In her opinion, she looked good. With regular exercise, she'd managed to remain a solid size twelve since college. She didn't wear heavy makeup; her skin was smooth, the color of double-creamed coffee. She maintained a tight form; nothing hanged or sagged lower than it was supposed to. She kept her skin soft with scented oils and creams. By her own judgment, she wasn't drop-dead gorgeous, but worth a second look. So what was wrong with Derrick? She couldn't help but wonder if it was more than her not ovulating that stopped him last night. Is it possible to grow bored after only one year? "God, please let my husband still be attracted to me," she found herself begging once again.

Staci carefully set the twenty-by-twenty-eight-inch frame on her desk, then hit the intercom button. "Can I have a moment of your time? I have something to show you," she sang into the speaker when Marcus answered.

She couldn't wait to show off her new painting. Both she and Marcus had been eyeing it. Now that she had it, she had to be a good sister and rub it in his face.

"Be right there." Marcus didn't question her; Staci intended for him to come to her and not the other way around. Otherwise, she would have barged into his office like she used to barge into his bedroom.

"How was your anniversary?" Marcus asked, entering her office and taking a seat.

"You tell me." When Staci lifted the painting around, Marcus jumped up.

"My boy picked that out? I can't believe it. I thought he would have written you a check," he chuckled.

"You're just mad because I got the original work and you didn't."

Marcus waved his hand in the air and dismissed her comment. "I'm just happy the man remembered his anniversary."

Staci offered her brother a half smile. She wouldn't dare tell him Derrick had indeed forgotten. Suddenly bragging wasn't important anymore.

"Are we still on for this weekend?" she asked. They were scheduled to meet at Brian and Lashay's for dinner and a basketball game.

"As long as my baby is up to it." As always, Marcus's face broke into a wide grin at the mention of his queen, Shannon. "She's been very tired lately, but I think we'll be able to make it." Marcus paused, like he was debating his next question.

"What is it?"

He continued. "Is Derrick coming? He's been missing in action lately. Is everything all right with him?"

Staci stood with the painting, mainly to avoid her brother's gaze. "He's been busy at the office during the week. You know your boy is an overachiever; always has to be the best."

Marcus and everyone else in the family knew about Derrick's insecurities. That's why he was concerned. Ever since learning of Shannon's and Lashay's pregnancies, Derrick had been acting indifferent toward the family. He always came up with reasons why he couldn't attend gatherings. He also wasn't attending church on a regular basis any longer.

"As long as you're happy." It was a question.

"Can you help me hang this?" Staci asked, before she ended up divulging how miserable she really was.

"Sure." Marcus hung the painting without pressing her for an answer.

Four days later, Staci roamed around her cousin's house wishing she had stayed at home.

"Will the two of you cut it out?" Staci scolded, and then smiled. Marcus and Shannon were at it again, hugging and kissing like the newlyweds they were. "Don't you think you've done enough of that already?" Staci's eyes fell to Shannon's slightly extended belly.

"I can never get enough of my baby," Marcus said, before kissing Shannon again.

Staci dismissed them with a wave of her hand and went into the kitchen only to find Brian and Lashay huddled at the sink. Finally, she walked into the den where Derrick sat. He was so engrossed in the basketball game he didn't notice her come in.

"What's the score?" she asked, then scooted next to him.

"Seventy-nine to sixty-five, Kings."

When his arm didn't automatically rest on her shoulder, she leaned closer into him. Still nothing. Desperate for some type of affection, she exhaled loudly and took his hand in hers.

"Staci, did you want something?"

She finally had his attention, but before she could answer, Marcus and Brian came into the den and booted her out.

"Why don't you run along into kitchen with the womenfolk?" Brian teased.

"That's right. A woman's place is in the kitchen during basketball season," Marcus added.

"And football and baseball seasons," Brian tagged on.

"Fine!" Staci rolled her eyes at Derrick. "There's nothing cooking out here anyway."

Now of all times, Derrick decided to say something. He always agreed with whatever Marcus and Brian said, like he didn't have a mind of his own. Staci hated that.

"All right, little woman, run along before I bend you over my knee and tame you," Derrick warned.

"Please do," Staci purred, before she went into the kitchen.

Derrick grinned, but she hoped he didn't miss her real meaning. Staci was becoming more frustrated and irritated with his lack of consistency. If he thought after the other night she understood enough to tolerate his distant behavior, he was sorely mistaken. She loved him, but at the moment, she didn't like him very much.

Chapter 7

Sunday morning Staci found herself on the second row of True Worship Ministries, alone. Derrick opted to go golfing instead of attending church service. Staci prayed all the way to church for Derrick. It was not like him to miss five Sundays in a row for no apparent reason. When she questioned him about it, he brushed off her concerns.

"I don't have to go to church every Sunday to be saved," is what he told her.

"I know that, but you don't even pray or read your Bible anymore," she countered.

"I may not pray as much, but I do pray. Unlike you, God understands my heart."

Derrick's put-down struck a nerve. "If you would share your heart with me, maybe I would understand! But you won't talk to me!"

Derrick slammed the refrigerator door shut and left her standing alone in the kitchen.

Now, in the midst of praise and worship, she regretted losing her temper. Derrick needed to be in church. When his spiritual life was on track, he was a different person. He was still introverted, but not nearly as withdrawn. Every major mistake he'd made in his life was committed after he'd slacked up in his walk with God. Including the time when he and Staci were weak and convinced themselves it was all right for them to have premarital sex.

Hurriedly, she wiped the corners of her eyes and hoped no one, especially her family, would ask her about Derrick's absence. As hard as she tried, she couldn't fully enjoy praise and worship. She was too worried about the future of her marriage.

Today, Pastor Reggie, who was also her uncle, took his text from Numbers 23:19.

"Don't abort what God has told you. Even when everything and everyone seems to be against you, hold on to what God has spoken to you."

I know you told me Derrick is my ordained mate, Staci conversed with God.

"No matter how long it takes, don't give up. God doesn't make empty promises. He doesn't play with our emotions. If He said it, it shall come to pass."

When, God? How long, God?

"His Word is for an appointed time. Some of us move out of God's time, then become frustrated when our plan doesn't work. We then want God to quickly deliver us, when in the beginning, all we had to do was believe the words He told us and trust Him to bring them to pass in His time."

Staci bowed her head and cried softly. She'd known she'd married Derrick too soon. Derrick was a loving and caring man, but he was controlled by his insecurities. There wasn't anything she could do about it now other than suffer patiently and pray constantly.

Before service was over, Pastor Reggie sent word by an usher that he wanted to speak with her after service in his office. She prolonged the discussion she knew would be centered on Derrick's absenteeism by chatting with fellow church members and her family. Sister Jones, the head of the education department, was trying to convince her to chair the annual scholarship banquet when the pastor and first lady beckoned for her.

"I'm sorry, Sister Jones, but I have to go." Staci walked away so fast she nearly tripped over her feet. She wanted to chair the scholarship banquet about as much as she wanted to walk barefoot on a bed of nails. Chairing the event meant hours of solicitation and dealing with church members who were gifted to complain about everything.

"Hi, Auntie." Staci hugged the first lady, Julia Simone-Pennington. Julia was her father's sister and Lashay's mother and also the owner of the development that housed MS Computers. Pastor Reggie invited her to have a seat, then sat behind his desk. Julia stood beside him.

"Staci, how are you?" Pastor Reggie began.

"I'm okay."

"How's Derrick? I haven't seen him in a while, and he's not returning my calls."

Staci shifted in her seat. There wasn't any need for her to put up a front, not to them. They would see right through it.

"Uncle, Derrick and I are having a hard time right now. He doesn't communicate that much with me, so I don't know what's really bothering him. He spends most of his time at the office, even on the weekends. Today, he's out golfing."

Pastor Reggie leaned back and laced his fingers together. "I'll be honest with you, Staci; I am worried about him. He's been on my mind all week, and I was hoping to see him today. I'll give him another call. I'll even get on his dental appointment schedule, if I have to."

"Thanks, but I don't think it'll help," Staci said solemnly.

"Staci, you haven't given up on him, have you?" Pastor Julia asked.

Staci took a moment to ponder her aunt's question. She hadn't given up, but she didn't know how much more she could stand. She was tired of being in a marriage by herself.

"No, Auntie, I haven't, but it's getting difficult. Being married to Derrick is not what I expected."

"Neither is life, but you can't give up," Pastor Julia pressed. "You've only been married a year."

"I know, but it feels like forever." Staci's eyes watered. "I guess because I'm always alone. It's like he only comes home because he has to."

Julia walked around and stood at her side and took her hand. "Staci, do you believe Derrick is your ordained husband?"

"Yes, I know he is." That was the sad and honest truth. Derrick was her soul mate.

"Then don't give up. Fight for what's yours. You're a Simone and a child of God. The fight is in you."

"What about him? Why do I have to do all the fighting? He's supposed to be the head of the house." Staci accepted the box of tissue from her uncle.

Julia spoke gently. "Staci, he is the head of the house, but the head can't turn without the neck, and the neck supports the head. Right now, you're stronger than Derrick spiritually, but when he accepts himself for the powerful man he is, you won't have to worry about fighting."

Staci remained quiet.

"Stop focusing on what's wrong. Focus on the good things. Focus on what you love about him and build on that."

Maybe her aunt was right. Maybe if she stopped complaining and just waited patiently for Derrick to come to his senses things would change. What did she have to lose?

***

When Derrick came home late that evening she didn't ask him where he'd been or what he had been doing. She simply asked if he wanted something to eat. When he said no, she didn't complain about how she'd spent most of the afternoon cooking dinner. She didn't say anything except good night and went to bed.

That went on for a whole month. She didn't say much to him, and he didn't say much to her. She still cooked and made sure he had everything he needed, but at night, she cried herself to sleep. Derrick didn't seem to notice that every day she withdrew further and further away from him. If he did notice, he didn't mention it.

Chapter 8

"Good morning, beautiful." Derrick strolled into the kitchen bright-eyed and grinning.

Staci looked around the kitchen to see who he was talking to.

"Come on, I haven't been that bad, have I?" he asked after he kissed her on the cheek.

"Yes, you have," Staci answered after taking a sip of her tea, totally unmoved by his touch. She took note of his tailored suit and adjusted his tie for him. "What are you so happy about?"

"I have a very important meeting this morning," he paused, "that I can't tell you about until later."

"Of course, you can't," Staci smirked and walked to the double sink to rinse her breakfast dishes.

Derrick stood behind her and wrapped his arms around her waist. "How about I tell you all about it over dinner tonight? I'll even cook, or if you want, we can go out."

Staci turned to face him with eyes laced in defeat. "Derrick, it doesn't matter anymore. It's your life, and you can see whomever, go wherever, and do whatever you want."

He watched her somberly climb the stairs but didn't go after her. If he wanted her to know how much he loved and appreciated her, he didn't show it. The small gap between them had grown enormously, but he made no effort to bridge the gap. For now, his agenda took precedence.

***

Staci was shocked, to say the least, to see Derrick's SUV in the driveway upon returning home midday to change clothes after an accident at work.

"Derrick?" she called as she stepped into the living room. When he didn't respond, she quickly climbed the stairs to their bedroom. She selected a new ensemble and began changing.

"Derrick? What are you doing in here?" She finally saw him seated on the side of the bathtub. When he held his head up to answer her, his facial expression was one of confusion and despair. When he didn't answer her, she asked again. "Derrick, what are you doing home this time of day?"

"I didn't know there were time restraints on when a man can be in his own house." His brash tone shocked her, and she took a step backward.

"I'm just surprised to see you, that's all." Staci studied his face. "Derrick, is something wrong?"

"What do you think? Of course, there's something wrong with me. I'm not from the perfect family like you are."

Slowly, Staci zipped her skirt and tried to control her temper. "Derrick, what does my family have to do with your bad attitude?"

He just stared at her with cold eyes.

"Derrick, talk to me. What's bothering you?"

"I'm tired of this!" he yelled, then walked to his closet and removed a suitcase.

Staci stared at him like he was an alien with two heads. It took a minute for his actions to register in her brain. He was packing his clothes.

"What are you talking about? You're tired of what?" Staci's voice was steady, although her body trembled.

"I'm tired of everything. Life. This house and you!" He continued packing.

Staci leaned against the door frame to keep from falling. "How can you be tired of me? You haven't been with me."

He continued packing without responding. Staci watched in silence as he grabbed things from the closet, then the chest and the bathroom. With every item he packed, she felt like he was taking a piece of her. She felt her world crashing down on her, like she was sinking into darkness. She didn't realize she'd slid down the door frame and was now sitting on the floor until her hands touched the carpet.

That's how she was when Derrick finally looked back in her direction: sitting on the floor with tears streaming down her face. Derrick's facial expression softened, but just slightly.

"Staci, I just need a break." His tone was more gentle, but his resolve the same. "I need some time to think about my life and what I want."

"And you can't think here, in our home?" she questioned, searching his eyes for the Derrick that used to love her. The one who vowed to love her until death. The Derrick she loved. "You don't want me anymore? There's someone else." It was meant to be a question, and his answers were supposed to assure her that he loved only her. His prolonged silence, however, made it a statement of fact. She turned her head away from him, not wanting him to see how deeply he'd hurt her.

"I just need some time alone," he whispered, then grabbed his luggage and left.

Staci remained quiet on the floor. When she heard the front door close, her body shuddered. She didn't allow the sobs that would tear her spirit to shreds and leave her gasping for air to come until after she heard the SUV drive off.

"Oh God!" she screamed over and over. Nothing in her life ever hurt like this. The pain was too much. She lay on the floor in the fetal position crying and holding her stomach until everything went black.

Chapter 9

Staci stretched and looked up at the ceiling. The florescent lights quickly reminded her that the nightmare was indeed real. Derrick had left her. She crawled to her bed and used it to support her weight as she tried to stand. She was too weak and collapsed on the bed.

"Why, God?" she asked with a new batch of tears. "I did everything I knew to do. How could he just leave?" When the silence didn't answer, she turned over and bawled some more.

Her cell phone rang, and she jumped up and ran to the dresser to answer it. She didn't check the caller ID, believing it was Derrick, saying he'd made a mistake and was on his way home.

"Derrick!" she yelled into the phone.

"No. Where are you?" It was Marcus. What was left of Staci's heart sank. "Staci, did you forget the meeting with the attorneys?"

Staci looked at the clock on her nightstand. It was four o'clock. She must have stayed on the floor for two hours. "I'm sorry," she said between sobs. "I'm at home. I can't make it."

"Staci, what's wrong?"

She couldn't answer him.

"Staci," he yelled into the phone. She still didn't answer. The line went dead.

She summoned the strength to clean her face and went downstairs and unlocked the front door. It didn't take a genius to know Marcus was on his way over, and probably with her younger brother, Craig. The two had always been very protective of her.

The sunken living room was one of Staci's favorite places, with the marble fireplace and hardwood floor. The sage walls usually gave the room a warm, cozy feel, but now the room felt cold and hollow, like she felt. Derrick's leaving had left her empty of more than his company. She'd become accustomed to not having his company, but he took her heart with him this time.

She walked into the kitchen, the same kitchen he'd promised to make her dinner in just hours before. Although she skipped lunch, she wasn't hungry. She made a cup of chamomile tea. She needed something to help her stop trembling. She was halfway through the first cup when Marcus and Craig walked into the kitchen.

"Staci, what's going on?" Craig asked, noticing her red, puffy eyes.

Marcus walked from the kitchen into the living room and back. "Where's Derrick?"

"He's gone," she whispered.

"Gone where?" Marcus pressed.

"I don't know, but he's not here. He's gone." When Staci broke down, Craig put his arm around her.

Marcus sat down at the table. "Tell me what happened."

It took her awhile, but Staci finally shared with her brothers how her husband had walked out on her. She couldn't bring herself to tell them that her husband didn't want her anymore. She just shared that he needed some time.

Part of Staci was glad Derrick was not there. Despite his smaller size, Marcus would have attacked him. Derrick was his boy. Since the day he married Staci, Marcus considered and treated Derrick like a brother. They shared a bond, but that wouldn't prevent Marcus from physically harming him for hurting his only sister.

As if reading his thoughts Staci said, "Marcus, please stay out of this," then turned to Craig. "Promise me you guys won't jump Derrick or vandalize his vehicle." That's exactly what they had done in their younger days when a guy disrespected their sister.

"Okay, but I might douse him with gasoline and strike a match," Craig answered seriously. "He's not so big that he can't be taken down."

"Please, this is hard enough to deal with." Inwardly, Staci hoped this was all temporary. Derrick said he needed space. Maybe after a couple of nights away, he would come back.

This time Marcus read her thoughts. "Maybe this separation is only temporary. I know he loves you."

Staci couldn't tell her brother that she didn't know if Derrick still loved her or not. She hadn't heard or felt those words in months. "Maybe." Her faint smile didn't hold much expectation.

Before Marcus and Craig left, they made her call their parents and tell them what was going on. "You should talk to Mom," Craig told her. Staci agreed. She could use the comfort of her mother, but what she really wanted was the arms of the first man she ever loved, her father. She needed him to hold her and tell her she was beautiful and make her feel special again.

After telling Carey what happened, there was a long silence on the phone. Unlike her brothers, her father grew quiet when angry. She could imagine his fair skin turning a shade of red. It was only after Derrick promised her father he would love his daughter and give her at least the same care and respect Mr. Simone had given her, did Carey give his blessing on their marriage. Carey recognized Derrick's issues and had voiced his concern, but he also knew his love for Staci was genuine. Carey treated Derrick like a son. He boasted about Derrick's success just as much as he did Marcus's and Craig's. Now, Derrick had disappointed him by leaving his baby girl alone and unprotected. Staci could tell from her father's grunts that he would deal with her husband man to man, real soon.

"Baby girl, why don't you come home for a few days?" her father suggested.

Tears rolled down her cheeks. She loved her daddy for always wanting to protect her. "I would, Daddy, but I have a lot of work to do with this expansion." She really wanted to stay around just in case Derrick returned.

"Derrick will know where to find you," her father responded.

"I think you should spend some time with Mom." Marcus's opinion confirmed her father's suggestion.

"Besides," Carey continued, "Marcus is the CEO. He's home now. Let him run his own company for a few days."

Her father was right. If Derrick did have a change of heart, the first place he would check would be her parents. And Staci really didn't want to stay in that big house all alone. The six-bedroom house wasn't meant to be lived in alone.

"I'll see you in a little bit." After her brothers left, Staci went upstairs to pack, all the while praying Derrick would come back or at least call. An hour later and without any word from him, she set the alarm, locked the house, then left.

Chapter 10

Staci pulled into her parent's estate and found her father waiting outside in the circular driveway for her. Fresh tears threatened to fall. Carey Simone was her hero, always there to rescue her. Before Staci turned the engine off, he was at the car door waiting to open it for her.

"Everything is going to be fine, baby girl," he said as he held her in his strong arms after she stepped from the car.

She buried her face in his shirt. "Promise, Daddy?"

"I promise. With God's help, you'll make it through this, and you'll be stronger because of it," Carey answered, then led his only daughter into the house.

Staci followed the onion and celery aroma into the kitchen where Alaina stood preparing homemade chicken soup. As far back as Staci could remember, Alaina used the soup to soothe any pain. "Hi, Mommy."

Alaina laid the ladle on the spoon rest and welcomed her daughter into her arms. There was something about Alaina's mothering arms that made Staci want to cry all over again and have her mother wipe her tears, but Staci didn't cry because that would have made Alaina cry too. It had always been that way. If Staci cried, Alaina cried.

"Why don't you go upstairs to your old room and take a hot bath. You'll feel better after some aromatherapy. I'll bring you some soup later."

"Thanks, Mommy." Staci slowly walked down the hall and up the winding staircase to the room she once called hers. Carey followed close behind with her suitcase.

"Remember, baby girl, everything is going to work out," Carey said before leaving after placing her bag on the queen-sized bed. Staci wished she shared her father's confidence. She wondered what the words, *everything will work out*, really meant. Did it mean everything would work out with Derrick, or did it mean without him?

"Thank you, Mommy," Staci whispered after she closed the door to her former room. Her mother had thought of everything. Aromatherapy candles burned and soft music floated from the CD player. Inside the bathroom was an assortment of bath oils and salts and, of course, a pack of Handi Wipes. For as far back as Staci could remember, Alaina always kept a pack of Handi Wipes with her for everything from dirty hands to public restrooms.

While hot foam filled the tub, Staci slowly undressed. She caught a glimpse of herself in the mirror and nearly tripped and hit her head.

"Oh my God!" she said as she took in her reflection. Her eyes were red and swollen. Brown streaks stained her face from the many tears she'd shed. Her lips looked ashy, and her shoulder-length hair was twisted into what looked like a knot. Good thing she had the hair texture that would soften in water, making it easier to comb through.

Once in the tub, the hot water and fragrant smells did wonders for Staci's stiff muscles but didn't touch her broken heart.

"God, what did I do wrong? Why did he leave? I did everything I was taught to do. The only thing I didn't do was carry his seed. Maybe that's the problem. Did he leave me because I didn't get pregnant? That must be it, because I haven't gained weight or let myself go."

The unanswered questions hung in the air as Staci tried to rationalize why her husband had walked out on her.

"God, I know you forgave me for fornicating and for having an abortion. So why I am going through this?"

"Because you didn't listen to wise counsel," a still voice whispered back.

Staci's mind immediately went back to the conversation she'd had with her mother a month before her wedding.

"Staci, I'm not saying Derrick isn't the one God has for you. All I'm saying is wait until the time is right. Let him work through his insecurities first."

"Mama, I love Derrick, and he loves me. That's enough to handle every problem we may have."

Alaina tried a different approach. "Staci, I know you're afraid of losing him again, but you can't rush into marrying him. Don't overlook his problems. Allow him time to work through them. If you don't, you're going to add to the trials you're already going to have."

"I hear what you're saying, Mama, but I know what I'm doing."

"No, you don't. You don't really understand how deep not having a father has affected him. I see it every time he's around your father and brothers. He works extra hard to be accepted by them when he doesn't have to."

There was some validity to her mother's words, but Staci didn't want to wait. She was afraid of losing him again.

"Mama, I can help him face his issues. I can—"

Alaina's voice, filled with frustration, cut her off. "Stacelyn, you can't help Derrick face anything he's not willing to face on his own."

In hindsight, Staci wished her mother had locked her in the basement to keep her from marrying Derrick. If she had, she wouldn't be going through this heartache now. Staci recognized early in their relationship that Derrick was insecure. He didn't express his feelings for her until after Staci expressed hers. Then periodically, Derrick would ask her if she was sure she really loved him. Then he would ask why she loved him. If he brought her a gift, he would ask her repeatedly if she liked it. And after they agreed to commit fornication, she had to constantly reassure him she enjoyed being intimate with him. Then when she had the abortion, he told her he felt like she had rejected him.

That was then. Since marrying him, Staci did everything a good wife was expected to do. At times when he didn't meet her expectations, she still catered to him. When she knew the only reason he desired to make love to her was to impregnate her, she submitted to his demands without mumbling a word. No matter how inconsiderate he was in bed, she never used a headache as an excuse.

Staci closed her eyes and squeezed the sponge on her face just as Alaina knocked on the bathroom door.

"Can I come in?" Alaina asked.

"Sure. I was just about to get out."

Alaina handed Staci a towel after entering the bathroom. As Staci dried herself, Alaina picked up her dirty clothes. She made an attempt to lighten the mood. "You're almost thirty years old, and I'm still picking up your clothes."

"I don't know why you're complaining. You know you love looking after your only daughter." Staci smiled slightly. She figured her mother had really come in there to make sure she didn't drown herself. "I know I looked and felt a mess when Daddy brought me inside. I feel a little better now, but I have a long way to go."

"You probably don't want to eat, but I brought you some soup."

As she tied the belt to her robe, Staci's eyes glanced at the clock above the sink. It was eight o'clock and still no word from Derrick. She wondered where he was and what he was having for dinner. Staci tried to contain her emotions, but couldn't. When she slumped over the sink, Alaina put her arms around her and led her to the bed.

"Mama, this hurts so much," Staci cried.

"I know it does, baby."

"Mommy, make it stop hurting, please. Make today go away. Please bring my husband back."

Alaina held her tightly. "Baby, the only one who can fix this is God," she answered and wiped away tears of her own. "Let's talk to Him about it." Alaina closed her eyes and bowed her head. "Heavenly Father, I ask that you comfort my baby right now. Let your love consume her and overtake her. Give her your perfect peace and understanding. Help her to lean on you for strength and not faint. Lord, turn this pain into ministry.

"God, I ask that you help Derrick and heal him of his past hurts. Help him to see that you did not make a mistake when you created him. Help him to see that you love him and that Staci loves him and that we love him. Help him to realize that he can't make it without you. Lord, turn his heart back toward you, then back toward his wife . . ." Alaina prayed and prayed until Staci fell asleep in her arms.

Chapter 11

"Oh, God, how did I get here?" Derrick cried with his face buried in his tear-saturated hands. He looked around the small hotel room, making sure he avoided the mirrors. He couldn't look at himself. He was too ashamed.

"I left my wife. I left my wife. How could I do that?" he asked in a barely audible voice.

"You left me," the still small voice Derrick had been trying to ignore answered.

Derrick's horrific sobs echoed through the room. His world was crashing down on him, and he couldn't do anything to stop it. It was happening too fast. This morning he was on top of the world, and now, the world was on top of him and crushing him with a vengeance. This morning he wanted to live; now at this moment, he wanted to die a quick death.

He walked over to the second-story window and looked down into the parking lot. He shook his head, thinking the worst that would happen if he jumped would be a broken leg. Instead, he walked back to the bed and plopped down, then asked a question he didn't have a reasonable answer to. "What am I going to do?"

"Come back to me. It's only in me that you live, move, and have your being."

Derrick shook his head, then hurried into the bathroom and started the shower. The steam released more tears.

He didn't sleep that night. Not feeling Staci's warm body next to him underneath the stale covers depressed him more. Every time he managed to doze off, his mind would replay the scene from that afternoon and conclude with a picture of Staci sitting on the floor of their bedroom trying to make sense of his erratic behavior. He accepted defeat and threw back the covers. Finally, he picked up his cell phone and called for help.

A few hours later, Derrick sat in the hotel's restaurant sipping a cold cup of coffee with Pastor Reggie. They'd been in there since Derrick phoned his pastor before dawn. He began by apologizing for avoiding his phone calls. To Derrick's surprise and relief, Reggie dismissed his behavior and agreed to meet him.

After a few minutes of listening to Derrick, Reggie stopped being his pastor and uncle. He became his friend.

"Derrick, you can't keep holding on to this. You've got to turn this over to God and let Him work it out. You have to make Him head of your life again."

"It's not that easy. I've struggled with this all of my life."

"And now you're making Staci struggle."

Derrick blinked his eyes. He was trying unsuccessfully to block an image of Staci sitting on the floor, heartbroken.

"Derrick, you've done to Staci what your father did to you. You rejected her and placed your insecurities on her. The difference is, you know Staci loves you, but yet, you're willing to hurt her instead of dealing with your issues."

"I love her, too. She's my heart," he added sadly.

"Then go home and tell her that. Share your heart with her. Tell her the truth about what happened."

Derrick listened. What Reggie said made sense, but he couldn't do that right now. He was too vulnerable. Sure, Staci loved him, but would she once he unleashed the skeletons in his closet?

Chapter 12

The next afternoon Staci went for a walk with her father along the man-made lake that ran adjacent to her parents' estate. Carey looked over at his daughter walking in silence with her head hung down and put his arm around her shoulder. She relaxed and rested in the safety her dad provided.

"Baby girl, hold your head up."

"Daddy, it's hard," she replied, with her head still down.

"I know it is, but you're a strong woman. I raised you that way."

"Maybe if it didn't hurt so much."

"Stacelyn, it only hurts because you love Derrick." Hearing her birth name, she instantly lifted her head. Carey almost never referred to her by her given name. She was simply his "baby girl."

"Derrick loves you too," her father continued. "He just doesn't know how to show it yet. I'm not trying to minimize the severity of his actions. In fact, I'm angry at him. But I also understand that he's battling a war within himself."

"Where does that leave me?" she asked and blinked back tears.

"Unfortunately, it leaves you hurt and wounded," her father sighed. "Sometimes no matter how much we try not to, we still hurt the people we love, the same way others have hurt us. That's what's happening to Derrick. But, baby girl, I promise you, you'll get through this. Hopefully, Derrick will come around, but even if he doesn't, you will get through this."

"How, Daddy?" she whined.

"By taking one day at a time. If it's easier for you, take an hour at a time. Do what you have to do, but don't stop living your life. Love Derrick, but don't stop living because he's not there."

"But, Daddy, I want him here. I want him with me," she moped.

Carey stopped walking and locked eyes with his daughter. "Do you want him with you if he's not willing to be there for you 100 percent? Do you want him here not knowing how to love you back? Do you want him here before God settles him?"

Staci didn't answer because that's exactly what she had now.

"Baby girl, this was a hard lesson for you to learn, and an even harder one for your mother and me to watch. But I think you've got it now."

"I thought Mom would be the one to say, 'I told you so.' Staci half-smiled.

"We're not concerned about taking credit for warning you. We just want to make sure you learn the lesson." Carey narrowed his eyes, and Staci knew he was waiting for her to recite the lesson, just like he'd done throughout her childhood.

"'God is the only one who can change people. And anything that is not in God's designated time is out of time.' Oh, one more. 'You can not hurry God; neither can you help Him out.'"

"That's a good start," Carey said, then kissed his daughter on the cheek.

"Daddy, there's more?" Staci whined.

"Oh, there's much more, but you're on your way."

***

Monday morning, after a hearty breakfast of pancakes, bacon, and eggs, Staci left her parents' peaceful home and set out to face her tumultuous life. As she drove down Highway 37, the wind from the sunroof blew her hair and she actually felt good. It had been an entire week since Derrick had left. She hadn't heard one word from him. Today that would change. She'd planned to stop by his office in hopes of spending his lunchtime talking about their marriage. She'd prayed fervently every day and hoped for a quick reconciliation. If that didn't happen, she would do what her parents instructed. She would keep living her life one day at a time.

Before heading to his office, she went home to change into something more appropriate and appealing, like the red and gold pantsuit he'd bought her for Christmas. Funny, Derrick couldn't coordinate his own clothing, but could select flattering outfits for Staci with ease. Walking into the house knowing no one else lived there was kind of creepy at first. She turned on the sound system, and the atmosphere warmed a bit.

Inside her bedroom, she noticed Derrick had been back and had removed more of his clothing. She swallowed the bile that threatened to erupt from the pit of her stomach and quickly changed clothes and applied light makeup to highlight her natural features. Before leaving, she sorted out Derrick's mail and tucked it into her handbag.

"Hello, Mrs. Garrison."

"Hello, Phyllis," Staci greeted Derrick's office manager and the other staff members present. "Is my husband available?"

"He's in with his last patient before lunch, but you can wait for him in his office."

"Thank you, Phyllis." Phyllis buzzed her inside the back office, and Staci slowly walked down the hallway that led to Derrick's office. With each step, she wondered if this is what the death-row inmates across the bridge at San Quentin felt like. It was like walking to her execution; the end of the world.

"Excuse me, Mrs. Garrison." Derrick's colleague, Dr. Hunt, bumped into her.

"It's my fault. I wasn't looking where I was going," Staci said and repositioned the handbag strap over her shoulder.

"I'll tell the big guy you're here," the elder gentleman offered.

"No need. I'll just wait for him in his office. I have a key." Staci was afraid Derrick would leave if he was alerted to her presence. She hurried on before Dr. Hunt could comment.

Staci entered the office quietly. She placed her purse and Derrick's mail on the desk. Out of habit, she walked around and checked the stock in his minirefrigerator. Mentally, she made a list of things to pick up at the grocery store. Then her eyes traveled to their wedding picture, still in its place on his desk. Her optimism returned. She picked up his picture and was outlining his face with her fingertips when Derrick walked in, leaving the door slightly ajar.

At first she thought she saw a slight smile on his face, but he froze too quickly for her to be sure. Her heart nearly leaped at the sight of him. She had missed her teddy bear so much. He just stared at her, so she spoke first.

"Hello, Derrick." She placed the picture back on the desk.

"Hi."

She inhaled and exhaled in metered breaths before saying, "Do you have any plans for lunch?"

"No." His monosyllable answers made his mood hard to read.

"I was hoping we could talk during your lunch break."

Her expectations fell when he walked around her and sat at his desk, then asked, "What do you want to talk about?"

"I want to talk about our marriage, or what's left of it," Staci answered, still standing next to his desk and forcing herself to maintain eye contact.

Derrick closed his eyes and rubbed his forehead.

"Derrick, I need to know if we still have a marriage or not."

"Staci—" he didn't get to finish.

"Derrick, I'm going to Zito's for lunch. Would you like to join me?"

Staci turned her head to see the female who'd rudely interrupted her time with her husband. She looked at the twenty-something female long and hard, but didn't recall seeing her before. She then looked at Derrick for an explanation.

"This is Rhonda. She's the dental assistant I hired a few months ago," Derrick explained. "Rhonda, this is Staci."

Inside her head Staci counted to ten—quickly. Derrick had just introduced her to an employee as simply Staci and not as his wife. He didn't seem to even notice his error. Staci wanted to remind him that California is a community property state, which meant half of this office belonged to her, including the employees.

"Hi, Staci," Rhonda said, then leaned against the door frame and waited for an answer from Derrick.

"That's *Mrs.* Garrison," Staci corrected and shot hot daggers at Derrick. When she looked back at Rhonda, her facial expression remained hard. "Rhonda, tell me, when did it become appropriate for an employee to barge into her employer's office and address him by his first name?" Staci didn't crack a smile. Derrick appeared nervous. He fumbled with his hands, then brushed them over his mustache.

Rhonda stood there with her mouth ajar. She'd been calling Dr. Garrison by his first name from the beginning, and he had never corrected her. Nor had he mentioned his wife.

"I'll meet you at Zito's," Derrick answered, and Rhonda made a quick exit.

Staci turned away from Derrick to gather her emotions. He had chosen to spend time with another female over her. He'd chosen to accept an impromptu lunch date with an employee instead of talking about their marriage with his wife. Now it was time for her to make some decisions of her own. At that moment, she made several. She was not going to beg Derrick to talk to her. She was not going to drill him on the nature of his relationship with Rhonda. If he wanted to spend his time with Rhonda instead of her, then so be it. She was not going to chase after him. She was hurt, but still had her pride.

"I won't keep you from your lunch date," she said when she finally turned around. "Here's your mail." She pushed the mail on the desk toward him. "I don't work for the postal service. I will not sort or deliver your mail to you in the future. I suggest you put in a change of address with the post office."

"Staci, we don't have to do all that."

"Yes, we do." She strapped her purse on her shoulder. "Derrick, I came here to talk to you about our marriage, and you just proved to me that our marriage is not important to you. I should've known that when you left a week ago. Our marriage is not now or ever has been important to you. I'm just sorry it took so long for me to see that."

In her heart, Staci waited for him to tell her she was wrong, that their marriage did matter to him. But he didn't.

"Good-bye, Derrick." As she turned to leave she gave in to her anger. "One more thing," she said after opening the door. "The next time you would like to enter my home to pick up the rest of your belongings, call first. I live alone, and I don't want strangers roaming around the premises."

Staci managed to stay composed all the way to her car. Once inside, she waited for the tears to come, but they didn't. They didn't come on the ride home either. Sitting alone in her bedroom and taking off her wedding ring, there still weren't any tears. That's when Staci decided she'd cried all the tears she was going to cry over Derrick Garrison. She had given him her best, and he had given it back. That hurt; it really hurt. But like her father said, in the end she would be fine. It would take some time, but her life would go on without Derrick. The sun would still continue to shine whether Derrick was in her life or not.

She placed her wedding ring into her jewelry box and looked down at her watch. It was only one o'clock in the afternoon. She grabbed her briefcase from the closet and decided it was time to go back to work.

"Dr. Garrison, your patient is ready." This time Rhonda knocked on the door before entering. Instead of stopping in the threshold, Rhonda walked in and leaned against his desk in the identical spot Staci had occupied earlier.

Derrick shifted in the chair but didn't make eye contact. "I'll be right out."

"I missed you at lunch. I brought you something back for later."

That's when Derrick noticed the plastic bag containing a Styrofoam container in her hands. "You didn't have to do that."

"I know, but I wanted to. I can't have my gentle giant passing out from hunger." Rhonda placed the food inside the refrigerator. "See you in a few."

After she closed the door, Derrick leaned back in his chair and picked up his wedding picture. "You've always mattered to me," he whispered to Staci's image. Why he couldn't voice the words in Staci's presence he didn't know.

Derrick had been stuck in his seat since Staci left an hour ago. He didn't mean for their first meeting since his leaving to go so badly. When he saw her standing at his desk, he wanted to hold her and tell her how much he'd missed her, but fear gripped him. Then Rhonda came in and everything went downhill from there. There was nothing going on between him and Rhonda, although she would like for it to be. She'd made several advances toward him, and honestly, he enjoyed the attention.

He owed Staci an explanation, but he just didn't know how to talk to her. His normally steady hands shook as he punched her number. Her voice mail picked up on the third ring.

"Hello, you've reached Staci Simone. I'm sorry, but I'm unable to accept your call at this time. Please leave a brief message and I'll return your call shortly."

Derrick felt like he'd been sucker punched in the gut. Staci had removed his last name from hers. What he feared most was starting to happen; Staci was removing him from her life. Derrick steadied his voice enough to speak.

"Staci, I'm sorry about today. It's not what you think. There's nothing going on between me and Rhonda. I just wanted you to know that."

Chapter 13

"You did what!" Miss Cora yelled.

"I've moved out of the house." Derrick shrugged his shoulders like it wasn't a big deal.

"You can't be that crazy. How could you leave Staci?" Her son's stupidity was enough to make her sit up in bed. She'd been feeling weak all day, but the anger brought on by her son's revelation gave her a much-needed energy boost.

"Mama, you don't understand."

"What is there to understand? You left your wife and for what?"

Derrick stood there with his hands in his pockets and his head lowered, just like he'd done all his life after he'd done something wrong. Like the time he loaned Miss Cora's car to his so-called friends who, in turn, participated in a street race, getting the car impounded.

"Baby, sit down." Miss Cora patted the space beside her on the hospital bed placed in her home. Derrick quietly obeyed. "Derrick, I'm not going to be around much longer," she began. "I need you to really hear what I am about to say."

"I'm listening, Mama."

"Derrick, I want you to forgive me for you not having a father around."

"That's not your fault," he protested.

"Yes, it is partially my fault." Miss Cora nodded her head. "Baby, I knew before I lay down with John Archer that he was a married man with no intentions of leaving his wife. He told me the first day he flirted with me that he was only curious. I was well aware that he kept coming back because of the sex and not because of me. He didn't love me. I was playing with fire, and I got burned, but not in a bad way. I got you. Derrick, you have been the joy of my life."

Derrick smiled. "I know, Mom. You tell me all the time right after you call me certified crazy."

"Baby, I should have picked a better father for you or at least provided a positive role model for you, but I didn't and for that, I'm sorry. If I had, you wouldn't be so insecure and screwed up right now."

"Mama, what are you talking about?" He disagreed with her. "I never said I'm insecure."

"That's the problem; you won't admit it. But not having your father has left you with a fear of rejection and insecurity."

Derrick turned away from her. She was right, but he wasn't ready to hear it, not yet.

"That's why you keep shutting Staci out; you're afraid that if she sees the real you, she'll reject you. That's why you won't share your feelings with her. That's why you left her, but baby, you're too late. She sees the real you just like I do, and she accepts you. I accept you. It's time you for you to accept yourself for who you are, so God can heal you."

She sounded like Pastor Reggie. "Mama, it's not that easy."

"And losing your wife is?"

Derrick's jaw flexed, and his eyes darkened. Why didn't his mother understand how he felt? Why should she?—he really didn't understand himself.

Miss Cora continued. "Derrick, go home and talk to your wife. Staci's a good wife. Don't make her suffer for my and John's shortcomings."

Derrick swallowed hard, but didn't say anything. Miss Cora gently touched his arm. "Baby, I know it's hard, but with God, it's possible."

Derrick couldn't admit to his mother he hadn't talked to God in so long, God probably wouldn't recognize his voice. He couldn't tell his mother that he felt like a failure as a Christian since he and Staci committed fornication. He couldn't tell her how he felt guilty about the abortion. He couldn't tell her he was afraid. He couldn't tell her any of that. What he did was kiss her on the cheek, told her he loved her, then left.

On his way back to his studio apartment, he stopped by his house. He was both relieved and disappointed when he didn't see Staci's car. Inside their bedroom, he fought and won over the urge to break down. He missed his home so much. In the three weeks he'd been gone, nothing had changed except the closet he once occupied was now completely empty. His chest and underwear drawers were empty also. His tie rack was bare. Staci had boxed up his remaining clothes and personal belongings. Before locking the door after loading the last box into his SUV, he grabbed a framed picture of Staci from the mantle. The peaceful image would have to be enough for now.

Chapter 14

Staci spent Saturday morning housecleaning and trying to keep herself from crying. When she returned home last night, the boxes she'd pack for her estranged husband were gone. The hot anger she had when she packed them had dissipated and now was replaced by an overwhelming emptiness.

Staci was determined to move on with her life despite how hard the task was. The nights were the worst. No matter how distant they'd become, she and Derrick always slept with his arms around her. Now, her king-sized bed was cold and uninviting. She tried unsuccessfully to substitute his lack of presence by changing her bedding and traded in the black and gold motif for an emerald green jacquard design. She thought the warm green would add warmth to the bed, but it didn't. The sheets were still cold.

She'd been tempted to call and tell her estranged husband off on a few occasions, but what would that solve? It definitely wouldn't bring him home. With each day he was gone, she wondered if she really wanted him back. After service on Sunday, she did, but by Tuesday, she didn't care if she ever saw him again. Then last night, she wished she'd been there when he came so she could see his face and hear his voice, or perhaps feel his soft hands against her skin.

Staci had just finished cleaning the refrigerator when she received a call from Miss Cora, apologizing for, as she put it, "her crazy son."

"Staci, this doesn't change our relationship. If I'm still living, I want to see you at my birthday party," Miss Cora told her. "Hopefully, by that time, you and my son will have worked everything out. Honey, I know he's going to come around, but before you let him back into your good graces, make him beg. Make him think he's never going to get back into your bed. That way, he'll appreciate you more when you do open up to him."

Staci laughed at her mother-in-law's reference to sex.

"I'm not playing. Hold out as long as you can."

I'm going to miss her when she passes on, Staci thought sadly after she hung up. Miss Cora was something else. She was the one who gave Staci handcuffs at her bridal shower.

"I should've used those handcuffs to keep his behind at home," Staci grumbled in frustration.

No sooner had she sat down in the den with the remote in hand, her doorbell sounded. To her surprise and delight, it was Shannon and Lashay, carrying grocery bags.

"What are you two doing here?" Staci relieved some of the bags and walked toward the kitchen. They followed.

"Checking on our girl," Shannon answered, after placing the remaining bags on the counter.

"That's nice of you, but what's with the groceries?"

"This is for the slumber party," Lashay smiled after hugging her cousin.

"What?"

Shannon explained. "We're sleeping over tonight. Marcus is away at an engagement this weekend. His plane doesn't land until eight o'clock in the morning."

"And what about Brian?" Staci questioned.

"He's on a ministry trip with Reggie. So that leaves us with some time alone to cheer you up," Lashay smiled and patted her shoulder.

Staci smiled too, but her smile didn't last long. In no time, she was leaning over the counter crying. "Thanks so much for stopping by, but you really don't have to stay," she managed between sniffles.

"We're more than relatives; we're friends, and right now, you could use your girlfriends," Shannon said. "So stop protesting and sit down. We're going to handle everything."

Lashay began unloading the bags. "We're making tacos and s'mores. You can't have a slumber party without something to drink so we brought this to help you drink your troubles away." Staci smiled when Lashay pulled out three bottles of her favorite sparkling pear cider. "We also have pickles and peppermint sticks and ice cream. The pickles and peppermint are for us, but you can eat the ice cream; it's Ben & Jerry's."

"For our viewing pleasure, we have five of the hottest DVDs. One each: drama, comedy, action, suspense, and love story." Shannon fanned the disks in her hand.

"You guys have thought of everything." Staci was about to cry again, but Shannon stopped her.

"No more crying. We're here because we love you. Now go on into the den and sit down."

Staci quietly obeyed and thanked God for a cousin and a sister-in-law like Lashay and Shannon. Their company was a welcomed distraction.

In record time, the two pregnant women prepared the food and the girlfriends feasted on chicken tacos. Afterward, Staci propped pillows on the floor and they roasted s'mores in the fireplace. Each had a flute of cider in hand.

Staci sat relaxed with her eyes closed as she leaned against the marble fireplace. The sounds of Kenny G played in the background.

"What happened?" Lashay finally asked. "I mean, I thought you and Derrick were happy."

Staci opened her eyes and took a sip of cider before answering her cousin's question.

"We haven't been happy, at least I haven't been, since the first month of our marriage," Staci answered honestly.

Lashay swallowed a chocolate marshmallow and probed further. "How could that be?"

"I married Derrick too soon. He wasn't and still isn't ready to share his life with anyone."

"Is it because he's insecure?" Shannon asked.

Staci wasn't going to mention it, but since it was out there, why deny it. "How did you know?" she asked her sister-in-law.

"I recognized that awhile ago. He displayed some of the same characteristics I'd displayed when I was fearful and insecure."

"I thought when you guys got married he was over it," Lashay added.

Staci took another sip. "Unfortunately, he wasn't, and now he says he needs time to figure out what he wants." She swallowed hard. "Hopefully, at the end of the day, he'll want to remain married. If not, I'll live my life without him just fine."

"I'll drink to that," Lashay stated and took a sip of cider.

Shannon touched her arm. "Staci, give him the time he needs. He'll figure it out the same way I did when Marcus proposed to me and I turned him down."

"What?" Lashay asked. "You turned my cousin down?"

"Is that why you guys had that riff?" Staci questioned.

Shannon nodded. "Marcus proposed to me on his birthday, and I said no because I was afraid and didn't think I deserved him. I was an outcast in my family, and I didn't think I was worthy of his or anyone else's love."

"No wonder he was so messed up; you kicked him to the curb on his birthday." Staci shook her head. "My conceited brother needed to be knocked off of his high horse. Now I'll drink to *that*." Staci savored the bubbly pear flavor.

Shannon further explained. "That was before I knew who I was and accepted myself for who I am. Once I became secure with myself and loved myself, I literally begged Marcus for another chance."

"You did *what?*" the two cousins laughed.

"I am not ashamed to admit it. I begged my boo for another chance, even got down on my knees."

Lashay's eyes widened. "Girl, no, you didn't!"

"Yes, I did, and it was the best move I ever made," Shannon smiled, rubbing her stomach. "I'd just come to grips with who I was and what I wanted. I wanted Marcus, but he said he wouldn't propose again, so I proposed to him. When he refused, I finally told him he didn't have a choice." All three of them laughed at that.

"I don't think my brother wanted a choice. All he wanted then and still wants now is his 'Queen Shannon.'"

"I know," Shannon paused, "but I wasn't able to fully accept that until I settled the war within myself. Now, I can't imagine my life without him. Sometimes I think I love him too much. It's the same way with Derrick. Once he gets healed, he'll spend the rest of his life loving you with everything in him. Unfortunately, he can't please you until he's first pleased with himself."

"Maybe you're right," Staci pondered. She remembered Shannon's insecure days very well. She refilled her glass before she added, "I sure hope you're right."

"Staci, I don't understand something," Lashay questioned. "Why did you marry Derrick if you knew he wasn't ready?"

"Well, to be honest, I was afraid of losing him again. We had just gotten back together, and I was afraid that if we waited, I would lose him. I knew then and still know now that he's my ordained mate, so I figured, as long as he's the right one, the timing didn't matter." She took several sips. "Boy, was I wrong."

"I know if I had married Brian before I matured, it would have been a disaster. I was way too childish," Lashay stated.

"We can all drink to that. You don't have to remind me. I was there," Staci said, then looked at Shannon. "As I recall, you had a lot to do with the game playing."

Shannon lifted her hands in surrender. "Guilty as charged. See, that's what I'm talking about. When you're insecure, you will do things that don't make sense. You will go after things you really don't want and do things you really don't want to—but you can't stop because you're driven by the fear of rejection and insecurity of who you are. I was so mixed up. I completely ignored Brian's constant rejections. The sad part is I didn't really like Brian that way. He didn't like me; I didn't like him. I was just wasting time, chasing after what wasn't mine and delaying my real blessing—Marcus. But Staci, you're not wasting time with Derrick. He loves you. That's what will bring him back."

"I agree with that," Lashay added. "That's what brought me and Brian back together. We loved each other. We were afraid to tell each other, but we loved each other almost from the day we met. It's our love that helped us through the bad times and taught us how to appreciate each other. And you know what? I wouldn't trade anything for what we have now.

"One day you'll feel the same way about Derrick. You'll look back on this and be thankful it happened." Lashay took a bite of s'mores, then asked Shannon. "Did I ever thank you for trying to break me and my boo up?"

Shannon threw a pillow at Lashay. "You know your crazy butt didn't."

"Thank you, girl. I wouldn't be married to the finest lawyer in the world and pregnant without you," Lashay laughed and threw the pillow back.

Staci laughed at her girls. She loved them both, but how much they loved each other amazed her, considering how they met. While Lashay was away in graduate school, Shannon had tried unsuccessfully to steal Brian. In the end, Shannon found Jesus and moved on. Maybe they were right. If God could work out their relationships, He could certainly work out her marriage.

Before the night was over, the three women danced and sang like teenagers, then watched a tearjerker love story.

Staci had to admit, she still felt the emptiness every time she looked at her girls' protruding abdomens. What she would give to have a baby of her own. The decision to abort her child seemed the right thing to do at the time, but she'd since acknowledged that it had been her emotions talking and not her heart.

Around midnight, Staci couldn't fight the urge to talk to Derrick any longer. She left the peppermint-pickle-eating women in the den and went upstairs into her bedroom and dialed his cell number. He answered on the third ring.

"Hello."

"Sorry, I didn't mean to wake you," she spoke just above a whisper.

"Staci, is that you?"

"Yes."

He hesitated before asking, "Is everything all right? Do you need anything?"

"Everything is fine. I just wanted to hear your voice." *Why make up an excuse*, she thought. *He's still my husband.*

"Really?" he sounded surprised.

"I miss you." *There, I've said it. But at least I'm not begging like Shannon did,* she rationalized.

"I miss you, too." His voice was softer than normal. "I'll call you sometime, if that's okay?"

I would much rather have you come home. "That's fine, Derrick." She was going to take Shannon's advice and give him some time. At least he agreed to call. "I'll let you go back to sleep; bye." There was a long pause before the line went dead.

Derrick couldn't go back to sleep. Hearing Staci's voice left his longing for her stronger than it had been hours before. He'd spent most of the evening trying to get her out of his mind. Then, just as he dozed off, she called. He had to see her. He had to hold her. In record time, he was dressed in sweats and in his SUV driving down Highway 24. He didn't know what he was going to say to her; he'd figure it out once he got there. His expectations plummeted, however, when he saw Shannon's and Lashay's cars in the driveway. There was no way he could say what he needed to say with them there. It was 1:00 A.M., too late for them to drive home so he could have some privacy with his wife. He backed out of the driveway and drove back down Tunnel Road.

Chapter 15

Staci nearly strained her neck looking around the sanctuary for Derrick. He hadn't given any indication he would attend church today, but after she'd hung up with him last night, she prayed fervently for him to come. As praise and worship came to a close without Derrick's presence, so did her hopes. That didn't dampen her mood, though. Derrick had said he would call. The sooner they talked, the sooner this mess would be resolved and he'd be back home and in her arms.

No sooner had the minister said the May the Lord watch between me and thee benediction, Staci turned her cell phone on in hopes of a message from Derrick. A smile crept across her face as she checked her voice mail. The smile remained as she listened to her father's message, but she still felt disappointed inside. *"Remember, baby girl, keep your head up. I love you."*

"I love you too, Daddy," Staci mumbled before pressing the number seven key to delete the message. She closed her cell phone and slipped it back into her purse, then she walked across the half-empty sanctuary to join the rest of her family on the dais.

"I'm surprised to see you at church today," Staci smiled at her younger brother.

"Miracles do happen," Craig smiled before giving Staci a hug. "Besides, Mama has been calling me every day leaving prayers on both my home and cell phones. You know the power of a praying mother."

The Simones laughed at the rebellious I-can't-be-saved-yet-because-I'm-still-having-fun Craig.

"It's not funny. Every time I try to do something, I can hear Mama saying, 'You are going to preach one day.' I feel so convicted that I can barely stand to sin anymore."

"Little brother," Marcus joined in, "I've got two words for you: Give up! This is one battle you will not win, trust me. Been there, done that, and got Jesus to prove it."

"I should've had Mama put some prayer on Derrick," Staci laughed, but couldn't conceal the seriousness from her tone.

"We're all praying for Derrick," Pastor Julia said, then in an effort to lift the dark cloud that had instantly settled over them, asked, "Staci, what would you like to do to Derrick?"

"Huh?"

"As long as you want to do bodily harm to him, that's fine, but if you start feeling like you want to see blood or stomp him ten feet in the ground, then we have a problem," Julia explained. "If you feel like you want to throw hot grits or hot grease on him, that's normal." Staci's eyes lit up at that suggestion. "You just want him to feel pain because you feel pain. But, if you start dreaming about his funeral or contemplating running him over with your car or bashing his head in with a sledgehammer, then we all need to lie out in sackcloth and ashes right now!"

Staci laughed. "It's not that bad, Auntie."

"I know; that's why he was at the 8:00 A.M. service," Julia smiled. "He's trying to sort things out."

Both relief and sadness washed over Staci. At least her prayer had been answered. He'd come to church, but she didn't get to see him.

As she walked through the parking lot to her car, Staci felt lonely. Every one of her family members had someone to go home to. Auntie Julia had Pastor Reggie. Lashay had Brian. Marcus had Shannon. She was sure Craig had one or maybe two hopeful young ladies waiting for him. But her house was empty.

Staci waited all week for a call that never came. Every day, she woke up with hope that this was the day Derrick would call and they would start working on their marriage, but that didn't happen. She started to call him, but decided against it. If he wanted to see her, he knew where she lived. If he wanted to talk to her, he had all of her numbers. By Saturday, she came to the realization Derrick didn't want her anymore.

She accepted the sad reality that she was on her way to becoming a single woman. Being single was foreign to her. She'd only been married for a year, but she and Derrick had been a couple since college. When they broke up, her heart still belonged to Derrick; therefore, she didn't consider herself single because she hoped they would reconcile. Staci wasn't afraid of being single; she just didn't know how to do it. She didn't know the rules anymore.

She walked into the kitchen and looked inside the refrigerator. The remnants of a Thai meal from two nights ago didn't appeal to her. She didn't feel like bothering the pizza man tonight, and she didn't feel like watching another DVD. She'd watched them so much she'd begun to memorize dialogues. She'd completed the work she had brought home from the office earlier in the afternoon. There wasn't really anything she needed to do. The house was clean, and the clothes, washed and folded.

Staci stepped out on the lanai. The weather was cool, but bearable. Since whatever she would eat for dinner had to be purchased, she decided to take herself on a dinner date. Back inside her bedroom, she pulled three sets of clothing from her closet. After holding them against her body in the full-length mirror, she selected the purple mélange pantsuit and matching four-inch sling-backs.

She showered and applied light makeup. At the last minute, she pulled the curls from her shoulders and pinned them neatly on the top of her head, leaving a few loose curls hanging down the side of her face. Once dressed, she checked herself in the mirror. "You look good, girl," she said to her reflection.

Staci backed out of the driveway and unto Tunnel Road without any idea of where she was going. When she saw the Interstate 80 turnoff, she decided to check out the new Mexican restaurant at Emery Bay. Using her parking pass, she pulled into her reserved parking spot in the Emery Bay garage. Before pressing the alarm button on her key ring, she buttoned her coat and strapped her purse on her shoulder. The mid-March evening air was average in temperature for this time of year. She inhaled the cool air and could still smell the rain from the night before.

The brick-paved streets of Emery Bay were cluttered with people. This was the norm on Saturday nights. The sixteen-screen movie theater always attracted a nice weekend crowd. This weekend, the latest animated flick released caused couples to flood to the theater with their young children. The plaza was lined with stores and specialty shops and restaurants. It was the perfect place to take a date. It was the kind of place couples could enjoy a delicious meal, then hold hands and stroll the plaza and feast on spectacular views of the Golden Gate and Bay bridges along with the San Francisco skyline. Staci attempted to ignore the passing couples who were doing just that, holding hands and sitting on the iron benches, cuddling. She opted instead to look into the windows of Abercrombie & Fitch, Ann Taylor, and Ethan Allen.

Staci reached her destination and quickly stepped inside the busy restaurant, hoping to eradicate the emptiness that had crept over her. Inside, the wall-to-wall crowded restaurant resembled a Mexican village. Waiters dressed in colorful ponchos scurried about trying to quickly satisfy the noisy crowd with huge trays loaded with the biggest margarita glasses she'd ever seen

"*Hola, señorita,*" the host, wearing a huge sombrero to accompany his poncho, greeted her.

"*Buenas noches*. Table for one, please." Staci felt hot from the sudden change of temperature. She'd just untied the belt on her coat when the host informed her of the half-hour wait. The only thing she had waiting for her was a vacant house, so she gladly took a seat in the already-packed waiting area and stared straight ahead.

I should have brought a book, she thought ten minutes into her wait after the pair seated next to her started kissing. She focused her attention on the tropical fish inside the aquarium opposite her. Every other minute she glanced at her watch until the host offered her a complimentary margarita while she waited.

"No, thank you, but I would like a virgin strawberry daiquiri." Within minutes, the host returned with the frozen fruit drink topped with whipped cream. "Thank you." Staci took a long swig, closed her eyes, and let the cold liquid glide down her parched throat and cool her insides.

"Good evening, beautiful lady. Mind if I sit next to you?"

She didn't see the gentleman who approached her. Staci opened her eyes and looked around and behind her to see who the man was talking to. Once she realized she was his subject, she gave him a brief visual inspection. He wasn't that small, about five feet ten, which is what she was in heels. He was no match for her giant husband, though.

"Certainly you've been called beautiful before," the man said, when she didn't respond to him. "Do you mind if I wait next to you?"

Staci moved her coat onto her lap and made room for him, then turned her attention back to her drink.

A few minutes later, the gentleman intruded on her solitude again. "What is a beautiful woman like you doing dining alone?"

Staci stopped sipping her drink. "Excuse me, Mr. . . ."

"It's Malcolm Leblanc," he answered.

"Mr. Leblanc, how do you know I'm dining alone?" Staci smiled, but her tone wasn't pleasant. The restaurant was hot and stuffy and now dark chocolate Mr. Leblanc was starting to get on her nerves.

"I saw you come in, and I heard you ask for a table for one."

Staci thought the man was nosey, but didn't verbalize it. "Mr. Leblanc, I'm trying to enjoy a peaceful evening alone, but you seem determined to sabotage my plans."

Malcolm appeared to be insulted and backed away. "Sorry, miss, I was just trying to hold a conversation with a beautiful woman to pass the time. Sorry if I offended you." He turned his back to her.

Staci had been out of the game so long that she couldn't tell the difference between flirting and causal conversation. Maybe she was being too hard on him. All the man said was hello.

She tapped his shoulder to get his attention. "Mr. Leblanc, I apologize if I was rude. Thank you for the compliment."

He turned and smiled again. "Please, call me Malcolm. I know there are a lot of predators out here, but I'm not one of them. I haven't bitten a woman in two weeks."

"If you try that now, I'll pour this drink on you," she replied and raised her glass.

Malcolm's chuckle revealed a pair of straight, almost white teeth. "I know, and you'll probably hit me with your purse too."

Staci looked at her watch, and then at him, but remained silent.

"Does the beautiful lady in purple have a name?"

Staci hesitated before answering, "You can call me Staci."

"It's a pleasure to meet you, Staci. Are you from around here?"

"Napa Valley," she answered, before stirring her drink.

"Really? I love Napa Valley. A friend of mine owns a winery there." Malcolm paused. "Maybe I'll take you there one day."

Staci almost choked on her drink. "Malcolm, you don't know me, and you're talking about taking me somewhere?"

"Maybe I'm being a little presumptuous."

"You think?" she replied sarcastically.

"I'll ask you again after we have dinner."

Malcolm smiled again, and this time Staci noted he had a nice smile enclosed by a full set of lips. "Malcolm, I'm not having dinner with you. I'm eating alone."

"So was I," he answered, not fazed one bit by Staci's sassiness.

The thought of having dinner with a man other than Derrick never occurred to Staci. Maybe it should have. She'd been alone most of the time when Derrick was home, anyway.

"*Señorita* Staci, your table is ready," the host announced.

Malcolm stood. "What do you say, beautiful?"

He's called me beautiful four times in the last twenty minutes, Staci mentally noted. She stood and gathered her coat. "Malcolm, I don't think that's a good idea." She paused. "I'm married."

"I didn't ask you to marry me; just to enjoy a meal with me."

Staci studied the man she stood eye level with. What would it hurt to have dinner with him? A little conversation would help take her mind off of Derrick. She hadn't come here for this, but it was a nice diversion.

"Promise not to bite," Staci teased.

"Scouts honor." Malcolm held up the honor sign.

"Just in case your honor doesn't hold up, I have mace and pepper spray."

"It wouldn't surprise me if you had a piece of steel in that purse," Malcolm said, as he followed her to a booth in the far back corner.

Seated across from him, Staci second-guessed her decision. Being in close proximity with a man other than Derrick didn't feel right.

"Is your husband an old man?" Malcolm asked once he settled into the booth.

The question surprised Staci. "Why would you ask that?" she stuttered.

"Because a man would have to be either old or blind to let a beautiful woman like you leave the house alone without your wedding ring."

Staci quickly looked away, hoping the sadness she felt didn't show on her face. "My husband and I are separated," Staci finally responded, then took a sip of her drink. This was the first time she'd said those words out loud, and they sounded foreign to her.

Malcolm appeared to study her face while taking a drink of water. "Sorry to hear that. How long were you married?"

"A year," she answered just above a whisper.

"*Hola*. May I take your order?" the waitress asked, much to Staci's relief.

After the waitress took their orders for steak fajitas and chicken tacos, Malcolm leaned back and relaxed his arm on the back of the booth. "Staci, tell me about yourself."

Staci caught herself just before she rolled her eyes at him. Hadn't he asked enough personal questions already? "What do you want to know?"

"What brought you to the Bay Area?"

"My job," she answered, without giving any details.

Malcolm leaned forward after the waiter set a basket of warm tortilla chips and salsa on the table. "Let me guess; you're in sales," he asked before dipping a chip.

Staci arched her eyebrows. "Could be. What brought you to the Bay Area?"

"I'm a stockbroker at Smith & Lowe." Malcolm's pride in his job showed through his beaming smile.

Good thing I don't have any accounts there, Staci thought. For some reason the thought of someone as nosey as Mr. Leblanc having access to her financial information didn't sit well with her.

"Do you live here in Emery Bay?" Emery Bay was saturated with luxury apartments and condos populated by urban professionals.

"I could. Where do you live?" Once again she avoided answering his question.

"I live in the new lofts in Jack London Square."

"That's a nice area."

"So you've been there?"

Not only had Staci been there, her Aunt Julia was the developer and Staci and Derrick were invested in two of the luxury lofts. "Once or twice," she answered nonchalantly.

Malcolm watched her dip a chip and admired her ability to control the conversation. "How is it that I ask the questions, but you get all the answers?"

"I've answered every one of your questions." Staci dipped another chip.

"Yet, I don't know anything about you," he responded.

"You know my name, and that I'm a married woman."

Malcolm touched her arm, and Staci stopped chewing. "Staci, you're a beautiful woman. Why are you so tense? And why do you keep reminding me you're married? It's obvious it wasn't a good marriage to have ended in a year."

Staci's cheeks burned with anger. She was angry at herself for sounding like a fool and angry at Malcolm for accurately analyzing her marriage. Suddenly, she wasn't hungry anymore.

"Mr. Leblanc, I wish I could say it was a pleasure meeting you, but that would be a lie." She reached inside her purse for her wallet.

Malcolm waved his hands. "Dinner is on me."

Staci cut her eyes at him. "I don't need any favors from you." She threw two bills on the table to cover food she'd never see, then grabbed her purse and left. She was halfway to her car when she heard someone calling her name. She turned to see Malcolm waving her coat in the air. Staci was so mad she hadn't realized she'd left it.

"You might need this," he said, once he caught up with her.

"Thank you, Mr. Leblanc," she managed through gritted teeth. At that moment, the wind decided to blow, chilling her to the bone.

He held the garment open, and she slid her arms inside. "I'm sorry if I said something wrong back there. I was only trying to help you relax."

"It's not your fault. I should have stayed home," Staci said and tied her belt.

Malcolm observed her eyes change from angry to sad. "Staci, how long have you been separated?"

Staci couldn't explain it, but she felt a sudden calmness draw her to this stranger. She wanted to open up to someone; why not Malcolm? It wasn't like she would ever see him again. "It's only been a month."

"Do you regret leaving him?"

Malcolm's voice was so alluring; Staci couldn't help divulging her personal business. "I didn't leave him. He left me," she whispered, then turned away from him. She was embarrassed to admit she wasn't able to hold her husband's interest. Malcolm turned her face back to him, and she jumped at his warm touch.

"Staci, you're a beautiful woman, and any man who would leave you is a fool." His voice changed from soft to firm. "It's not your fault he left."

She took a step backward. "Thank you, Malcolm, but I really should get going," she stuttered.

Malcolm reached inside his jacket and handed her his card. "I'd like to keep in touch with you." Staci hesitated before accepting it. "I know separation is a hard thing. Sometimes all you need is an ear to listen and a shoulder to cry on. I know we've just met, but I'd like to be that person for you."

Malcolm's presence confused Staci so much, she didn't know if that was a good idea or not. What she did know was that she would love to have someone other than a family member to talk to. What she did next went against what she'd been taught about relationships, but what could it hurt? Maybe God had sent her there to meet Malcolm. Maybe he could offer her a male perspective and help her understand Derrick.

Staci ignored the warning her conscience sent and handed him her business card.

"Wow," Malcolm said, after reading her card, "Chief operating officer? Beauty and brains. Simone." Malcolm repeated her last name a few times, like he was trying to remember something. "Are you related to the gospel artist, Marcus Simone?"

"Could be," she smiled, then hurriedly walked away.

On the drive home, Staci was more confused than ever. The closer she got to her home, the more she regretted her decision to connect with Malcolm. At least she hadn't given him her home number, she reasoned. She made a mental note to have Chloe screen her calls. To make sure she didn't call him, she threw his card away.

It wasn't until after she was home and had changed into her pajamas did she notice the message light on her answering machine. She savored a spoonful of Chunky Monkey before pressing the Playback button.

"Hello, Staci, it's me. Just calling to see how you're doing. I miss you. Talk to you later."

"If you really wanted to talk to me, you would have called my cell," she mumbled and at the same time deleted Derrick's message. She'd totally forgotten she'd left her cell phone at home. She was not going to call him, at least not tonight. She'd waited an entire week for him. Now he could wait for her.

Chapter 16

The intercom interrupted Staci's train of thought. "Mr. Leblanc from Smith & Lowe is on line one."

"Shoot!" Staci grumbled. She'd totally forgotten about having Chloe screen her calls. At church yesterday, she'd prayed and felt peace about her marriage being mended back together, but that peace soon faded when Derrick didn't answer her call last night. "Oh well, if Derrick won't talk to me, someone else will," she decided and picked up the extension.

"Hello, Malcolm," she answered cautiously.

"Hello, my new friend."

The jubilance in his voice made her smile. "Still presumptuous, don't you think, considering we've just met?"

"Staci, Staci. I'm going to have to do something to make you relax."

"What do you have in mind, Mr. Leblanc?" *Oops. Am I flirting?*

"Dinner and a movie."

Staci sounded surprised. "Are you asking me out on a date?"

"Of course not. I wouldn't dare ask a married woman out on a date, but I would ask a friend."

"Whether therefore ye eat, or drink, or whatsoever ye do, do all to the glory of God. How am I getting glory from you dating?"

Staci reasoned with the still small voice. *What can an innocent dinner and movie hurt? Nothing out of order is going to happen. Malcolm knows I'm a married woman.*

"When?" she finally responded to Malcolm, after shifting the phone to her right ear.

"Now we're making progress. You pick a night." Malcolm didn't make any attempt to hide his excitement. "I'm available anytime you need me to be."

Staci had a thought. "What about your significant other?"

"I'm not married, and I don't have a girlfriend, if that's what you're asking."

Staci wondered why she felt happy to hear that, but didn't linger on the thought. "How about Thursday?" She didn't want to miss her Wednesday night Bible Study.

"Perfect. Where shall I pick you up?"

Staci hadn't thought about that, but under no circumstances would she allow him to come to her home. "Why don't I just meet you somewhere?"

"Do you like surf & turf?"

"I love it."

"Good, I'll meet you at Skates at six o'clock."

"I'll see you there," she said, wondering what on earth she was doing.

"Staci," she heard him call before hanging up.

"Yes."

"Feel free to use my number any time. I'm always available to you."

"Thank you. I'll see you on Thursday." She couldn't remember the last time Derrick was available to her for anything other than occasional sex.

Staci sat at her desk and wondered if she'd lost her mind. Why in the world had she agreed to have dinner with a man she barely knew? She really didn't want to go anywhere with Malcolm Leblanc. In actuality, she didn't care if she ever spoke to the man again. She wasn't attracted to him at all. He wasn't ugly; he just wasn't her type. But he was available.

She looked at her watch and thought of Derrick. By now, he was probably busy with his morning patients.

"I'll call him later," she whispered, before packing her briefcase and preparing to meet the contractor at the new Corte Madera site. But she couldn't wait. She missed him too much. No sooner had she merged onto Interstate 80, she dialed his cell phone.

"Hello, Staci."

Hearing his live voice made her so happy, she almost giggled. "Hi. Did I catch you at a bad time?"

"No, you can never catch me at a bad time." Actually, his first patient was a root canal that took longer than expected. Derrick was running thirty minutes behind. "Sorry I called at a bad time last night."

Then why didn't you call me this morning, she was about to ask, then remembered on Mondays she doesn't turn her phone on until ten o'clock. Staci listened to him breathe on the phone for a few seconds.

"How are you doing?" he asked too calmly for her.

"What on earth do you mean? How am I doing at work? How am I doing at church? How am I doing with my new exercise routine? Or do you want to know how I'm dealing with the fact that you left me?" Staci didn't mean to sound bitter, but how could he ask her that knowing he was the reason her world had been turned upside down?

"Staci, I am sorry about all of this. Please try to understand I need some time to figure things out. I wish there was something I could do to make it up to you."

Staci conceded, "Derrick, I don't want you to do anything you don't want to do."

"Thanks for understanding."

Her smile was gone, now replaced with the silent tears she vowed never to shed. Derrick was supposed to say he missed her and wanted to come home, but he didn't.

"Anytime," she whispered before pressing the red End call button.

"Derrick, I brought you some lunch." It was Rhonda. "I knew you wouldn't have a chance to go out, so I picked up some Zachary's."

Derrick was starved. He'd worked straight through lunch, forgetting he no longer had the arsenal of edible treats Staci normally stocked in his refrigerator.

"Thank you, Rhonda. Come on in. How did you know Zachary's is one of my favorites?"

"I've been watching you, and, Derrick, you're a simple man to figure out."

"You think so?" Derrick questioned, just before he opened the box containing the spinach and chicken Chicago-style stuffed pizza. "My wife wouldn't agree with you."

Rhonda pulled up a chair alongside his desk and sat only a few inches away from him. "You don't talk about your wife. Why is that?" she asked, placing a slice on her paper plate.

Derrick looked confused. "What do you mean I don't talk about my wife?"

"I know you're married from your wedding picture, but you never talk about her, and you don't wear a wedding band," Rhonda pointed out before cutting into her slice.

"I can understand the ring part because you work with your hands, but what about the day she showed up and you introduced her as only Staci and not as your wife. Then you made a lunch date with me. You never showed, but I bet she doesn't know that." Rhonda smiled. "We've had several conversations since, and you haven't mentioned her at all. What's that all about?"

He didn't like her summary of him, but it was the truth. "Since you think I'm so easy to figure out, why don't you tell me?" He took a bite of pizza and listened.

"It's obvious you're not happy at home, and you want out. I think you're attracted to someone else who has piqued your interest. Someone you work with and who is definitely interested in you." She let the words digest. "I would even venture to say you don't love your wife. Perhaps it's one of those 'cheaper to keep her' things, considering your profession." Rhonda arched an eyebrow and simultaneously rested a hand on his thigh. "Am I right, Derrick?"

Derrick dropped his pizza onto the plate. The bile in his stomach wouldn't allow him to eat another bite. Rhonda was right. He wasn't happy, but it wasn't Staci's fault. It was his. Derrick removed her hand and stood straight up.

"Rhonda, let me get something straight. I love my wife and will always love her. As long as she lives I will love no one else. No matter how many lunches or conversations you and I share, nothing will change that. And you can keep your hands to yourself. I am not now, nor have I ever been, attracted to you. I enjoy your company, and you stroke my ego, but I love Staci with every cell in my body. I wouldn't be half the person I am today if it weren't for her and the love she gives me."

Rhonda's mouth opened and closed several times before she was able to form words. "Well, I didn't mean to upset you, but thanks for the feel. I'd love to see that muscle in a pair of shorts." She stood and gathered her food. "I'd better get going." Before she opened the door she turned and said, "I have one question for you. If you love your wife so much, why do you live in the studio above the office? One would think with all that love going on, you'd live under the same roof."

Derrick didn't have an answer for her, at least one that he wanted to give. "Rhonda, my relationship with my wife is none of your business. If you want to continue working here, I suggest you remember that."

After Rhonda left, Derrick leaned back in his chair with his eyes closed. He rubbed his forehead and reflected on his earlier conversation with his wife. He didn't mean to make her cry. Sure, she tried to hide the tears, but he had heard the sniffles.

"Why can't I stop hurting you?" he asked her photo image.

"Because you can't stop hurting yourself." The voice was back.

Staci deserved better than he was capable of giving her. He made a decision right then and there: he wouldn't talk to her again until he was able to do so without causing her more pain.

Chapter 17

"Thank you," Staci said and accepted the hard hat from the foreman. She followed aimlessly behind him as he showed her the inside of the new store. His mouth was moving, but she didn't have a clue about what he was saying. Her mind was cluttered with her latest brief conversation with Derrick. She wanted to do something to him so he would hurt like she hurt. Something to make him understand how much she needed him. On the way to Corte Madera, she started to turn around and head to his office to tell him off, but she missed the last exit before crossing the San Rafael Bridge. It wouldn't have solved anything anyway. Just would have made her look like a fool.

"Miss Simone, are you satisfied?" the foreman asked.

"Excuse me?" Staci hadn't heard one word he'd said. "I'm sorry, but my mind wandered off."

The foreman's twisted facial expression said he wasn't too happy about her having wasted his time and breathe. He repeated himself. This time Staci pushed Derrick out of her mind and paid close attention.

"Did you understand me this time, Miss Simone? Or do I need to repeat myself again?"

The foreman smiled, and Staci wanted to slap the silly grin off his face. She was mad at her husband, but Mr. Foreman had just earned the right to take the wrath meant for Derrick.

"Mr. whatever your name is," she began, "would you speak to my brother or any other man in that manner?"

"A man would have understood me the first time," the foreman smirked.

"Oh really? I have something for you to understand." Staci paused, then said, "You're fired! Do you understand that, or do I need to repeat it? Maybe I should find a man to explain it to you!" Staci removed the hard hat and pushed it against his chest, then stomped away.

When she returned to her office she was still mad. Chloe waited until the smoke settled from the heat of her slamming the door before giving Staci her messages.

"Thanks," Staci said, without looking up.

"Staci, are you crazy?" Marcus stormed into her office. No doubt Mr. Smart-mouthed Foreman had phoned. "You can't fire him after he's completed most of the work and without good cause."

Staci rolled her eyes. "He shouldn't have gotten smart with me."

"What did he say?"

Staci told him.

"You don't think the man had a right to be a little upset after spending all that time showing you around when you weren't paying any attention?"

"I was too mad at Derrick to focus on that weasel," she snapped.

Marcus folded his arms across his chest. "So you fired a very good contractor, whom, I might add, has stayed well under budget—without cause—because you're mad at Derrick?"

Staci leaned back in her chair. It was her time to fold her arms. "Maybe I didn't handle that properly."

"Do you really think so?"

"Big head, you can save the sarcasm." She rolled her eyes once again.

"You better stop rolling your eyes before they get stuck."

Staci conceded. "Look, I know I overreacted. I'll call him tomorrow."

"No need. I hired him back after I apologized for your irrational behavior. To keep this from happening again, from here on out, I'll deal with him." He gave a look that dared her to protest.

"Whatever, big head; you're the boss. Now get out of my office." Staci picked up the stapler from her desk and raised it in the air, aiming for Marcus.

"Is this any way to treat your brother *and* the man who pays your six-figure salary?"

"Get out!" She lifted the stapler higher.

"I'm leaving, but baby girl, you really need to separate work from your personal life. I know it's not easy, but you have to try. If you don't, you're going to let this situation with Derrick destroy you. You're stronger than that. You can handle this."

After Marcus left, Staci lay her head on the desk. "God, please help me deal with this," she prayed. Sifting through her messages, she started to return her mother's call first, but then she saw his message. Malcolm had called and left his number.

Staci stared at his number. Maybe this was God's way of helping her deal with the situation. She'd thrown Malcolm's number away, and now when she needed someone to talk to . . .

"I am not the author of confusion. Talk to me."

Staci ignored the voice and dialed the number. Hearing Malcolm's voice come on the line, she started to hang up, but it was too late.

"Hello," he said for the second time.

"Malcolm, it's me, Staci."

"You sound sad. Is everything all right?"

"I've been better," she sighed.

"You sound like you need a boost. I can meet you in an hour if you want to talk about it," Malcolm offered.

Staci pondered his suggestion. It wasn't a good idea. "I don't think I should do that."

"Why not? You want to."

Staci couldn't deny that she wanted to talk to someone. When she didn't respond, he continued. "I'll meet you at the new Mexican place in an hour, and this time, stay for the entire meal. It'll give me the chance to redeem myself." Before she could answer, the line went dead. When she called him back, he didn't answer.

"What am I doing?" she asked herself. She asked the same question again an hour later when she walked through the doors of the Mexican restaurant. This wasn't right. She couldn't fill the emptiness like this. Staci decided to leave, but before she could turn to leave, Malcolm approached her carrying a floral bouquet.

"Good evening, my beautiful friend." He bore such a jubilant smile, Staci couldn't help but return his with one of her own.

"You're awfully happy this evening."

"I'm always happy to be in the company of a beautiful woman." Malcolm's dark eyes captured hers as he stepped closer. "You're more beautiful than I remember."

A shiver ran down Staci's back at the sound of his voice, and she redirected her eyes to the flowers. "Who are those for?"

"For my friend, of course." Malcolm held the flowers out to her.

"Thank you." She accepted them and tried to remember the last time Derrick had given her flowers, but couldn't.

"Our table is ready." Malcolm delicately placed his arm around her waist and led her to the booth. His touch made her uneasy, and she stepped out of his grip. Once they were seated and had placed their orders, Staci relaxed.

"Tell me what's on your mind," Malcolm said, offering Staci his full attention.

She sipped her virgin Strawberry Daiquiri. "You go first."

"Tell me about Mr. Simone."

His request confused her. Why did he want to know about her father? "What?"

"I want to know everything about the man, so I can make sure I don't follow in his footsteps."

It was then she realized he thought Simone was her married name. She didn't deem it necessary to correct him. "What footsteps might that be?" Staci said, before taking another sip.

"The ones he used to break your heart," Malcolm answered, before taking a sip of his drink.

Staci didn't like hearing those words, although it was the truth. Derrick not only broke her heart, he'd crushed it. "You don't have anything to worry about. We're only friends, remember? Besides, there isn't much to tell about my husband."

Malcolm wasn't convinced. "How did you meet Mr. Simone?"

"We met in college."

Malcolm appeared to ponder. "Let me guess. He was a ballplayer, and you were captain of the cheerleading squad."

Staci was taken aback at how close his guess had been. She wasn't captain of the cheerleading squad, but she was certainly number seventy-two's biggest fan back then. "Something like that." She dipped her chip into the salsa.

"What happened? What made you stop cheering?"

"People change," was her reply, but inside, she knew Derrick hadn't changed that much. She had just overlooked his issues back then. Her feelings for him hadn't changed either. If he walked into the restaurant right now, she'd run into his arms.

"You didn't answer me the other night. Is your husband the gospel artist?"

"No, he's not." Malcolm didn't need to know Marcus is her brother and business partner. "He's not a musician; he's a dentist." Relief washed over her when the waitress delivered her chicken Caesar salad; she was tired of his questions. "Tell me about your family. Where are you from?" she asked after saying grace out loud. Malcolm sat back and watched.

"I grew up in Fresno. I'm an only child. Both of my parents are deceased," he answered before cutting into his steak.

"Sorry to hear that."

"Don't be."

Staci didn't care for the way he dismissed the passing of his parents, but let it pass. The rest of the meal she shared vague details about her family, but what Malcolm seemed to be interested in most was her relationship with her husband.

"You've known your husband since college. Does that mean he's the only lover you've known?"

Staci choked on a tortilla strip and had to wash it down with water. "Malcolm, the number of lovers in my past or present is none of your business."

"You're right. It's none of my business." Malcolm studied her face. "What happened? What made the two of you grow apart?"

"Stop talking!" the voice warned, but Staci ignored it.

"Several things. For one, we stopped communicating; then he stopped spending time with me," Staci answered against her better judgment. She went on to tell Malcolm about the late nights and his refusal to communicate with her.

Malcolm took a sip of water before planting the seed. "Do you think he's having an affair with someone at his office? Or maybe he's gay."

Staci shook her head. "No, my husband is not gay, of that I'm certain. He's not having an affair either." The idea of Derrick and Rhonda being intimately involved had crossed her mind, but she believed Derrick when he assured her nothing was going on between them. Derrick was an introvert and selfish, but he wasn't a liar.

"Are you sure?" Malcolm placed his hand on top of hers. "Why else would a man choose to spend all of his time away from home when he has someone as beautiful as you at home waiting for him?"

Staci snatched her hand away. "I'm positive." She wasn't going to tell him about Derrick's insecurities. "My husband may be insensitive and inconsiderate, but he's not a cheat."

"I don't mean to upset you, but it does make sense."

"That's because you don't know my husband." Staci amazed herself. Derrick walked out on her, and here she was defending him.

Malcolm must have sensed he wasn't going to get anywhere and changed the subject. "Tell me, what do you like to do for fun? Do you have any hobbies?"

Fun, that's something she hadn't had in a long time, at least with a man. She and Derrick used to enjoy attending art festivals or touring Napa Valley from a hot air balloon. Sometimes they would go rollerblading, then have a picnic in the park. What she loved most were the long drives up Highway 101 into the mountains. During those times, they would talk and laugh and share each other's dreams. They shared their first kiss parked on the shoulder in the midst of the California Redwood Forest.

"That depends on what area you're talking about. I have fun at church, but I also have fun working." She thought that was a safe answer. Malcolm didn't need to know her recreational activity.

"I wouldn't consider attending church and going to work every day fun."

Staci chuckled. "You would if you attended my church. As for work, I'm the COO, remember? I don't have to work every day. I do it because I enjoy my job."

Malcolm tried another jab. "Why do you work? If I were your husband, the only work I'd want you to do is on me."

The thought of doing anything sexual with Malcolm Leblanc made her stomach turn. "That's why you'll never be my husband, or boyfriend, for that matter," she responded and watched the smile on his face disappear. "I work because I have the brains to do the job and because I want to."

"So the money you make has nothing to do with it?" he asked.

Really it didn't. Staci was from a wealthy family. Having money was nothing new to her. She lived very comfortably off of the six figures Marcus pays her, considering she didn't have a mortgage or car payments. With her trust fund, real estate investments, stocks, and Derrick's income, Staci was a multimillionaire. But Malcolm didn't need to know all that. "Like I said, I work because I want to."

"Not me. I work because I enjoy making money. The more money I make, the more power I gain," Malcolm explained.

Staci didn't agree with that assessment.

"I have enough money to make you forget all about that little dentist salary," he said once again, referring to her husband's deficiency.

"I wouldn't exactly consider a dentist salary little, but it doesn't matter. I didn't marry for money." She took a sip of her drink before bluntly stating, "Malcolm, you don't have enough money to buy me. I am not for sale. There's nothing you can do for me that I can't do for myself. There's nothing you can buy me that I can't buy myself. In fact, I won't accept any gifts from you because I don't want you to think I owe you anything."

Malcolm's jaws flinched. Never before had a woman insulted him like that. Women usually worshipped him after he told them how much money he made, but not this one. She'd basically told him he wasn't good enough for her. He wouldn't use the word *confident* to describe Staci. *Arrogant* was more like it. Malcolm didn't like arrogance in anyone, other than himself, but he'd tolerate it from Staci since she was the sexiest woman he'd been with in a while.

"Staci, I wasn't trying to buy you," he finally responded in an even tone.

"Then we have an understanding." The cocky smile lacked warmth.

"Is it acceptable for me to pay for dinner, or would that be considered an attempt to buy you?" he asked when the check came.

Staci laughed and tilted her head to the side. "It would take a lot more than a chicken Caesar salad to buy me. I'll allow you to pay for dinner—this time."

He placed enough money on the table to cover the bill and a hefty tip.

They stepped out into the plaza as the sun was setting. "I'm not ready to go home," Staci announced, then turned to Malcolm. "Are you in a hurry? I would love to catch a movie."

Malcolm's feelings were still hurt, but the thought of sitting next to her in a dark theater excited him.

"Sure, Miss Simone. I'll take you as far as you want to go."

"I don't believe it!" Rhonda exclaimed.

"What are you talking about?" her sister asked.

Rhonda pointed toward theater twelve. "That's my boss's wife over there with that man in the tan suit."

Her sister looked in the direction. "I assume the man she's with is not your wonderful and fine Dr. Garrison?"

Rhonda waved her hand at her sister. "Girl, please, Dr. Garrison is much bigger and more gorgeous than that Martin Lawrence look-alike."

Rhonda observed how much attention the man gave Staci. For sure he wasn't her brother or close relative. The look in his eyes said he wanted her, and the smile on Staci's face said she didn't mind his affections. After Derrick's "I'm so in love" speech that afternoon, Rhonda thought it best to leave Dr. Garrison alone. Based on what she observed now, Mrs. Garrison didn't share those amorous feelings for Derrick as he had for her. "There's a chance for me after all," Rhonda told her sister.

Chapter 18

Staci caught the phone on the fifth ring after checking the caller ID. "Hello, Mom," she answered and dropped her jacket and briefcase on the bed.

"I didn't wake you, did I?" Alaina asked.

"No, I'm just getting in." No sooner had Staci said those words she wanted to take them back. It was nearly midnight, and her mother would want to know what had kept her out so late on a weeknight.

"It's not the end of the quarter, is it?" Alaina questioned. Normally, at the end of each quarter, Staci worked longer hours, but that wasn't the case today.

"No, Mama. I went and saw a movie."

On the other end of the phone, Alaina remained silent. Staci just knew her mother's discernment was about to kick in. "How did it feel to go the movies alone?"

Staci stuttered. "I didn't go alone; I went with a friend."

By the time Alaina started her speech, Staci had stepped out of her clothes and was ready for the shower.

"Staci, I know you're a grown woman, and I know I raised you right. So I know you know better than to go out on a date while you're married."

"Mama, it wasn't a date." *Or was it?* she thought. "He's just someone I met the other evening at the new Mexican restaurant near the store."

"You shouldn't be starting new male friendships while you and Derrick are separated."

"It's okay, Mama. I told Malcolm I'm married."

"That doesn't matter. How would you feel if Derrick made new female friends and sat in a dark theater next to them all evening?"

At the moment, Staci didn't care what Derrick did. Like Malcolm had said, Derrick was a fool for leaving her.

"Mama, why don't you have this discussion with your son-in-law? If he hadn't walked out on me, I wouldn't have this problem," Staci snapped.

"No, if you had listened to me and waited until Derrick was healed before you married him, you wouldn't have this problem!" her mother snapped right back. "Staci, you're wrong, and you know it."

She did know it, but what was she to do now? She and Malcolm had plans for Thursday, and tonight they had decided to drive down, on Saturday, to Monterey to the aquarium. How was she supposed to cancel without hurting Malcolm's feelings? To be honest, she didn't want to cancel. She enjoyed the company and attention.

"Mama, you're right," she sighed. "I shouldn't be spending time with Malcolm." *And after this weekend I'll stop,* she added inwardly.

"You do want your marriage to work, don't you?" her mother asked.

A month ago, even earlier today, Staci would have immediately said yes. But at this moment, she wasn't so sure. Her emotions were in such turmoil, she couldn't think straight. She'd once prided herself on her ability to make sound solid decisions. But today, the combination of hormones and a broken heart had her brain twisted like a pretzel.

"I want whatever the will of the Lord is for my life," she finally answered.

"Then don't complicate things by involving an unnecessary third party."

Staci half-listened to her mother lecture a few minutes more before saying good night and ending the call.

Following her shower, she was too tired for her nightly Bible reading. The next morning, she did say a quick prayer before leaving. She didn't notice, but she didn't mention Derrick in her prayer.

Derrick,

I'm sorry if I crossed the line yesterday. Please accept my apology.

Enjoy.

Derrick placed the card on his desk and opened his refrigerator. Rhonda had stocked it with his favorite snacks. He hated to admit it, but Rhonda did know him very well. She knew what he liked, and she was a good listener. He could talk to her without her asking too many questions he didn't want to answer. She didn't hold him accountable for anything, unlike his wife. Staci wanted his soul.

He picked up the phone and called his office manager. "Phyllis, can you bring me fifty dollars from petty cash?"

"Be there in a minute." Phyllis was always extraperky and efficient. That's what made him hire her in the first place. "Here you are, Dr. Garrison." The middle-aged woman's smile showed nearly all of her teeth.

"Thanks." Derrick retrieved the cash from Phyllis. "Will you send Rhonda in, please?"

"Not a problem," Phyllis answered, but instead of leaving, she added, "Dr. Garrison, I think Rhonda likes you."

"I know she does," Derrick responded with a shrug.

"I can talk to her, if you want," Phyllis offered.

"Thanks, but I'll handle this one myself, but for potential legal reasons, I need you to stay and witness this."

Phyllis disappeared, and Rhonda entered a moment later wearing a big grin. "You wanted to see me?" she asked and helped herself to a chair, not realizing Phyllis had come in behind her.

"Yes," Derrick began. "I wanted to pay you for going shopping for me. In the future, that won't be necessary." He watched her smile vanish. "Here is fifty dollars." He held the money out to her. "This should cover the bill and something for gas."

"You don't have to pay me, Derrick," Rhonda started to protest, but stopped when she heard Phyllis clear her throat. She suddenly turned, and Phyllis gave her a warning stare.

"I mean, Dr. Garrison," Rhonda corrected.

"Yes, I do. Shopping for me is not part of your job description."

Rhonda's face distorted, and Derrick wondered if she wanted to scream and ask if having lunch with him and listening to all that crap about how much he loved his wife was part of her job description.

"And Rhonda, no more lunches either. From here on out, Phyllis or I will handle my lunch plans and my shopping."

"No problem, Dr. Garrison." Rhonda left without another word.

Chapter 19

"This is so good," Staci said after biting into her Cajun shrimp, while seated at a table overlooking the bay. She loved Bubba Gump's as much as she loved the movie *Forrest Gump*.

"I'm glad you like it," Malcolm said.

After talking on the phone every day and dinner at Skates, they were spending the day in the beautiful seaside town of Monterey. Monterey was a beautiful, historical town, where sea and land literally kissed. Monterey was once a thriving seaport for the sardine-packing industry. Now it was home to world-famous restaurants and specialty shops, along with world-class wines.

The first part of the morning they toured the two-story renowned Monterey Bay Aquarium overlooking the clear blue peninsula and the California coastline. While strolling down the waterfront district on Cannery Row, Staci browsed the art galleries and boutiques and purchased a few items for her home. She even treated herself to some saltwater taffy, something she hadn't had in years.

Malcolm's eyes bulged when she purchased a sculpture with a $5,000 price tag and a painting that carried a $10,000 tag. He didn't like it when she asked him to wait outside before placing her credit card on the counter and giving the store owner the shipping address.

"You were right, Staci, there's nothing I can buy you that you can't buy yourself," he said when she joined him on the sidewalk. "Are you sure Dr. Simone won't mind you spending money like that?"

"Not at all." That was true. Derrick had always encouraged her to buy what she liked, as long as they could afford it, and they could. Despite the separation, Derrick still made his deposits into their accounts as if he was home.

Malcolm watched her devour the shrimp and became more fascinated with her. Who was she, really? Never before had he met anyone like her. She was beautiful and had more independence than he liked. Would she be able to walk away from the obvious life of luxury her husband provided? In the past, his women were needy and gullible. All he had to do was show them his platinum card or a wad of cash and they would do anything he wanted, but not Staci. She wouldn't even tell him where she lived and wouldn't exchange her home number. But he did manage to get her cell number after dinner on Thursday.

She wouldn't let him touch her either. Whenever he reached for her hand, she'd ignore it. If he placed his hand around her waist, she'd step away from him. Right now, he wanted to reach over and kiss her lips. That's what a good friend would do, he smirked.

Staci, too engrossed in her own thoughts, didn't notice the smirk on Malcolm's face. Her mother's words warning her not to get involved with Malcolm bombarded her thoughts. She'd planned to end communication with him after today, but there was something about him that wouldn't let her. In a short period of time, she'd gotten used to his company and conversation. In fact, she'd gotten so relaxed, an hour ago, while walking along the beach, she confided in him about how unfulfilling her sex life had been. That was a definite no-no, and she knew it, but the more she talked to Malcolm, the easier it became to divulge Derrick's shortcomings.

It also became easier to talk negative about her husband. That's something she'd never done before. In the past, she would cover Derrick no matter what. Now, she found herself referring to him as sorry and pitiful, much to Malcolm's agreement.

Derrick had been gone for five weeks. At first she thought she wanted and needed him. She'd prayed for him and tried to understand his need for space. But after one week of knowing Malcolm, she wasn't sure she wanted Derrick back. In fact, she wasn't sure she still wanted to be married. Malcolm constantly made it clear to her that Derrick didn't want her. At first, she didn't agree with his assessment, but the more she heard it, the more it made sense.

"Staci, when are you filing for divorce, or have you already?"

She stopped eating. Filing for divorce had never crossed her mind. If there was going to be a divorce, she wasn't going to file for it.

"I'm not divorcing my husband," she answered frankly.

"Why not? You can't stay separated forever. You have to go on with your life."

Her father had told her the same thing; he just didn't mean go on by spending time with another man.

"I am going on with my life, but my husband is very much part of my life," she answered. *I can't believe I said that!*

"But he's a lousy husband, and he left you," Malcolm retorted.

"Can't argue with you there, but he's still my husband, and I love him." Staci's declaration of love surprised both her and Malcolm.

"How can you still love him after he's made it clear he doesn't love you?"

Was it clear? Staci wasn't so sure. True, Derrick hadn't told her he loved her in months, but the thought that he really didn't love her anymore was too much for her to consider.

"I'm not sure my husband doesn't love me. If he doesn't, he'll serve me with papers. Until that happens, I'm not doing anything."

Malcolm started to leave her sitting in Monterey, but remembered he didn't drive his car. Staci had insisted on taking her car, thinking if Malcolm turned out to be crazy, the authorities would be able to locate her because of the tracking device in her Benz.

Again, recognizing his inability to control his environment, he exhaled deeply in frustration. He had to figure out how to remove her absent husband completely from the equation. That, or get Staci in bed with him. Malcolm liked the second option.

"Girl, where have you been?" Lashay asked upon stepping into Staci's living room.

"I think a better question is, what have you been doing, and with whom?" Shannon corrected.

"Whatever you've been doing, I hope you've been doing it with Derrick," Lashay added with a raised eyebrow.

Staci loved her girls, but sometimes they acted like her mother. Staci was a grown woman and didn't owe either of them an explanation.

"What are you talking about? I've been around," she replied to Lashay's and Shannon's questions, knowing full well what they were referring to.

"You've been around where? We haven't seen or heard much from you in three weeks."

They were right. Staci had been spending most of her time with Malcolm. When they weren't physically together, they talked on the phone.

"And you've missed church and Bible Study two weeks in a row." Lashay narrowed her eyebrows. "Please tell us you've been having private study time with Derrick."

Staci smacked her lips and simultaneously waved her hand. "Please, I haven't seen or talked to that sorry half Negro in weeks."

Lashay and Shannon looked at each other, then back at Staci. "Then *who* have you been spending time with?" Shannon asked.

Staci walked over and sat on the couch. "He's just a friend."

"He?" the two women asked in unison.

"His name is Malcolm, and he's just a friend."

"Then why is he taking up all of your time?" Shannon wanted to know.

"We have a lot of things in common. He's single. I'm single, so we hang out together," Staci answered, shrugging her shoulders.

"Staci, you're not single. You're a married woman," Lashay reminded her.

Staci jumped up and walked around the living room, then the kitchen. "Do you see my husband around here?" she asked, looking around. "Of course, you don't. He left me, remember?"

"What happened to you giving him time to work through his issues?" Lashay asked.

"I am giving him time; I'm just keeping busy in the process. Besides, he could have changed his mind about wanting to be married. Or maybe he's found him a friend to pass the time with." Staci used two fingers for quote marks to emphasize the word *friend*. "For all I know, he could be living with a woman."

Inside, Staci prayed that wasn't the case, but like Malcolm had said, it made sense considering Derrick hadn't called her in weeks, and he never told her where he moved to.

"Staci," Shannon shook her head, "in your heart you know that's not the case."

"No, I don't!" Staci screamed. "All I know is that I was a good wife to him and he left me!"

"Cuz, what you're doing is wrong, no matter how much you try to justify it." When Lashay tried to touch her shoulder, Staci jerked away.

"Lashay, what do you know? Has Brian ever left you? Have you spent one day or a minute, for that matter, wondering if Brian still loves you?" Staci didn't allow her to answer. "Or course, you haven't. Your husband acts like he can't use the bathroom without you!"

"Staci, don't say that." Shannon attempted to calm her down.

"You don't know anything either, Shannon. My brother worships you. All he talks about is 'Shannon this . . .' 'my baby Shannon . . .' 'I love my boo.'" Staci imitated Marcus's voice. "You don't know what it's like not to remember the last time your husband said he loved you." Staci wiped the lone tear that managed to escape.

When Lashay placed her fists at her waist, her stomach looked even larger; like she was overdue. "We don't know that because we had enough patience to wait until our men were developed before we married them." Lashay's words slapped Staci smack in the face. "Instead of criticizing what we don't know, you need to ask God to deliver you from that impatient spirit that controls you before you create a bigger mess!"

"You said yourself you married Derrick because you didn't want to wait," Shannon added. "Now you're willing to break your vows because you don't want to wait for him to get healed. That doesn't make any sense."

"I'm not going to break my vows." Staci slid back on the couch. "Malcolm knows I'm married."

Shannon waved her hands. "Rewind. This man *knows* you're married, and he *still* wants to spend all this time with you?"

"Yes, I told you we're just friends."

"Just how often do you see each other?" Lashay probed.

"At least three nights a week and the weekends."

Lashay wouldn't let up. "How often do you talk to him?"

"Every day."

"Friends, nothing. You are in a full-fledged relationship with his trifling behind," Lashay said before positioning herself in the chair. "And you're trifling too for having a boyfriend on the side."

"How many times do I have to tell you, we're just friends!"

"He is *not* your friend. He's a void filler for you. You're using him to fill the emptiness left by Derrick," Shannon plainly stated. "And he's waiting for you to get lonely and weak enough to invite him into your bed."

Staci disagreed with that. Well, at least the last part. "I've told him repeatedly that nothing is going to happen between us."

"It doesn't matter what you say if you keep spending all of your time with him," Lashay explained. "If he wasn't trying to get you into bed, why do you have to keep repeating it? You would only have to tell a legitimate brother once."

"And a legit brother would encourage you to talk to your husband and not to him," Shannon added.

Staci remained quiet. Her girls were right. Malcolm constantly threw sexual innuendoes. Like the other day when he said he had a taste for something sweet while looking at her breasts. She always ignored him, but she had to admit it felt good to know that she was still desirable to someone. He also never corrected her when she spoke negatively about her husband. Malcolm still didn't know his name, but what Malcolm did know from Staci was that her husband was lousy, both in and out of bed.

"You're right," Staci finally conceded. "I am in a relationship."

"You've got to end all communication with him. That is, if you want your husband back."

"Lashay, I don't know what I want," Staci admitted. "Some days I want him back, other days I don't know. I wish he would talk to me."

Shannon arose from her seat, rubbing her belly. "He will when he's ready, but, girlfriend, you need to talk to God about this. You need to ask Him for direction. Most important, you need to pray for Derrick. Pray for his healing."

"You're right, and I will."

Before she went to bed that night, Staci started to pray, but her cell phone rang. It was Malcolm. She didn't pray that night or any other night. Neither did she stop communicating with Malcolm.

Chapter 20

While parked across the street from Miss Cora's house, Staci replenished her lipstick one last time, using the visor mirror. She then fingered her curls once more. Her hand shook upon contact with the door latch. "Why am I nervous?" she asked herself. "He's just a man." But he wasn't just any man; he was her husband.

She hadn't seen Derrick since that day in his office three months ago. She'd known he would be here. Under no circumstances would Derrick miss his mother's birthday. The family was certain this was Miss Cora's last one. Staci believed that too. Every day Miss Cora grew weaker, and lately, her appetite had declined. As much as she hated to admit it, Staci worried about how Derrick would handle it. How does one really prepare to lose their only parent? Derrick didn't have many real friends. The ones he had he'd isolated himself from. Like his boys. According to Marcus and Brian, he hadn't spoken to them since the separation.

During their daily phone conversation, Malcolm warned Staci against attending Miss Cora's birthday party.

"Staci, this man left you," he'd said. "Don't allow him to use his mother's illness to keep you dangling around. He hasn't spoken to you in months. Don't allow him to parade you like a trophy in front of his family."

Staci wasn't worried about that. What she was looking for was some sign from Derrick that he still wanted to be married to her; that he still cared.

The first thing she noticed after stepping from her Mercedes was Derrick's SUV in the driveway. Her heart palpated, and her palms sweat. "You can handle this," she told herself.

Before retrieving the flowers from the backseat, she straightened her clothes one last time. Instead of ringing the bell, Staci used her key.

"If the two of you don't stop arguing, I'm going to hit you with my cane!" Miss Cora declared.

"Mama, tell him to leave me alone," Keisha begged.

"Tell her that dress shows too much cleavage," Derrick pleaded with his mother.

"I'm a grown woman. I can wear what I want!"

"Not as long as I'm your brother."

"Some things never change." Staci's voice startled everyone, especially Derrick. The words he had for his sister were quickly forgotten once his eyes beheld Staci.

Staci diverted her eyes away from him. "Happy Birthday, Miss Cora. How are you feeling today?" She hugged and kissed her mother-in-law.

"Thank you, baby. I was doing fine until Bonnie and Clyde showed up."

Staci laughed, then embraced Keisha. "I love that outfit. Girl, you are wearing that dress."

"Thank you. At least someone in the family, besides me, has taste." Keisha stuck her tongue out at her brother, but Derrick didn't notice. His eyes were glued on his wife. Her presence brought out a longing in him that nearly brought him to his knees. Keisha stepped back to allow room for Derrick and Staci to greet each other.

"Hi, Derrick." Staci's greeting was curt and impersonal. Without waiting for a reply, she turned to Miss Cora and said, "I'm going to put these flowers in a vase for you," then turned to leave.

"Derrick, aren't you going to speak to your wife?" Keisha questioned.

Once again, Staci didn't allow him to answer. Upon stopping in the doorway, she turned and said, "Your brother and I are no longer together."

Miss Cora shook her head, and Keisha's mouth hung open.

"Sister-in-law, what are you talking about?"

"Derrick and I are separated." Staci pasted the smile back on her face and left the room.

"What did you do?" Keisha asked at the same time punching Derrick's arm.

"What makes you think I did something?"

Keisha didn't say a word, just folded her arms and twisted her face.

"Whatever." Derrick waved her off. "You still need to change that dress."

Derrick watched Staci from the doorway as she cut flowers over the sink. No woman could wear a pair of jeans like his wife. His missed her so much, he wanted to wrap his arms around her and never let her go. Right before she stooped to pull the step stool from the utility closet, he walked up behind her and retrieved the vase for her.

"Thank you," she said, without making eye contact. She went on cutting the stems as if he wasn't there.

She smelled so good; like a ripe Georgia peach thanks to her favorite body cream. He wanted to hold her, kiss her, and . . .

"How have you been?" he asked.

"Fine."

Her short answers were tearing him apart. His eyes roamed her body and focused on the exposed part of her neck. He smiled slightly, remembering the first time he tasted its nectar. The smile disappeared when his eyes traveled to her left hand.

"Staci, why aren't you wearing your wedding ring?"

This time she made eye contact, and he wished she hadn't. "Why should I wear a wedding ring when I don't have a husband?" She shrugged, then continued with her task.

Derrick would have preferred for her to have stabbed him with the scissors than make that statement.

"Staci, don't say that."

"It's the truth. You have never been a husband to me." She smirked, "At best, you were a bad roommate."

"How can you say that?"

Staci ignored the hurt she heard in his voice. "Derrick, I didn't come here to discuss your inability to be a man. I'm only here to celebrate your mother's birthday." Her voice dripped with sugar. "If you would like to discuss anything else, call me on Wednesday. That's the day I deal with foolishness."

He watched her leave the room and wondered, who was that woman? That was not his Staci. She sounded like her, even walked like her, but that person wasn't his wife. This woman was angry and bitter. "What happened to my wife?" he asked the question audibly.

All day he watched Staci interact with everyone but him. Whenever he started in her direction, she went the other way. She held conversations with his uncles, aunts, even the neighbors, but said nothing to him. She danced with his uncles, but wouldn't even shake Derrick's hand. Everyone noticed the distance between them. Nearly all of his relatives questioned him about why they weren't together anymore.

"Dental school suctioned all of your common sense. How could you leave that woman?" his uncle Jimmy asked. Like always, Derrick didn't have an answer.

When the time came for Miss Cora to cut her birthday cake, Staci helped her position herself at the table.

Miss Cora was so weak; Keisha had to help her hold the knife.

Derrick accepted for certain that his mother wouldn't be around much longer. He and Staci locked eyes, and her eyes misted when she saw the sullen expression on his face. She looked as if she wanted to reach out to him and would have if Miss Cora hadn't touched her hand. Miss Cora turned and beckoned for Derrick to come stand next to Staci, but his emotions overwhelmed him and he left the room. Staci excused herself and practically ran into the bathroom.

Outside on the porch, Derrick couldn't contain himself. It was more than seeing his mother so frail. For the first time, he realized his need for space had cost him his wife—permanently. He'd known his mother was dying, but he didn't know the love Staci had for him had already died. Every look she afforded him was one of anger and contempt. How could nearly eight years be gone so quickly?

"You rejected her."

As hard as he tried, Derrick couldn't ignore the soft still voice any longer. "That's not what I meant to do," he replied audibly.

"You haven't talked to her; you've completely shut her out of your life. Now she's shutting you out of hers."

"I'm not shutting her out. I just need some time to figure things out."

"You've had three months, and nothing has changed. You're not talking to me, and you're not talking to her. You're still sitting around feeling sorry for yourself. You haven't been honest with yourself, and you haven't been honest with me." The voice grew more forceful. *"You've rejected me, telling me I didn't know what I was doing when I created you. You've insulted me by*

looking for approval and validation from men instead of allowing my love for you to become your validation."

Derrick couldn't stand the tongue-lashing anymore. He jumped into his SUV and sped off.

Inside the bathroom, Staci turned on the faucet to hide the sound of her sobs. Seeing Derrick today was harder than she'd thought. The entire day had been like a roller-coaster ride with all the twists, turns, and dips she felt inside of her. When she first saw him, she wanted to run to him, to touch him. But he didn't move, so she put up a guarded front. Even in the kitchen she waited for him so say something, anything that would let her know that he still cared, but he didn't. All he cared about was her wedding ring. She thought back to what Malcolm had said earlier about not allowing Derrick to use her as a trophy in front of his family. Witnessing him walk away from her once again was the breaking point.

"God, please show me how to stop loving him. I don't want to love him anymore." She said the prayer, but knew chances were God wasn't listening to her since she hadn't prayed or read her Bible much since meeting Malcolm.

She dried her face and unclipped her cell to phone Malcolm. Without saying a word, he listened to her tell him about Derrick's behavior and how now she was ready to divorce him.

"What are you doing tonight?" Malcolm asked.

"Go home!"

Staci blocked out the voice. "Nothing. What do you want to do?"

"Why don't you stop by here? I'll make you dinner."

She'd never been to his loft, but he'd bragged constantly about what a great cook he was. "I'm not hungry. I just want to enjoy a quiet evening alone."

"We can have that here. I have an extensive collection of DVDs and digital cable."

Staci placed a hand over her ear in an effort to quiet her conscience. "I'll be there in forty-five minutes." She committed the loft address to memory. "Shall I bring anything?" she asked, before hanging up.

"Just yourself," he answered sheepishly. "And an open mind."

Before leaving, Staci sat with Miss Cora for a few minutes. For some reason, she felt this might be her last time seeing her alive.

"I hope you had a good birthday, Miss Cora."

Miss Cora sighed. "Every day I wake up is a good day, but I was hoping this day would have been better. I don't know why my son left like that."

Staci hunched her shoulders, but didn't say anything. She didn't know what to say.

"I wish I could be around for your twentieth wedding anniversary. I might ask the good Lord to send me back, just so I can say, 'I told you so.'"

Staci didn't have the heart to tell her mother-in-law that she and Derrick weren't going to have a second anniversary, let alone a twentieth.

"Miss Cora, if we make it to twenty, I'll ask the Lord to send you back." Staci laughed, but Miss Cora remained serious.

"I'm not going to physically see it then, but I can *see* it now."

Staci secretly wished she could see half as well as Miss Cora, but right now, her vision was clouded with anger and blurred by hurt.

Staci hugged her again. "I love you, Miss Cora."

"Staci," Miss Cora called before she opened the door to leave, "don't forget what I told you about making him beg."

Chapter 21

Derrick had barely made it inside the studio apartment above the dental office before he fell to his knees. He didn't even turn the lights on. How he made it home, he didn't know. He did remember nearly hitting at least two pedestrians as he drove like a maniac down International Boulevard. He couldn't get rid of the still voice that kept asking him questions he couldn't answer.

"Why are you running from me? We used to have sweet fellowship. What happened?"

Heavy tears rolled down Derrick's cheeks and met at his chin. He accepted the fact that he couldn't fix things on his own. He needed God back in his life. Beyond his need for Staci, he needed God.

"Why do you refuse to accept yourself for the awesome individual I made you? Why don't you love me enough to let me be your father? I made you. Why can't you trust that I know what's best for you?"

"Because I don't like who I am. I don't like myself. I don't like not having a father." Derrick finally answered the voice honestly, between sobs that shook his body.

"I know the thoughts I have toward you, Derrick. Thoughts of peace and not evil, to give you an expected end. I gave you everything you needed to be a secure man, but you gave it back to me and went after man's approval."

Derrick's face fell to the floor and before he knew it, he was lying prostrate with his arms stretched out.

"Derrick, my son, you are fearfully and wonderfully made. Before I formed you in your mother's womb, I knew you. I didn't make a mistake in selecting your parents, and I didn't make a mistake in creating you. I am God! I don't make mistakes."

As he lay there, Derrick felt God's love covering him with the warmth of an electric blanket, something he hadn't allowed himself to feel in a very long time.

"Come back to me, my son. Come back."

Chapter 22

Staci blasted the satellite radio in her Benz on her way over to Malcolm's loft. It wasn't that she enjoyed the music so much; she was trying to drown out her conscience. It wasn't safe for her to be with Malcolm right now, and she knew it. "What could be wrong with watching a movie?" she asked audibly. She knew what was wrong. The same thing that was wrong when she and Derrick had done it a few years ago. The quiet evening turned into breakfast in bed and lunch in the afternoon. "I don't have anything to worry about, because I'm not attracted to Malcolm." As the words left her mouth, doubts surfaced. She may not have been attracted to Malcolm, but she craved the pleasure he offered.

The elevator ride to Malcolm's third-floor loft felt like an eternity. She thought it was ironic that the song playing in the elevator was Marvin Gaye's "Let's Get It On." She only had to knock once before Malcolm opened the door.

"Good evening, beautiful."

Malcolm's sensual smile confirmed her earlier doubts. He was wearing what appeared to be silk pajamas. The warm vanilla aroma engulfed her the second she stepped inside the unit. Malcolm had scented candles all around and soft music playing through the surround sound stereo system.

"It smells heavenly in here. How did you know I like vanilla?"

"You told me, remember?" he answered.

"I also told you I wanted a quiet evening, not a romantic interlude."

"Staci, relax. I'm just creating a cozy atmosphere so you can get today's events off your mind." Malcolm reached for her hand, and she allowed him to lead her to the bar, where he had champagne chilling.

"Malcolm, you know I don't drink alcohol." Once again, she glimpsed his outfit. "Why are you wearing pajamas?"

"Staci, stop worrying. The champagne is nonalcoholic, and this is what I wear when I'm lounging around."

"Just as long as you understand nothing is going to happen between us tonight," she said, before accepting the drink.

"Of course, Staci. Nothing will happen here tonight that you don't want to happen."

"Good."

Staci took a sip of champagne and walked around the loft. The floor plan was similar to the ones she and Derrick owned. It was a simple place, decorated typically the way a single man would decorate. The furniture was nice, but it was simple in design. Probably something he'd picked out from IKEA. Most of the walls were bare, but the hardwood floors were gorgeous. Staci, too engrossed in the self-tour, didn't notice Malcolm wasn't drinking with her.

She closed her eyes and started swaying to the music. Malcolm stood back and watched her succumb to the atmosphere. "You're beautiful and too sexy for your own good." He extended his hand to her after she finished her drink. "Dance with me, Staci." When she hesitated, he pleaded. "Come on, I won't bite."

Staci was so relaxed by now she didn't care if he did bite. The music, the warm vanilla scent, the glow of the candles—all had an intoxicating effect on her. She accepted his hand and in no time they were slow dancing to Boyz II Men's "I'll Make Love to You."

Staci closed her eyes and rested her head on Malcolm's shoulder. Flowing to the music she thought of Derrick. He was the only man she'd danced this close to before. The more friction they created, the more she thought of Derrick.

Malcolm stroked her back. Starting at the top and working his way down lower, lower, until he was gripping her and pressing her body against his.

She moaned and imagined Malcolm's touch felt like Derrick's touch. She inhaled his scent and willed Malcolm to smell like her husband. Staci let her hands run across Malcolm's shoulders and down his arms. She gasped. Malcolm was nowhere near the size of Derrick, but at that moment, in her mind, his body felt like Derrick's.

"Beautiful, Staci," he whispered when he kissed the side of her face.

The illusory game worked too well. Derrick loved to call her, his "beautiful Stacelyn." She felt light-headed as fantasy and reality collided. She knew she was with Malcolm, but he felt so much like Derrick she wanted to be with him in the most intimate way.

Malcolm whispered the words to the song in her ear. *"I'll make love to you like you want me to."*

He even sounded like Derrick. She wouldn't open her eyes for fear he would look like her husband. She tried to break the embrace, but she was too weak. Suddenly, the day's events drained her physically.

"Der—I mean, Malcolm, please stop." Her voice sounded as if it came from someplace far away.

"Staci, you know you want this. You need this." He moaned and trailed kisses along her neck.

Staci couldn't protest. She did want this, but not with him. She tried pulling away, but he strengthened his grip. She knew if she didn't leave soon, she would end up in bed, or worse, on the couch with him. At the moment, the hardwood floor was a viable option. She had to get away from him, but somehow didn't have the strength.

God, forgive me for not going home, she prayed inwardly. Somehow in the grogginess that enveloped her, it made sense for her to pray. She couldn't do anything else while Malcolm continued grinding against her and exploring her neck with his tongue and lips.

God, please help me get out of this. Somehow in her sedated state, she remembered a scripture. "God is our refuge and strength, a very present help in trouble."

"I'm in trouble, Lord. Please send help now," she whispered the prayer.

Malcolm unfastened the first button on her blouse, then jumped back. The vibration from her cell phone startled him, but it made Staci perk up. With record speed, she unclipped her phone from her waist and answered it before Malcolm could protest.

"Hello," she almost screamed into the phone.

"Baby girl, how are you? You've been on my mind all evening. Just thought I would give you a call. I hope I'm not interrupting anything."

Staci vigorously shook her head as to clear it. Once again, her daddy was her hero. She stepped away from Malcolm.

"Daddy, your timing is perfect. Thank you so much for calling me." She fastened her button and quickly retrieved her purse. She still felt groggy, but she had to get out of there now.

"Baby girl, are you sure you're okay? You sound funny."

"Staci, wait!" Malcolm called when she opened his front door, but she continued on.

Once outside the unit, she answered her father. "Daddy, this phone call kept me from making a major mistake."

Carey's tone deepened. "Staci, where are you? And who is that yelling your name?"

The elevator opened just as Malcolm stepped outside into the hallway. Staci shook her head at him and stepped inside the elevator.

"I'm somewhere I shouldn't be," she answered her father while looking at Malcolm. She was very fatigued, so she couldn't be sure, but she thought she saw fire in his eyes.

When she reached her car, she didn't think it was safe for her to be driving. She was too sleepy, but she refused to stay there. "Daddy, can you talk to me until I make it home? I'm very tired."

"Sure, but you'd better stop tempting the grace of God."

"Don't I know it."

Chapter 23

Derrick sat on the floor at the foot of the bed with his opened Bible in his hand. He'd been down there for hours. He cried a lot, releasing the feelings of hurt and insecurity he had buried deep inside of him. Then he listened to God comforting him and encouraging him. He prayed too. He prayed for courage, stability, and acceptance. Not from people, but for him to accept his life as it is. For him to stop trying to conform himself to what he thought he should be and accept what God had made him. Then he prayed for forgiveness.

"Father, have mercy on me; for I acknowledge my transgression and my sin is ever before me. I have not been honest with my wife. I have tried to build our marriage on deception in order to cover up my own shortcomings. I know you desire truth in the inward parts. Wash me thoroughly from my iniquity and create in me a clean heart. Restore unto me the joy of my salvation. Help me to take responsibility for my actions and grant me the grace to handle the consequences. Amen."

By 7:00 A.M. Derrick was dressed and ready for church. He hadn't slept all night, but he wasn't tired. Even if he was, it didn't matter. He was going to church today, and he wasn't going to hide in the balcony. Some kind of way, he would get through the pending loss of his mother and find his way back home to Staci, but first, he needed to rededicate his life to God. That's the only thing that mattered to him. Everything and everyone else was secondary, including Staci. His experience last night showed him the reason his life started spiraling downward was because he left his first love.

Since childhood, he had a relationship with God. He learned about Him in Sunday School and Vacation Bible School. In high school, he used to get teased because he always blessed his food and carried a Bible in his backpack. In college, it was the same thing until he fell in love with Staci. Shortly after they'd met, God had shown him in a dream that Staci was his ordained mate. Derrick insisted they wait until he finished dental school before they married, and she quickly agreed. That being the first real relationship for both of them, they didn't know how to handle the sexual tension that arose. From the moment he yielded to his flesh, his life started unraveling at the seams. That night everything changed; he changed. He'd been running ever since.

Staci could barely open her eyes. From the brightness of the sun, she knew she had overslept past her usual 6:30 A.M. start time. *Maybe I'll catch the second service,* she thought. She liked the 11:00 A.M. worship service better anyway. She stretched once again, and this time finally opened her eyes to check the time.

"Oh my God!" she exclaimed. It was after one o'clock in the afternoon. How in the world did I sleep so long? she wondered. She remembered dragging into the house extremely tired and sleepy. So sleepy that she didn't bother changing her clothes, having slept on top of the covers in the same clothing she'd worn to Miss Cora's birthday—and to Malcolm's loft.

Staci shook her head when she thought of the big mistake she'd almost made last night.

"Lord, I will never let that happen again," she vowed. Just thinking about Malcolm touching her, kissing her, made her feel dirty. She hurried into the bathroom and started the shower. Instead of throwing her clothes into the hamper, she threw them into the trash, underwear included.

Things were without a doubt going to change as far as Mr. Leblanc was concerned, she decided as the hot pellets rejuvenated her body. Last night, he'd crossed the friendship line. He didn't bear the blame alone, though. She shouldn't have been there in the first place. In retrospect, there were a lot of things she shouldn't have said or done. She should've listened to her mother months ago, but she didn't, and because of that, she nearly committed adultery. She felt like she had.

God, thank you for being so merciful to me last night. I know I haven't been faithful to you lately, but as always, you've extended your unconditional love toward me. Forgive me for my disobedient actions.

As Staci dried off, she made a sound decision. She was going to stop using Malcolm as a Band-Aid and a cushion. On his best day, Malcolm couldn't replace Derrick, and she didn't want him to. She would have to find another way to handle the emptiness left by Derrick. It was difficult, but yesterday helped her accept the fact that her marriage was damaged beyond repair.

"Did I tell you that?"

"No," she audibly answered the voice.

"Nothing is over until I say it's over."

Staci's mind wandered back to Miss Cora, who believed without a doubt she and Derrick would celebrate twenty years of marriage. The drugs she's taking must have hallucinogens in them, Staci figured.

She was about to head to the kitchen to brew some tea when the phone rang.

"Who would be calling me on a Sunday? It'd better not be Malcolm," she grumbled.

"Girl, where are you? You won't believe what happened today!" It was Lashay with Shannon in the background. Their excitement was contagious.

"What happened?"

"Guess!" Shannon yelled into the phone.

"Oh my God, you didn't have the baby without calling me, did you?" Staci asked.

"No, nothing like that. Guess who rededicated their life to Christ today?"

"Craig?" Her younger brother was the only person who came to mind.

Lashay smacked her lips. "Please, you have to have once been dedicated in order to rededicate."

Staci didn't have a clue as to whom they were talking about. "I give up."

"Derrick."

"Who?"

"Don't tell me you've forgotten your husband's name already," Lashay laughed.

Staci was stunned. "Are you sure? True Worship has over five thousand members. It could have been someone who looks like him."

"Is she crazy?" Staci heard Lashay ask.

"You've known her longer than I have. I just married into the family. That's your blood relative," Shannon responded.

"Staci, how many people are six feet five, two hundred fifty pounds, and look like a rerun episode of *Magnum, PI?*" Lashay asked.

"I guess you're right," she responded, trying to suppress the smile threatening to break forth. "What happened?"

"One of the ushers told me he came to the eight o'clock service," Lashay started, "but I saw him when I came to the second service. This time he didn't hide in the balcony. He sat on the main floor, front-row center. Then when Reggie made the altar call in the eleven o'clock service, Derrick was the first one to come forth."

"You should have seen him," Shannon added. "He was on his knees with his hands raised, just crying and praising God."

Staci didn't know what to say. The Derrick she saw yesterday didn't sound like the same person they were talking about. However, the description did sound like the Derrick she'd met almost eight years ago.

"Girl, your man is back!" Lashay exclaimed.

Staci had been let down too many times to be that optimistic. Besides, today, she didn't want Derrick back.

"I wouldn't say all that, but it's good he's getting his life in order."

"She *is* crazy," Lashay whispered, but Staci heard her.

"I'm not crazy, I'm real. Derrick and I are not getting back together."

"Welcome back, son," Pastor Reggie said when Derrick joined him in the office after service.

"It's good to be back." Derrick really meant that. For years, he hadn't felt the inner peace he was now experiencing. Derrick went on to share his midnight encounter with Reggie.

"God is so good, and He knows how to get our attention," Reggie laughed. "How does that old song go, 'You may be high, you may be low, but when the Lord gets ready, you've got to move.'"

"Believe me, He knows how to move you," Derrick chuckled.

Reggie's expression turned serious. "Are you ready to talk to Staci?" Derrick knew he was referring to telling her the truth about what happened the day Staci ended the life of their child.

"Almost, but first, I need some uninterrupted time with the Lord. For the next seven days, I'm consecrating; then I'm going to talk to her. That is, if she'll listen."

"I think that's a good idea. I would also like to see you once a week for one-on-one counseling."

Derrick smiled. He himself was going to suggest something like that. There were many things he wanted to get off his chest, and Pastor Reggie was one of the few people he felt he could trust with his feelings. "Thank you." Derrick paused. "I don't know what's going to happen with Staci. Based on what I saw yesterday, it may be too late."

Reggie leaned his elbows on his desk. "Derrick, what do you want to happen?"

"I want to go home to my wife."

Chapter 24

"Are we still on for dinner?" Malcolm asked, pleadingly.

"I guess so," Staci answered, halfheartedly. She hadn't seen Malcolm since the incident at his loft ten days ago. Instead of cutting him off completely, she'd cut their daily phone conversations down to twice a week. He wasn't happy about that, but she didn't care. She needed to put some space between them. Malcolm constantly apologized for crossing the line at his loft, hoping that would change her mind, but it didn't. Tonight, she only agreed to have dinner with him to tell him she didn't want to see him anymore at all. "I'll meet you at the restaurant in half an hour."

When she ended the phone call, her mind instantly went to Derrick. She still hadn't heard from him. Sunday, she didn't see him at the second service, but several members approached her and offered congratulatory remarks on Derrick's rededication. She started to call him and congratulate him herself, but decided against it. The next time she speaks to him, Staci was going to ask him for a divorce. It wasn't fair for him to keep her in limbo. She had allowed him sufficient time to straighten out his life. Now it was time for him to offer her the same courtesy. Staci was ready to move on. She was scared, but she was ready.

Since reducing the time spent with Malcolm, she'd been able to take an objective look at her life with Derrick. Neither of them had been happy in the marriage. Staci believed he still harbored ill feelings toward her for aborting their baby. She reasoned that was why he wanted a baby so badly, as a replacement. Staci didn't understand why she couldn't get pregnant; maybe she couldn't have any more children. If that was the case, it was best she and Derrick end things now. Derrick could find someone to have babies with, and she could find someone who would reciprocate the love she had to give. Having a baby wouldn't have solved their problems anyway.

Staci pushed back the lump she felt forming in her throat. It was hard for her to come to this conclusion, and she really couldn't imagine her life without Derrick. But the reality was she'd been without him for a long time. She didn't know who Derrick was anymore, and she was tired of trying to figure him out. She was drained from giving him more than he was willing to give her. Someday he would make someone a good husband, but she wasn't that person.

She packed her briefcase and was preparing to leave when Chloe announced she had a visitor.

"Mr. Leblanc is here."

"Malcolm, what are you doing here?" she asked when he stepped into her office carrying flowers. "I told you, I'd meet you at the restaurant."

"I know, but I wanted to escort you."

Has he always resembled Martin Lawrence? she asked herself. "Malcolm, I don't need an escort."

"I know, but I also wanted to give you these." He held the mixed bouquet out to her.

The arrangement of daffodils, irises, carnations, and lilies was nice, but she really preferred roses. Staci accepted the flowers and asked Chloe to find a container for them. When she turned her attention back to Malcolm he had his arm extended out to her. Ignoring the goofy expression on his face, Staci interlocked her arm with his and headed for the elevator.

Derrick's eyes were glued on the numbered circles above his head. One by one, each circle lighted as the elevator made what was, by his perception, a long, slow trip to the tenth floor. He shifted the long rectangular box from one arm to the other and checked his watch once more. Staci should be getting off any moment. He felt more like a teenager picking up his first date, than a married man making a surprise visit to his wife.

He didn't know how Staci was going to respond seeing him unexpectedly. He'd started to call first, but feared she wouldn't take his call. He'd picked today to start the rebuilding process because today was Wednesday, and that's the day she'd told him she'd deal with foolishness. Derrick didn't like her considering him foolish, but he had to admit, he had been a fool to leave her.

He twisted his face when he checked his reflection in the mirrored wall. The tan suit he wore made him look distinguished, but his tie was crooked. "Why can't my tie stay straight?" he grumbled. He knew the answer. It was because Staci didn't tie it. She always tied his ties perfectly. The frown on his face softened at the thought of his wife's soft touch. He knew that was afar off, but the thought calmed his nerves a bit.

He didn't know what he was going to say to her, other than he was sorry and he wanted another chance to explain the reason behind his actions; that he loves her more than life, and that his life is incomplete without her. That he misses her smile and the soft feel of her curls underneath his chin as she lay cuddled against him. He focused on the numbered circles again, eight . . . nine . . .

Malcolm wore that goofy expression the entire time he and Staci waited for the elevator. It wasn't until he winked at her did she realize he thought the look was sexy. *I'll be glad when tonight is over*, she thought. The bell sounded, and the silver doors parted.

"Excuse me," Derrick said when the box he carried bumped the couple entering the elevator as he was exiting. It took a few seconds for it to register that the woman with the average-looking gentleman was his wife.

"Staci?" He said her name like it was a question. On her face he saw that she was just as surprised to see him as he was to see her with her arm interlocked with the man next to her.

"Hi," she responded weakly, not sure of what to say. She studied his appearance and came to one conclusion. Despite her animosity toward him, Derrick Garrison was a fine man. No one could wear a suit like her husband. His thick curls were cut low, and his mustache trimmed. As always, his tie was crooked. She noticed the Conroy's label on the long box underneath his arm and knew inside were long-stem red roses. It was going to be harder than she imagined to let him go.

"What are you doing here?" she asked.

Derrick tried to focus on her, but the stranger captured his attention. Who was he, and why was he touching his wife?

"I'm here to see you. I was hoping we could have dinner and talk."

The elevator warning buzzer sounded, and Malcolm urged her to step completely inside the elevator before the doors closed. She did, and Derrick followed.

"Malcolm, Derrick. Derrick, Malcolm." Staci made the informal introductions before she answered her husband's request. "Derrick, I've already made dinner plans for tonight. Give Chloe a call tomorrow and make an appointment," she said, before pressing "L" on the instrument panel.

"Hello, are you Staci's brother?" Malcolm asked with his free hand extended to Derrick. Staci had forgotten she'd never told Malcolm her husband's name. She didn't think he needed to know that information.

For a moment, Derrick ignored Malcolm. He was still processing that he needed an appointment to have a conversation with his wife. Then to have this stranger, who was obviously displaying possession of Staci, think he was her brother enraged him.

"I am not her brother!"

Staci recognized the anger in Derrick's tone immediately. In an instant, his light complexion turned a shade of red, and his eyes darkened. Staci quickly removed her arm from Malcolm and prayed the elevator would speed up or at least stop so she could get out.

"What is your relationship? Are you her boyfriend?" Derrick asked, looking from Staci to Malcolm.

Staci wanted to punch Malcolm when he answered, "Something like that," with a smile.

"Why is this elevator so slow?" Staci grunted.

"Something like that?" Derrick repeated and stepped closer to Malcolm.

Thankfully, the elevator stopped, and the doors opened. Before Derrick stepped out into the lobby, he took Staci by the arm and placed her alongside him.

"I'm sorry you've wasted your time, Malcolm, but my wife will not be having dinner with you tonight or any other night."

Malcolm's face twisted at Derrick's statement, which sounded more like a command.

She'd never seen Derrick so jealous. *Men,* she thought. *They don't want you, and they don't want anyone else to have you.* Staci wanted to remind Derrick that he lost his right of ownership the day he walked out on her, but she feared for Malcolm's safety as well as her own.

"Malcolm, I'll talk to you later," she said.

Derrick shot her a look that said, "No, you won't!"

"Staci—" Malcolm started.

"Malcolm, please just go," Staci pleaded.

Malcolm conceded and retreated through the glass doors. No sooner had the doors closed then Staci snatched her arm away from Derrick.

"What do you think you're doing coming here like this?"

"What do you think you're doing with a boyfriend?" Derrick shot back.

Staci rolled her eyes. "Malcolm is not my boyfriend!"

"Then why were you about to have dinner with him?"

Staci fished her car keys from her purse. "Derrick, you gave up the right to know my business the day you left me."

"I am still your husband! I—"

She cut him off. "Derrick—" she was about to yell, but another elevator opened and emptied a full load. By the time the crowd passed, Staci was walking through the side garage entrance.

"Staci!" Derrick called after her.

She stopped abruptly and turned around. "What do you want? Why are you here?"

"I wanted to talk to you, but you're too busy with your boyfriend. Does he have to make an appointment also?"

"I've told you, Malcolm is not my boyfriend! He's about as much of a boyfriend as you were a husband!"

Derrick felt like he'd been slapped across the face, twice, but he wasn't going to let that stop him.

"How long have you known him? How did you meet him? Has he been in our house?"

Staci found the last question funny, even hilarious. She laughed the rest of the way to her car. She was still laughing after she put her briefcase in the backseat. When she started the car, more laughter poured from her. When she looked in her rearview mirror at Derrick standing there still holding the boxed roses as she drove away, she laughed the loudest.

Malcolm walked back to his car in a daze. Being able to put a face and name on his enemy made him nervous. He wasn't prepared to meet the man he'd planned on replacing. Staci's husband was nothing like he had expected. Malcolm pictured him to be a short, overweight, bald guy. At least that's how his dentist looked. Derrick was much bigger and stronger, and frankly, he frightened Malcolm.

Now that he knew who Derrick was, he'd have to change his approach toward Staci. He'd have to work harder to convince her he was the one for her. Not the mixed breed giant. The good doctor may have been a lousy husband, but he was what the sisters and even some of the brothers would call a good-looking man. Malcolm considered himself average looking. What he didn't have in the "fine" department, he made up for in the bedroom, and, of course, with his money.

He'd given up a long time ago on trying to impress Staci with his money, but the bedroom was another story. He'd almost had her that night in his loft. If only he'd remembered to slip her cell phone from her waist.

"That's the name she almost called me," he remembered, thinking back to that night.

He paused before inserting his key into his Lexus. "What if I'm already too late? What if she stays with him tonight?" Malcolm couldn't let that happen. Staci was his woman; his beautiful and sexy woman. She actually reminded him of his mother, but the things he wanted to do with her, he could have never done with his mother.

She'd never voiced any attraction for him, but from his experience, women used more indirect communication, than direct. If she didn't want him, why had she spent so much time with him? And if she didn't want to sleep with him, why had she told him so much about what she was missing from her husband in bed. She wanted him to meet her needs. If Derrick hadn't shown up tonight, he would have done just that.

"Tomorrow, baby, tomorrow," he said to the picture he kept of Staci on his dashboard, the one he'd taken while Staci stood next to the dolphin tank at the Monterey Bay Aquarium. "Tomorrow, you'll be mine, one way or another." This time he patted the plastic bag of white powder he had in his front jacket pocket.

Chapter 25

Staci hadn't had been home five minutes before Derrick walked through the door, still carrying the boxed roses. She wasn't surprised at all. She knew he'd show up if only to make sure she wasn't with Malcolm.

"I knew I should have changed the locks," she said and rolled her eyes at him. He followed her into the kitchen and watched her take items from the refrigerator for a sandwich.

"Staci," he began, his tone solemn, "I don't want to fight anymore. I want to talk to you. I need to talk to you." When she didn't respond, he added, "I bought these for you." He held the boxed roses out to her.

She accepted the box. "Thank you."

He thought her hostility toward him was softening until his eyes followed her to the garbage can. There, she opened the box and dumped the roses into the can, then continued making her sandwich. His cheeks burned, and his nostrils flared.

"Staci, why did you do that?" he asked in a controlled voice.

"Because I don't want anything from you, and I don't want you. Now would you please leave my house?"

"Staci, I'm still your husband, and this is still our home."

"Oh really? If this is our home, why have I been the only one living here for four months? I can write you a check right now from my trust fund," she said nodding toward her purse, "for your half of the house. As for you being my husband, that shouldn't be too hard to fix considering we've only been married eighteen months."

"What are you talking about?"

Staci thought she saw hurt in his eyes, but she didn't care. "I'm talking about reaching an agreement on how to divide our marital assets for the divorce."

Derrick turned his back to her. When she saw his broad shoulders slump, she almost felt sorry for him, but she was used to him running away from her. She expected him to run out the door any second. She continued eating her sandwich like he wasn't there.

"I don't want a divorce," he said sullenly.

"I don't understand. You don't want to be married, at least not to me, but you don't want a divorce?"

"Staci," he begged, "I do want to be married to you. That's what I came to talk to you about, among other things."

"Isn't this ironic? You finally want to talk to me, but now I don't want to listen. Save it for your next wife."

Derrick sighed and massaged his temples. There was no getting through to Staci, at least not tonight. She wasn't just being stubborn, she was angry and bitter.

"Staci, I will give you space and time, I owe you that. But we still need to talk."

Staci set her sandwich down and folded her arms. "Derrick, you can't give me back what you owe me. You can't give back eight years of my life. You can't replenish the energy I've wasted on you. You can't replenish all the tears I've cried for you. You can't reset the times you pushed me away and ignored me." She figured she'd stop before the tears fell. "But what you can do is give me a divorce."

When Derrick turned around his eyes were glossy and his breathing labored. He left without saying another word.

Staci waited until she heard him drive off before she moved an inch. She looked down at the turkey on wheat bread. She didn't feel like eating anymore. She felt like crying, which is what she did. Somehow asking Derrick for a divorce didn't bring her the closure she desired. The request brought on more questions. Was she ready to live her life completely free of her husband? Is that what she really wanted? Was she doing the right thing? She voiced the questions to the empty room.

The still voice answered.

"What did I tell you? Nothing is over until I say it's over, and I haven't spoken yet."

That was not what she wanted to hear.

Staci attempted to drown out the voice by turning on the sound system, but that didn't work. The satellite station played Hezekiah Walker's "Second Chance." The selection after that was Mississippi Mass's "Hold on Old Soldier." She gave up and went upstairs to her bedroom where her cell phone was ringing for the fourth time. She turned it off, knowing it wasn't anyone but Malcolm.

Chapter 26

Staci could barely keep herself from crying as she watched the home health nurse attempt to feed Miss Cora. She'd stopped by to visit her mother-in-law before heading to the office. After a few small bites of toast, Miss Cora refused to eat and sent the nurse away. She beckoned for Staci to come sit on the hospital bed next to her.

"Staci, you don't have to put on a strong front. I know it won't be long now." She patted her daughter-in-law's hand. "Me and the Lord had a talk awhile back. I told Him I wanted my children saved before I left." Miss Cora smiled. "Keisha called Sunday to say she got saved, and you already know about your husband. I told you he would come around. God wasn't going to let him get too far gone." Miss Cora leaned slightly forward. "Did you make him beg like I told you?"

Staci smiled slightly and nodded. She couldn't tell Miss Cora she and Derrick were divorcing. She'd let Miss Cora take her hope to the grave.

"Staci, I've always appreciated you for how much you love my son. At first, I thought you were a little crazy for loving him so much." Miss Cora laughed, but Staci wanted to cry. "What I figured out was, you loved him the way the Bible says. Patiently, kindly, and Lord knows, you suffered long." She squeezed Staci's hand. "But aren't you glad you didn't give up on him?"

Staci didn't know how to answer her mother-in-law. She moved her mouth to answer, but no words would come.

"I'm sure glad she didn't." Derrick's voice startled Staci. She turned her head to see him entering Miss Cora's room. "I thank God every day for blessing me with this beautiful woman that I in no way deserve. Thank you for not giving up on me," he added after squatting down beside Staci and taking her free hand in his.

Staci wasn't prepared for his sudden appearance and even less prepared for the words he'd spoken. She turned her attention back to Miss Cora, whose smile resembled the Kool-Aid mascot. She couldn't break the dying woman's heart, but she would tell her husband off later. Maybe wash his mouth out with soap for lying.

Derrick turned to his mother. "Mama, do you need anything?"

"Son, I have everything I need now."

The three made small talk for a while before Staci kissed Miss Cora's cheek and said good-bye. "I love you, Miss Cora."

"Love you too, baby." The lethargic voice pulled Staci's heartstrings. *Why must Miss Cora's life be cut short?*

Without Staci asking, Derrick walked her to the car. As if knowing she would have some choice words for him, Derrick opened the door and sat inside the passenger seat of her Mercedes. His assumption proved correct.

"I thought you were saved. How could you lie to your mother like that?"

"I didn't lie to my mother. Everything I said was the truth," Derrick answered calmly.

"Yes, you did. You made your mother think you and I are back together, and you know that's not the case. Did you forget I asked you for a divorce last night?" she yelled.

"Sweetheart, did you forget I told you I don't want a divorce? I know things aren't good between us now, but I know eventually they will be. It's true, I don't deserve you. I was speaking in the future."

"It doesn't matter in what tense you choose to speak," she snarled. "The shell of a marriage we had is over. And don't call me sweetheart."

Derrick sat quietly for a moment, determined not to crawl back into his shell. "Staci, will you have dinner with me tonight? I need to talk to you."

She chuckled and shook her head. "Some things never change. You didn't listen to me when we lived together, and you're not listening to me now. Unless you want to discuss the divorce, we don't have anything to talk about."

Derrick bowed his head and mumbled something Staci couldn't make out before addressing her again. "Staci, at some point, we're going to have to talk. There are some things I need to say to you. I'm not running away this time. I'll wait as long as necessary and do whatever I have to do in order to make things right between us. So for now, I'll play by your rules. I'll make an appointment with Chloe for next Wednesday." With that, he got out of the car and walked around to the driver's side and knocked on her window.

"Your tires are worn. I'll pick up your car this afternoon and have a new set installed," he announced, then left before she could refuse him.

While backing out of the driveway and onto Skyline Boulevard, Staci suppressed the hope stirring inside of her. He was right. After last night, she'd expected him to shut her out like always, but he wasn't doing that.

Maybe I will talk to him next Wednesday, she pondered and merged onto Highway 13.

When Marcus met Staci in her office for their meeting three hours later, he was excited. Staci figured it had something to do with Shannon and his unborn twins.

"Another ultrasound today?" she asked.

"No. I'm excited about the developments in your life. I'm still not happy with your husband, but if you're happy, I'll tolerate him," Marcus explained.

"Marcus, I'm not happy with my husband either, so what are you talking about?"

"Well, at least he's on the right track. He's back in church, and I know you can feel the difference at home."

Staci twisted her face. "Derrick and I are not back together," then added flatly, "and we're not getting back together."

Marcus was confused. "I assumed since you're driving his SUV, you two were living under the same roof again and trying to work things out."

Staci had forgotten Derrick had arranged to pick up her car. "He's changing my tires; that's all. The only things we have to work out are the details of our divorce," she explained.

Marcus frowned at that statement. He, along with the rest of the family, assumed now that Derrick had straightened out his spiritual life, the two of them would work on their marriage. Marcus disliked Derrick for deserting Staci, but he didn't want his sister to divorce him. In his opinion, that would be a major mistake and said as much.

"You're getting a divorce?"

Staci sighed. "Eventually. Right now, Derrick doesn't want one."

"Neither do you," Marcus said frankly.

Staci rolled her eyes at him before asking, "How do you know what I want?"

"Because I know you and I know Derrick. True, he made a major mistake, which I'm still mad at him for, but he does love you. And you love him despite how bitter you've allowed yourself to become."

Staci stood, and Marcus waited for the hand on the hip and neck rolling, along with the pointing of the finger to start. His sister didn't disappoint him.

"Marcus, you need to stay out of my business! You don't know how I feel. Let Shannon walk out on you after you've given her everything and see if you would welcome her back so easily!"

"I never said it was easy, but you owe it to him to forgive him and give him another chance. You do remember the vows you took, don't you? Oh, that's right. Your vows said for better only, not for worse."

Staci glared at her brother; she hated when he was right.

"Don't get me wrong. I don't agree with what he did, and right now, I don't agree with you pushing for a divorce. I think it's a rash decision, one which you will live to regret. You haven't done everything right yourself. If you had, you wouldn't have married him when you did. But you refused to wait, and now, you want to make him pay for your impatience."

Every word spoken by Marcus flowed through Staci's veins and filled her with rage. She slammed her briefcase on top of her desk and grabbed her purse.

"Marcus, I don't care what you think or what you say! You're my brother, but that doesn't give you the right to stick your nose in my personal business. I don't work for you so you can tell me how to run my life. In fact, I don't work for you at all. I quit!" she yelled and stomped toward the door.

Marcus stood and followed. "Quitting won't change the fact that you're wrong," he said before she slammed the door in his face.

Marcus walked into the reception area and instructed Chloe to reschedule Staci's remaining appointments for the following day.

"Sure thing." Chloe knew as well as Marcus that Staci would be back. In the last year, she had quit at least eight times after an argument with Marcus, only to return the next day.

Once in the parking garage and in the confines of Derrick's SUV, Staci admitted her brother was right. She was bitter and part of the blame for her shambled marriage could be attributed to her impatience. She felt strange sitting in the SUV. The vehicle reminded her too much of Derrick, and she started to feel a longing for him. "No! I can't do this!" she screamed.

The still voice answered. *"Yes, you can."*

"No, I can't!" she answered back. She placed her key in the ignition and shifted into reverse, but her cell rang before she could back out. She shifted back into park, then checked the caller ID. It was Malcolm. She didn't want to answer it, but she needed a distraction.

"Malcolm, what do you want?" she answered plainly.

"Hey, beautiful, how's your day?"

Staci shook her head and wondered what she was doing. Why couldn't she cease to communicate with Malcolm? She had no problem dismissing her husband.

"Malcolm, I don't have time to talk."

She could hear him breathing heavily. "Are you with him?"

"If you're referring to Derrick, no, I'm not. But I still don't have time to talk."

"I'd like to see you tonight, if that's okay with your husband."

"Would you like to call and ask him?" she retorted, knowing Malcolm was afraid of Derrick. She didn't miss the fear in his eyes yesterday.

"I don't want to talk to your husband. I want to see you."

"Malcolm, I need to see you too. It's time for things to change between us."

"Staci, I couldn't agree more."

When she heard the smile in his voice, she knew they weren't on the same page. It didn't matter, though. After tonight, he'd have a clear understanding.

"I'll meet you at the Mexican restaurant at six." She pressed the red End call button without saying goodbye. She then turned the engine off and went back upstairs to MS Computers Corporate Offices to resume her meeting with Marcus.

When she stepped into Marcus's executive office suite, he started talking about the grand opening of the Corte Madera store like she'd never left, then offered her half of his sandwich. From time to time he would stop and write down words and musical notes on a pad.

"What are you doing?" she asked.

"I'm writing a song about waiting on God," he answered. "I'm going to entitle it, 'My Baby Sister.'" He laughed.

"Do it and die," she warned.

At the end of the day Staci returned to the parking garage to find Derrick not only had new tires installed on her car, but he also had it washed and waxed. The inside detailed complete with a new vanilla air freshener. The silver E420 looked brand new. On the way to the restaurant to meet Malcolm, she called Derrick's office to thank him, but he was in with his last patient, so she left a message. That worked out better because she really didn't want to talk to him anyway.

Malcolm was already seated in a booth and had taken the liberty of ordering her a virgin strawberry daiquiri. The closer her steps got to him, the more she wondered how he was going to handle what she had to tell him. Settled inside a booth with the appetizer she'd chosen as her meal, Staci decided not to delay the inevitable any longer.

"Why haven't you touched your drink?" he asked.

"I'm not in the mood for a daiquiri tonight, but thanks anyway."

He leaned closer. "Just what are you in the mood for?"

She leaned back. "Malcolm, it's time I made some changes with our friendship, relationship, or whatever you want to call it."

The frown that instantly appeared on his face told her that he wasn't going to like what was coming next.

"This relationship consumes too much of my time and right now, I need space so I can clear my head and make solid sound decisions about my life."

"What are you taking about? I've given you your space these last two weeks."

"That's only because I made you after you almost seduced me," she pointed out. "But it wasn't your fault entirely. I should not have been at your loft in the first place."

"Admit it, Staci, you liked the way I made you feel."

She didn't miss the smirk on his face. "I did like it," she admitted, "but not for the reason you think. And I'm glad I left when I did."

That confused him. "Is this 'space' your idea or your husband's, because if you're adjusting your life for him, he's only going to hurt you again. He's proven once that he doesn't want you."

Staci's thoughts went back to Shannon's comment that any legitimate brother would encourage her to work things out with Derrick and not avoid him. Like Marcus had done earlier.

"Malcolm, this is my decision. It's what I want to do, what I need to do to decide what I'm going to do about my life."

What she was saying didn't make sense to him. This didn't sound like his Staci.

"Did you sleep with him last night?"

Staci almost rolled her eyes. "What goes on with me and my husband is none of your business, but I will answer you this one time. No, I didn't spend the night with him." She paused. "I asked him for a divorce last night."

Malcolm didn't try to hide his pleasure with that announcement. This was major progress from her stance three months ago.

"Don't get too happy; my feelings for you haven't changed. I'm not interested in a relationship with you either."

If Malcolm wasn't so happy about her divorce, he would have been offended.

"Malcolm, I hope you understand what I'm saying. I won't be seeing you or talking to you anymore."

"I understand," he answered, sounding as if he didn't believe any of it for a second. Like she'd be calling him within twenty-four hours.

They finished their meal with small talk; then Staci left without having touched the frozen drink.

That night she had the strangest dream. In the dream, she was seated in what appeared to be True Worship, but it wasn't a regular church service. She couldn't tell what type of service it was. Miss Cora was there, but she wasn't sick. She was healthy and dancing around the sanctuary yelling, "I told you so. His light is shining bright."

Keisha was there along with the rest of Derrick's family on the front row in the center section. She looked around. Derrick was nowhere to be found. Staci's family was there too. Everyone was smiling and singing; some were even dancing in the spirit, so it couldn't be a funeral. Or could it? Pentecostals do dance at funerals.

Pastor Reggie stood on the dais in his white cassock. Lifting his hands in the air, he prayed for the person below him. From her seat, Staci couldn't see who the person was. The person appeared to be lying down with their face concealed.

As Pastor Reggie prayed, Miss Cora continued dancing and yelling, "I told you so. His light is shining bright." No one but Staci seemed to have noticed her. Staci started to stand up so she could see better, but a little boy with a strong resemblance to Derrick stopped her. The little boy didn't say anything, just held unto her arm and giggled. Staci looked into the child's eyes. There was something familiar about them, but she didn't have time to figure it out. She wanted to know why Derrick wasn't anywhere to be found. And who was Pastor Reggie looking down at?

She tried to remove her arm from the little boy, but he wouldn't let go of her. "I'm yours, I'm yours," the little boy kept repeating. Staci was reciting those same words when she awakened the next morning.

Chapter 27

Derrick spent his last hour on Friday reviewing his new appointment schedule with Phyllis. He'd reorganized his work schedule so he would be able to stop working every day at 5:30 and have his evenings free with Staci. It was still premature, but he was making preparations for his return to his wife. There wasn't any doubt in his mind he and Staci would reconcile. He'd prayed about it, and the Lord had shown him it would happen. Derrick just didn't know how and when.

It was hard, but Derrick played by Staci's rules. He admitted his jealously of Malcolm and was mad at himself for creating the opening that allowed that man entry into his world. However, Derrick refused to sit back and give Malcolm full access to his wife. Derrick's presence in Staci's life would be visible. Like tonight, he'd planned on stopping by the house just to see if Staci needed anything—and to make sure Malcolm wasn't there.

On his way out, Rhonda caught up with Derrick and invited him to dinner with her, again. As always, he declined.

"You're consistent, but no thank you, Rhonda," he said, then added, "Do you know of anyone who would like to rent the studio? I'm moving back home soon."

Rhonda's fake smile failed to hide her disappointment. "That's wonderful. Staci's a lucky woman. I would say I'm happy for you, but that would be a lie."

"I don't want you to lie. You've been upfront about your feelings, and I appreciate that. I hope you'll eventually appreciate how much I love my wife."

Rhonda opened her mouth to speak, then closed it. She glared at him, then finally said, "I'll ask around about the studio."

"Thank you," Derrick said, walking away, knowing Rhonda was watching his back.

Staci was upstairs getting dressed to go out when he arrived at the house. The sound of Derrick's voice calling her from downstairs startled her. She rushed from her room to the staircase to find Derrick standing in the living room with a carton of Ben & Jerry's Chunky Monkey in his hand. *He's good*, she thought. *He knows I won't throw that away.*

"Derrick, what are you doing here?" she asked with her hands on her hips.

Derrick stared at her but didn't answer. She asked again, and when he didn't answer the second time, she followed his eyes. In her rush, she'd forgotten she wasn't wearing anything but a black lace bra with matching underwear. She turned and quickly walked back into her room. When she came downstairs, Derrick was in the kitchen drinking ice water. His bright skin had turned a shade of red.

"Derrick, what do you want? It's not Wednesday," she asked, while inserting silver hoop earrings.

"I just wanted to stop by and see how you're doing." His eyes focused on how well the black A-line dress with the side split that came up to her thigh accented her figure.

"Next time call first. I have plans for this evening, and like I said, it's not Wednesday. You know, the day I deal with foolishness."

"Okay," he said, still silently admiring the dress. "Who are you going out with?" He was not about to let her go out with Malcolm in that dress and have him undressing her with his eyes in the same manner he was now doing.

"Derrick, that's none of your business. You gave up the right to know my plans the day you left me."

Derrick swallowed hard trying to control his anger. He was willing to play by her rules, but not when it came to her looking sexy for another man. He set the glass down on the counter.

"Staci, I don't want you going out with Malcolm in that dress."

Staci rolled her eyes at him. "I don't care what you want. I will go out with whomever I please, and I will wear whatever I please."

"No, you won't," he said calmly, but firmly.

"Maybe if I'd worn this dress six months ago, you would have kept your behind at home." The contempt on her face antagonized him even more.

"Staci, I am still your husband, and I am telling you, you're not going to spend the evening with another man in that dress!" he restated. "And that's final."

"Derrick, shut up. You can't tell me what to do. I'm a grown woman."

"Staci, I'm warning you. You're not wearing that dress."

"Yes, I am." She turned her back to him and slipped her feet into her pumps.

"Don't say I didn't warn you," he said, then flung her over his shoulder and carried her upstairs.

"Put me down!" she screamed and beat him on his back all the way into their bathroom.

He finally set her down inside the shower stall and turned on the cold water. With one hand he held the shower head and sprayed her. With the other, he held the door so she couldn't get out. Staci was so angry she almost screamed profanities at him.

When he was sure he had soaked her enough to ruin the dress, he turned the water off and opened the door to let her out. Staci used her hand and covered her mouth to keep from cursing at him. "Get out!" she screamed.

Ignoring her, he helped her remove the drenched dress that now clung to her body, causing her to shiver. He then handed her a towel.

"Get out! Get out!" This time she punched his hard pectoral muscles. She was soaking wet and not about to give him the pleasure of seeing her stripped down to her birthday suit, not after what he had done.

"I'm leaving, but I don't want to have this conversation again. You're my wife, and your body is for my eyes only. Period."

"I hope your eyes had fun, because your hands will never touch this body again!"

Derrick shook his head and left.

When Shannon and Lashay showed up five minutes later and asked why she wasn't dressed, Staci huffed and puffed and recapped the shower episode.

"Why didn't you just tell the man you're riding out to my mother's house with us to help plan our joint baby shower?" Lashay asked once she stopped laughing.

"He doesn't need to know my business," Staci snapped.

Shannon dismissed that explanation. "That's not the reason, and you know it."

"What are talking about?" Staci's attempt at innocence didn't even fool her own self.

"Girl, please, you know you wanted to make him jealous," Shannon said after smacking her lips. "Why else would you have worn a dress that sexy in the first place?"

Staci laughed. Her girls knew her well. "I couldn't help it after the way he gawked at me in my underwear, like he wanted to sop me up with a biscuit. I wanted to remind him of what he gave up."

"Your little plan backfired," Lashay said. "Dr. Garrison reminded you that he hasn't and will not give up anything. You're his woman whether you like it or not."

"And girl, you know you like it," Shannon added.

Once again, Staci suppressed the spark of hope which flared deep inside her. Taunting him with her body was one thing, but she refused to let Derrick back into her heart. "I don't care what Derrick Garrison says. He doesn't own me. I will dress however I want," Staci proclaimed and stomped up the stairs.

"Uh-huh," her girls said. Neither one was surprised when Staci returned wearing jeans and an oversized sweatshirt.

Malcolm paced around his loft trying to figure out why Staci hadn't called him in two days. "Where are you?" he asked the picture of her that he kept on the wall. He'd heard her say she was going to stop seeing him, but he didn't believe her. She couldn't stop seeing him. She wanted him. He dialed her number again; still no answer. "Why didn't I make her give me her home number?" he said out loud. "Why didn't I get her home address?

"She's not getting rid of me that easy," he grumbled. "The good doctor had better watch his back."

Chapter 28

When Staci saw Derrick's SUV parked in the driveway, she started to keep right on driving and take up residence wherever she ran out of gas. She was still furious about the shower incident three days ago. If Dr. Garrison wanted an argument, he wasn't going to get one. He'd be lucky to get a hello.

Staci entered her home and found him sitting on the stairs in the dark with his head down. Because it was dark and she really didn't care what was bothering him, she stomped right past him and into her bedroom.

"Derrick, I don't feel like arguing with you today, and I don't need a shower," she barked when she heard him enter what was once their bedroom. To her surprise, he didn't respond and that caught her attention and made her turn and take a good look at him. "What's wrong?" she asked, noticing his sullen and damp face.

He didn't answer with his mouth, but his shoulders started to heave and the look in his wet eyes told her that something was very wrong. Derrick never cried. In that moment, all of the animosity she had toward him didn't matter. She had to find out what was wrong with her husband.

She walked over to him and placed her arm around him. "Baby, what's wrong? Is it your mother?"

He looked down at her, and his voice quivered as he said, "My mother died this afternoon."

"Oh, honey, I'm so sorry." She fought to keep herself from crying and failed. "I really loved your mother," she said between sobs. "Why didn't you call me?"

"I wanted to, but . . ." he let the answer hang and yielded to his pain.

They stood there crying side by side until Staci guided him over to the bed they once shared. As though it was a natural reaction, when Staci leaned back against the pillows, Derrick leaned his head against her and she held him tightly against her bosom and stroked his dark curls. By looking at them, no one would know the turmoil that ruled their marriage. It was impossible to tell that he had walked out on her, and she was counting down the days before she would be single again.

Maybe this is what the dream was about, Staci thought. *It was about Miss Cora's passing, but that wouldn't explain why Derrick wasn't there or the little boy in the dream.* She pushed it to the back of her mind and concentrated on Derrick.

After he calmed down, they rested back against the headboard and talked well into the night. She listened as Derrick told her how Miss Cora died peacefully with a smile on her face.

"I held her hand until she took her last breath," he said, sniffling. Staci grabbed a tissue from the nightstand and gently wiped his face for him.

"You're a good son," she whispered.

She couldn't recall the last time they had talked this long without it ending in an argument. Or the last time she'd been this close to him without wanting to wring his neck. All she wanted to do was comfort him, to make his pain go away. As she lay there, Marcus's words rang in her head. *You don't want a divorce.* She pushed that thought out of her mind and continued stroking Derrick's head and back.

Derrick asked her if she would accompany him to the funeral home and assist him with the arrangements. She quickly agreed and offered to help him make the necessary phone calls to his relatives as well.

"Keisha will be here in the morning. I hope you don't mind her staying here at the house. She's afraid to stay in Mama's house since that's where she died."

"That's fine, Derrick. We are family; for now anyway."

"I also plan to stay here." His statement was more of a question.

"Derrick, we don't have to put up a front. Everyone knows we're not together anymore," Staci answered. Then the thought occurred to her that he just didn't want to be alone and she really didn't want him to be alone. "But if that's what you want, you can stay in the guest room."

"Thank you for allowing me to stay."

"It's late," she announced, after looking at the clock alongside her bed. It was after midnight.

He watched her walk into the bathroom. Derrick took that as his cue and stood to leave.

"If you wake up in the middle of the night and want to talk, I'm here," Staci said after she returned from the bathroom with a robe in hand.

Derrick observed her carefully as she prepared for bed, making sure she didn't reveal any side of herself to him. His heart ached. There was once a time when she would have freely shown him every inch of her. She would have given him free access to everything. Now she kept everything hidden from him, like he was a stranger instead of her husband.

"Good night," she said after sliding between the sheets and bringing the covers just underneath her chin.

Derrick watched his wife lying there and fought the urge to risk climbing into bed with her. He wanted—no—he needed—to be next to her. He needed to feel the warm softness of Staci's body next to him, to reassure him that he wasn't alone in the world. Derrick needed her sweet voice to tell him that he would make it through this trying time. Due to his own actions, he wasn't going to get any of that.

Staci opened her eyes after she heard the door close. If Derrick had stayed one minute longer, she was sure she would have invited him into her bed. She didn't want to admit it, but it hurt her to see him in so much pain. As much as he had let her down and as angry as she was with him, she couldn't stand to see her teddy bear so wounded. When he cried, she literally wanted to kiss his tears away.

Chapter 29

While Derrick sat on the lanai and ate the breakfast Staci had prepared for him, Staci called the office and left instructions for her store managers on the things she wanted done in her absence. She then called Marcus.

"I'm sorry to hear that," Marcus said after she told him about Miss Cora's death. "How's your husband taking it?"

"Your boy is about as well as can be expected."

"Until he apologizes, he is not my boy. He's simply your husband, and he really needs you right now."

"I know. Anyway, I've left instructions with the managers regarding the expansion, but I'm sure you're going to check on them."

"Of course. I have to watch my money."

Staci looked out the window and saw Derrick approaching the patio doors. "Big head, I need to go. You can reach me on my cell."

In a surprise move Marcus said, "Let me know when the services are and give Derrick my condolences."

"Sure," she said before she hung up. The phone sounded a second later. She assumed it was Marcus calling her back, but it wasn't.

"Malcolm, I can't talk right now. My mother-in-law passed away yesterday."

The condolences he offered lacked sincerity. "Sorry to hear that. Does this mean I can't see you today?"

Staci closed her eyes and exhaled deeply. How on earth did I spend so much time with someone as inconsiderate as Malcolm? she wondered.

"Malcolm, I told you before, I'm ending our communication."

"I know what you said, but I miss you, and I know you miss me too. I know you have a lot to do, but just talk to me for a minute." Malcolm's voice sounded like it belonged on a 900 sex talk line. "I just need to hear your sweet voice for a little while," he practically moaned.

"I don't have time to babysit you. I have important business to take care of. Good-bye." Staci clipped the phone on her waist just before Derrick entered her home office.

"Marcus asked me to give you his condolences," she said, looking up at Derrick.

"I appreciate that. I'll call him later." She guessed Derrick meant that. She figured he really missed the few friendships he once had. It seems like he'd lost so much when he walked out on her. He probably didn't realize just how much until now, when he needed someone.

"Thanks for breakfast," he said just as she walked around the desk with her jacket fanned over her arm.

"Sure. Are you ready to go?" She avoided direct eye contact with him because she was starting to feel her heart opening to him again.

He reached for her, but she took a step back and at the same time shook her head.

"I'll get my keys," he finally answered and walked out.

Staci spent the entire day supporting Derrick. First stop, the San Francisco International Airport to pick up Keisha. Staci couldn't have imagined the drive back to Oakland would be so taxing. Keisha cried, nearly screamed from the moment Derrick stepped from the SUV at curbside. She was so distraught. Her big brother had to carry both the luggage and her. Staci's hands were shaking, and her ears ringing by the time she pulled into the mortuary parking lot.

Miss Cora had refused to talk about the type of service she desired, but she did select a funeral home and prepaid enough money to make sure her children would be able to give her a nice home-going.

Derrick ran every decision he made by Staci. For the next seven days, outside of personal hygiene, he didn't do anything without Staci at his side. He needed her for everything, from arranging the service to selecting clothing for his mother. Keisha didn't mind. She considered Staci a sister. Besides, she was too distraught to make any sound decisions on her own.

Derrick wouldn't even eat without Staci, which wasn't good, because she was so busy that she really didn't have time to eat. Some days he didn't eat until the evening when Staci finally had a chance to sit down and eat with him.

She was busy, but Staci had to admit she enjoyed feeling needed by her husband again and being touched by him again. He constantly held her hand, rested an arm around her, or leaned against her for support. A couple of times she gave him a quick peck on his lips before realizing what she'd done. This morning upon entering the kitchen, she greeted him with, "Good morning, honey."

Staci constantly fought the war within herself about her future with Derrick. Her stomach fluttered with hope all the while her rational thoughts were against reconciliation of any type. She liked how they were now, but it was only temporary. That didn't change how natural it felt though. But she couldn't allow herself to become vulnerable to him again. As soon as he finished grieving, Derrick would return to his usual withdrawn self. Staci believed that.

The night before the funeral, after the sedative a doctor prescribed for Keisha had taken effect, Derrick and Staci sat in their room talking and laughing like they used to do back when they were in college. They reminisced about their first date. To punish Staci for making fun of his lack of color coordination, Derrick flipped her onto the bed and tickled her until she begged for mercy. As Staci lay on her back giggling uncontrollably, Derrick's hands traveled upward from her abdomen and touched parts of her that made her instantly sober. She lay there with her eyes locked into his, debating if she should respond to his sensual touch or push him away. However, her cell phone rang, making the decision for her.

Derrick removed his hands and waited for her to answer the phone, but she didn't move. He guessed it was Malcolm and interpreted the look in her eyes as one of longing and wondered if she was longing for Malcolm.

He stood up. "I'll leave so you can return your call."

"You don't have to do that." She wanted him to both stay and leave.

He gave her a slight nod, but still left the room anyway. She never did check her phone.

She didn't see Derrick again until the next morning when he asked her to help him straighten his tie. For some reason, Derrick could never tie his tie straight.

"Some things never change," she stated, while working on his tie. She'd provided the exact same assistance for both his college and dental school graduations. How many more opportunities would she have to help him get dressed and coordinate his clothing? She didn't know. She really loved picking out clothes for him and seeing a smile of appreciation on his face. Staci was suddenly overcome with a sadness that showed all over her face. Derrick recognized the look, but wrongfully assumed it was due to the funeral set to start in an hour.

"Everything is going to be all right, sweetheart. I know Mama is in a better place."

Hearing the endearing term only made matters worse for her. "Derrick, let's keep it real today. My name is Stacelyn, and I'm the one you walked out on four months ago. We are married in name only, and after today, you will be going back to wherever it is you live."

"Staci, I meant—"

She held up her hand to stop him from speaking. "The limo's here. We should be going." On her way out, she quickly went over the instructions with the caterer. The repast would take place at the house following the burial.

When they stepped outside, Keisha was already in the limo. Staci sat opposite Derrick to allow Keisha some comfort from her big brother.

When they arrived at the church, Derrick refused to get out of the limo. Staci enlisted Keisha's help in attempting to coax him out. When that didn't work, Pastor Reggie sat inside and talked to him. She had no idea what her uncle said to Derrick, but whatever it was, it gave him the strength he needed to attend his mother's funeral, but not without Staci on his arm.

Staci nearly missed a step as they walked up the stairs leading to the vestibule. At the landing stood Rhonda, adorned in a red suit with a matching red hat. With red being Miss Cora's favorite color, the entire Garrison clan had dressed in red. Rhonda could have very easily been mistaken for a family member. Staci concluded that's exactly what she had intended.

Rhonda offered condolences as the couple passed by. "Hello, Derrick. Sorry for your loss." She didn't address Staci.

Derrick paused, but Staci responded for him. "Thank you, Rhonda. Please make a notation in the guest book, indicating you're an employee. Dr. Garrison and I will send out individual thank-you cards at a later date. Now, if you'll excuse us." Staci brushed past Rhonda and Derrick followed.

For the entire ninety minutes of Cora Ann Garrison's funeral service, Derrick kept physical contact with Staci. While listening to the choir sing, his hand rested on her leg. During expressions from family and friends, he placed his arm around her shoulder. When it was time for the final viewing, he held out his hand for her, then interlocked his fingers with Staci's. She stood right beside him, stroking his back as he said good-bye to his mother. To Derrick's surprise, so did Marcus and Brian. He didn't have a chance to acknowledge them; he had to quickly turn to catch Keisha before she fell to the floor.

Through his shades, Staci could still see the pain etched on his face, but he didn't cry. Instead, he played the strong role for his little sister, who was having a hard time letting go. Staci did hear a couple of sniffles coming from him, though, and felt the tenseness of his body.

When it was time for the funeral director to lock the bronze casket, Derrick turned his head so he wouldn't have to watch. He did the same thing at the cemetery. He couldn't stand to see his mother being lowered into the earth. It wasn't until he was back at the house and in the privacy of the guest room did he allow himself to break down. Staci heard his sobs when she walked past his door, but she didn't intrude. Derrick wouldn't have wanted that, so she thought.

When Derrick finally joined his family and friends outside on the lanai, Staci thought he looked like he had been run over by a truck, and then dragged down the street. Her heart instantly went out to him, and oddly enough, she wanted to take him upstairs to the confines of the master bedroom suite and comfort him. She watched him quietly take a seat next to Keisha, who shared a story with the Simones about their mother.

"Thank you," he said, after accepting the bottle of water from Staci. She remained beside him, playing with his curls.

Later, when he was alone, Carey approached him. Derrick hadn't spoken to his father-in-law in months, but he couldn't avoid him any longer. He owed him an apology for breaking his word to him. Derrick also needed to thank Carey for supporting him in his time of loss.

"Hello, Dad. Thanks for coming." He extended his hand, but Carey ignored it.

"Derrick, I thought we got past the handshake a long time ago." The Simones had a tradition of greeting family with a hug.

"We did." Derrick paused. "I just thought that since things are the way they are . . ."

"You mean since you broke your promise and walked out on my daughter?" Carey clarified for him.

Derrick swallowed hard. "Yes."

"Derrick, I'm not going to butt into your marriage. I don't like what you did, but the fact remains my baby girl loves you, and I know you love her. There's no need in me going off on you because eventually, the two of you will reconcile, and I'll still be mad. So, I'm praying for the two of you to work things out quickly, because I'm tired of seeing my baby girl's sad eyes, and I don't like seeing you so miserable either."

Derrick was so overwhelmed by Carey's show of support that he embraced his father-in-law before he realized what he was doing.

Staci watched from a distance with tears in her eyes. It was then that she recognized Derrick's need for a real father figure. *Maybe he was doing the best he could with me*, she thought.

"Now I'm speaking. Are you listening?"

"Not now," Staci grunted back at the voice.

"You still love him, don't you?" her mother asked and interrupted her thoughts.

"It doesn't matter, Mama. Things will never be the same again."

"Maybe things will be better," Alaina commented. "Have you considered that?"

Staci felt the vibration of her cell phone at her waist. "Maybe I don't want things to be better with him." Staci read the number, then walked inside the house through the patio door to answer Malcolm's call.

"What took you so long to answer?" Malcolm questioned when Staci finally said hello.

"I was busy."

"Doing what?" Malcolm sounded like he was interrogating her.

Staci stepped into the hall bathroom and closed the door. The last thing she needed was for someone to overhear her.

"Malcolm, I told you, today's my mother-in-law's funeral. Why am I explaining myself to you?"

"What does that have to do with you?"

"It has everything to do with me. I loved Miss Cora," Staci defended.

"Or is it her son you love?"

Staci pulled the phone away from her ear. She felt the answer to that question wasn't any of Malcolm's business, but didn't voice the words.

"Staci," Malcolm called out when she didn't respond.

"What did you call me for?" she finally said.

"I called to tell you that I miss you." His voice was gentle and soothing again. "I was hoping we could hang out. Maybe catch a movie."

Staci rolled her eyes as if he could see her. "Malcolm, I have a house full of grieving relatives, and you want me to catch a movie with you? Are you sure you're smart enough to be a stockbroker?"

After a pregnant pause, Malcolm apologized. "I'm sorry if I came off the wrong way. It's just that I'm worried about you. I know you have spent the past week tending to the needs of your family. I want to be the one who attends to your needs. I know you're tired, and I thought you could use a break, that's all."

Lately Malcolm had a strange way of showing his concern for her, but at least he was concerned about her, unlike her husband.

"That's nice of you, but I can't leave." Someone knocked on the door. "I have to go." She ended the call and flushed the toilet, then turned the water on to give the illusion she had been using the restroom.

Staci opened the door and saw Derrick standing there and instantly felt guilty. The look in his eyes when he saw the cell phone in her hand told her he knew exactly what she had been doing.

"I'm going to drive Keisha to the airport." Keisha's new job only allowed her seven days of bereavement leave. "I'll be back later. The caterer is looking for you," he said, never addressing the issue of the phone conversation with Malcolm.

"Okay," she said and started to walk past him, but he turned so that they were both stuck in the doorway, forcing her to look up at him.

"Derrick, will you move so I can get by?" She tried to sound irritated, but felt too ashamed to be effective.

"In a minute, but first there's something I need to say to you."

"What is it?" She looked away from him and shifted her weight from one foot to the other. Being this close to him with no one else around made her uneasy.

Derrick moved in closer and turned her head back to his and stroked the side of her face. "Thank you for everything. I'm sorry to say, but as always, you have been better to me than I have been to you." She took a step back, so that now she was leaning against the door frame. She both loved and hated his touch.

"Stacelyn," he whispered softly and moved in even closer. "I love you so much."

She opened her mouth to argue the point, but before she could get one word out, his lips were massaging hers ever so softly, just the way she liked it.

"No!" she tried to scream, but the words were trapped inside her head, along with the command telling her body to move away. She moaned faintly, and as if they had a mind of their own, her lips parted even more and fully welcomed him, holding him captive in one of the most passionate kisses they'd ever shared.

For a short while, Staci put the last year of her life out of her mind and enjoyed the feel of her husband holding her and kissing her, cherishing her. The longer they kissed, the more relaxed she felt. By their own accord, her hands traveled up his body and around his neck and began playing with his thick curls. Derrick deepened the kiss and Staci's knees buckled. He steadied her by lifting her body to his and squeezing her tightly. If Keisha hadn't interrupted them, there's no telling what would have happened in that doorway.

The feel of Staci's arms around him and the warmth of her mouth helped Derrick forget that she was just on the phone with the "other man." Her response confirmed for him that she still wanted him and that there was hope for reconciliation.

"I'll be right out," Derrick said to Keisha, trying to steady his breath after his younger sister told him she would be waiting in the car for him.

"We'll talk later," he said to his wife after kissing her again, then slowly backing away from her.

Staci's mind was so mixed up all she could do was nod. One question boggled her mind: *How could he still have that effect on me after what he's done?* She knew the answer. She still loved him and always would. Hearing him say the words she longed to hear for so long was all it took to make her temporarily forget about his shortcomings and enjoy his passion.

Staci splashed water on her face before she went looking for the caterer.

"Looks like the making up process has already started," her mother said when she rejoined everyone on the patio.

"What are you talking about, Mama?"

Alaina smiled. "Your face is flushed, and Keisha told me she caught you guys making out in the bathroom."

Staci shook her head. "Mama, it wasn't all that." She blushed.

"If you'd like, I can have Craig drive Keisha to the airport. Julia and I can tend to the guests, and Derrick can take you upstairs and make you scream." Alaina caught the attention of several guests when she laughed out loud. "I'll even turn the music up so no one can hear you," she whispered.

For the first time in a long time, Staci laughed at the thought of Derrick making her scream. "Mama, just pray for us." As soon as the words left her mouth, Staci realized praying for her marriage was something she hadn't done in a long time, a very long time, not since hooking up with Malcolm. "God, please help us," she softly, yet sincerely, prayed.

Chapter 30

With everyone gone and business settled with the caterer, an exhausted Staci headed upstairs to the serenity of her bedroom. While removing her earrings, her eyes fell on Miss Cora's obituary that lay on her dresser. Staci had been so busy with making arrangements and supporting Derrick, she hadn't had time to work through her own grief.

From day one, Miss Cora had been like a second mother to her. Even when Staci and Derrick began having problems, Miss Cora never blamed Staci for their problems. In fact, she always told her, "Baby, I know my son is off, but if you can hang in there with him until he works through his issues, he'll make you a good husband."

Staci removed her shoes and stretched across her bed and reflected on more of her conversations and interactions with her mother-in-law. Staci cried when she thought about how much she was going to miss her mother-in-law, then laughed out loud when she reminisced on the day Derrick accidentally slammed Miss Cora's front door, and she came running out of the house waving a baseball bat at him.

"You may be big, but this bat is the equalizer! Slam my door again and I'll knock you farther than a Barry Bonds's homerun!"

Derrick didn't know she owned a bat. All he could say was, "I'm sorry."

Staci had just returned from the bathroom where she had showered and changed into a nightshirt when Derrick entered the room. Immediately, she used her arms to cover herself.

Derrick smiled his admiration of her body through the transparent sheerness of the material.

"Did Keisha's flight leave on time?" she asked.

"Yes."

"How is she?" Staci wanted to divert his attention away from her. She sensed Derrick wanted to finish what he'd started earlier in the downstairs bathroom, but Staci wasn't having it. She went into the bathroom and returned wearing a robe.

"It may take awhile, but she'll be fine," Derrick answered and sat down in the chair adjacent to the bed.

Staci sat on the bed and looked around the room at nothing in particular. Derrick watched her every move. They sat there quietly, not knowing what to say to each other. They had known each other for almost eight years and had been married for eighteen months. But it seemed they didn't know what to say to each other now that they were alone in their bedroom.

"Staci, we need to talk," Derrick finally broke the silence.

Staci already knew he wanted to discuss the future of their marriage, but after the kiss they shared earlier, she wasn't sure she could have an objective conversation with him.

"What do you want to talk about?" She finally made eye contact with him.

Derrick leaned forward in the chair and took her hands into his. "I'm ready to work on our marriage. I'm ready to be a husband to you."

The sincerity in his voice touched her in a place she thought had closed long ago. But she wasn't ready to open up, not just yet. "Derrick, so much has happened, I don't know if that's possible."

"Staci, nothing has happened that can't be fixed. I know I made mistakes, and I've hurt you deeply. But, I'm ready to make restitution to you. I've settled the issues with my insecurities."

Staci's head jerked upward. This is the first time she'd heard him admit his insecurities.

"I know who I am now, and I accept me, just the way I am." He brought her hands to his mouth and kissed them. "I love you, and I'm ready to be your husband. I look forward to it."

Staci reclaimed her hands, then walked over to the window. The red taillights and white headlights going in and out of the Caldecott Tunnel only added to her blurred vision. Derrick had finally released the healing balm for her broken heart, but she couldn't apply the ointment.

"I don't know if I'm ready for this," she answered honestly.

Derrick stood directly behind her with his arms folded, appearing suddenly ready for a confrontation.

"Staci, what is the full extent of your relationship with Malcolm?"

Staci whirled around. "What?"

"Have you or are you now sleeping with him?"

"Why?"

"I need to know if he's the reason you're not ready. I need to know if there's a second party competing for your heart."

Staci hesitated before she answered, not sure of how much she wanted to reveal to her estranged husband about her outside relationship. She decided to just lay everything out on the table. She had nothing to hide. She's wasn't the one who walked out; he was.

"Staci, answer me," Derrick insisted.

"No, Derrick, I didn't sleep with Malcolm." She heard Derrick exhale loudly. "But I almost did," she finished.

Staci watched her husband's face distort with both shock and hurt. She quickly suppressed the satisfied smile that threatened to light her face.

Derrick stood frozen and attempted to reject the truth. Despite all of their problems, the thought of Staci in the arms of another man had never occurred to him until he saw her with Malcolm. He'd just assumed that while he was gone, she would just patiently wait for him to get himself together. Isn't that what a good, saved wife is supposed to do?

In the four months they'd been separated, he'd thought about being unfaithful. Rhonda was more than willing, but he couldn't bring himself to do anything because he loved Staci too much, and he had made a commitment to God. Derrick had to admit, though, that his commitment to God was shaky at best and wasn't enough to keep him at home with his wife.

"Staci, how could you? How could you even think of doing such a thing?"

Staci dropped her hands and glared at him. Derrick had the audacity to stand there and pretend to be the victim. Had he forgotten that he was the one who treated her with little regard, and then walked out on her because she couldn't get pregnant? If he had, she was certainly going to remind him.

"How could I?" Staci placed her hand on her hip. "Derrick, that was easy after the way you've treated me."

"What are you talking about? I mean, I know I've been gone for four months, but you knew that was only temporary. Didn't you?"

"Derrick, please. You may have physically left this house four months ago, but you left me a long time ago. To be honest, you have never really been here, at least not with me."

"Staci, what are you talking about? Up until four months ago, I was here every day."

She inhaled while trying to figure out a way to say the words without falling apart. "Since our honeymoon eighteen months ago, you've treated me like I was nothing more than a baby-making machine. The only time you touched me was on the days you figured I was ovulating and would conceive." She bowed her head and took another deep breath, determined to get everything she'd been holding in all this time out into the open.

"Derrick, did you even notice that I didn't enjoy the times we were intimate? Of course, you didn't notice," she said, shaking her head. "The only person you care about is yourself. Do you notice how you never refer to me as your wife? It hurt when you introduced me as Staci, and not your wife, to the employee that would love to give you some personal bedside care, if she hasn't already. Did you notice that up until today, you've only told me you love me three other times since our wedding day?"

The reality of those words broke Staci, and she had to turn away from him. She refused to let him see her cry over his abuse. "You're the one who stopped complimenting me and talking to me. When I didn't get pregnant, you stopped spending time with me, and then you left me. I don't even know where you have been living for the past four months. You vowed to love me forever, and then you left me. You never wanted me; all you wanted me for was a baby."

Her honest words shredded his heart. Derrick couldn't deny her summation of their marriage, but he needed to explain to her why he treated her the way he had. "Staci, I've always loved you."

She faced him and screamed, "Then why did you leave me?"

Derrick leaned back against the wall; he didn't have an answer good enough.

"Why did you put me in the position of wanting and needing the attention of another man? I only started spending time with Malcolm after you rejected me. I needed to feel like a woman again, and he helped me to do that by giving me the attention and respect and support I should have gotten from you."

Derrick remained stuck to the wall, watching Staci cry and in shock at the realizations she'd just brought to his attention. Everything she said was true. He had just refused to see it for what it was.

"You blame me for us not being able to have another baby. You think it's my fault because I aborted our first baby without telling you."

"No, I don't," he contested.

"Yes, you do, Derrick." She walked back to the bed and sat down, drained. "I know it doesn't matter to you, but it took me a long time to get over what I'd callously done. To this day, I wonder what it would have been like if we would've had a daughter with my curly hair or a son with your eyes. But I'll never know, and that's something I have to live with." Her face dripped with tears when she finally asked her husband, "God forgave me. Why couldn't you?"

Derrick turned away from her. He couldn't look her in the face when he revealed to her the real reason why he had been so adamant about conceiving another baby. At that moment, he regretted the decision he'd made more than he did deceiving her all this time.

When Derrick turned away from her, Staci took that as him rejecting her again. She sighed, absorbing yet another blow.

"Derrick, please leave," she asked calmly. "It's been a long day for both of us, and I don't want to talk about this anymore." Staci leaned back against the pillows with her eyes closed, wondering how it would feel to be a single woman again. At twenty-eight and attractive, she wouldn't have a hard time getting a man's attention. Malcolm Leblanc was proof of that. She wondered if Derrick would want to sell the house or would he sign the deed over to her? How would they split their stocks and bonds and real assets, the cars?

"Staci, I knew," Derrick's somber voice interrupted Staci's mental preliminary divorce proceedings.

"You knew what?" she opened her eyes, but didn't look at him.

Derrick turned around slowly. "I knew about the abortion," he said and lowered his head.

"What?" Staci said, sitting up straight.

"I heard you on the phone making the appointment at the clinic the week before."

Staci was at a loss for words at Derrick's revelation. All this time, she'd thought he'd been oblivious to her selfish plan.

"I knew when and where you were planning on having the procedure. I even followed you there on the day of your appointment."

Staci shook her head from side to side. "Why didn't you say something?"

"I sat in the parking lot the entire time trying to get up the courage to go inside and stop you."

"Why didn't you come inside?" Staci stood and walked over to him and tried to look in his face, but he wouldn't allow her eye contact.

"Staci, I was scared and confused."

"So was I, Derrick!"

"I've hated myself ever since that day. I hated myself for not being man enough to stop you from aborting our child. I've hated myself for becoming a coward like my father. I couldn't live with myself. That's why I left the first time."

Staci thought back to the yearlong breakup after the abortion. "That night, after the procedure, when I told you, you sat in my apartment and pretended to be shocked and angry. You said you couldn't be with me anymore, because you didn't trust me. You called me evil!"

"I said that because that's how I felt about myself. In order to deal with it, I placed the blame on you. I put my energy into blaming you so I wouldn't have to deal with myself," he said and finally met his wife's gaze.

Staci took a step backward. She wanted to get away from him. "Why did you marry me?"

"I wanted another chance at fatherhood. I figured if we got married, and then had a baby, God would be pleased. The guilt would go away, and everything would be fine." Then he added after a pause, "And because I love you, Staci. I've never stopped loving you."

"You don't know anything about love!" she screamed. "You have made my life a living hell because you love me? You placed your inability to stand up and be a responsible man on me. Then you walked out on our marriage—all because you love me? You left me open and vulnerable and wounded because you love me? Derrick, get out!" She pointed to the door. He didn't move, so she ran up and pushed him. "Get out!"

He stilled her arms. "Staci, I told you, I love you, and I'm ready to come home."

"Come home? We don't have a home. We have a house!"

"It's important for me to be here if we are going to reconcile."

"Reconcile what?" Staci couldn't believe her ears. "Our whole marriage has been nothing but an excuse for you not to deal with your conscience!" She broke free from his grip. "What makes you so sure that I want to reconcile with someone who's willing to leave me unprotected, and then walk out on me just so he won't have to deal with his own issues? Do you think I want to be married to someone who would willingly blame me for his issues and lack of ability to be a man?" She waved her hands and shook her head simultaneously. "No, Derrick, I deserve better than that. I deserve better than you. Now get out."

Derrick wanted to defend himself, but he couldn't. He was guilty as charged and as long as he lived, he would never forget the hurt he'd seen in his wife's eyes or the anger permeating her voice. He would spend every day showing her how sorry he was for letting her down. He had not only let her down as a man, but as a husband.

Notwithstanding his many failures, Derrick found solace in knowing Staci still loved him. If she didn't, she wouldn't have been right by his side throughout the ordeal of his mother's passing. During the past week, Staci had covered and protected him more than he had ever done for her. From this day forward, Derrick Garrison had one mission in life: to win his wife's trust and affection back.

"Staci, you're right, I have not been a husband to you. I haven't even been a good friend to you. I have treated you badly, and I was wrong for walking out on our marriage. It doesn't sound like much, but Staci, I really do love you, and I am sorry for all of the pain that I have caused you. I am sorry for not keeping the vows

I made to you, but I'm asking you to give me another chance to show you how much I love you and how important you are to me. Give me a chance to rebuild the trust that I've broken."

Staci turned away from him and walked back to the bed she once shared with him. She offered no words.

"I'm moving back home tomorrow," he said before turning and reaching for the doorknob.

"Derrick," she called after him.

Hoping she had a change of heart, he quickly turned around. "Yes, baby?"

"Lock the door on your way out."

Hours later, Staci gave up on sleeping. It was 5:00 A.M., and she had been tossing and turning all night. How could he do that? How could he take his faults out on her? Those questions kept her up most of the night. She'd always known Derrick had insecurities because he'd grown up without a father, but she had no idea he would allow those insecurities to intentionally hurt her. And what brought about this sudden change? Was he only sorry because he'd just lost his mother? Would he go back to his normal self after he finished grieving?

Staci was not going to open up her heart again to him, plain and simple. She had given him her heart, and he had proven that he didn't deserve her love. She just wished she didn't love him so much. Wished she hadn't said those "for better or worse" vows Marcus had reminded her of.

Staci threw back the down comforter and climbed out of bed. She started to pray, but she couldn't focus on anything but Derrick. She gave up and put on a pair of fleece sweats and prepared to go running down Tunnel Road. If she was lucky, the running spirit that possessed Tom Hanks in the movie *Forrest Gump* would also overtake her and send her on a long journey.

Chapter 31

"Ugh!" Staci grunted when she spotted Derrick's SUV in the driveway when she returned from the office the following evening. She rolled her eyes while at the same time hitting the garage door opener. She was not in the mood for any more drama; not today. The expansion in Corte Madera was wearing her out, and Marcus was pressing her for the quarterly report, and she had another argument with Malcolm about why she couldn't see him today.

"What are you doing with him that has you too busy to see your man?" Malcolm had questioned her earlier over the phone.

"Excuse me? Malcolm, you are *not* my man. Have you forgotten that I'm a married woman?"

"That never mattered to you before."

Staci couldn't defend that. He was right. Up until recently, she had been basically at his beck and call.

"Malcolm, I have to go. I'll call you in a couple of days." She hung up the phone before he could respond.

Now, she didn't need the added stress that came along with her sorry husband, but Derrick wouldn't go away.

"Derrick, what are you doing here?" Staci asked when she saw him in the kitchen setting the table for two.

"How was your day?" he asked with a smile and continued setting the table.

"What are you doing here?" This time she folded her arms.

"I'm setting the table for dinner," he answered again with another smile.

"Derrick, answer me!" she screamed. "Why are you in my house?"

Derrick remained collected. "Staci, I told you last night that I was moving back home today."

She had heard enough. "You also vowed to love, honor, and cherish me until the day you die, but you didn't do that. How was I supposed to know you would keep your word about moving back here?"

Derrick took a long, deep breath, but didn't say anything.

"Look, Derrick, I can't stop you from staying here; the house is half yours. But I don't have to pretend that everything is fine between us, because it is not. It never will be again," she yelled, then stormed from the kitchen and up the staircase.

Derrick planted his fists against the table and bowed his head in prayer. Pastor Reggie had warned him it was going to be tedious work trying to regain Staci's trust. Derrick just didn't realize how hard it was going to be until he saw the raw anger in her eyes.

"You have an uphill battle ahead of you. It's a winnable battle, but it's going to be a challenging one. You can't give up when things don't change as fast as you would like them to. You have to be patient and consistent and allow her to work through her emotions," Reggie had told him in their weekly counseling session.

Derrick made Staci a plate of food and carried it upstairs to her on a tray. Before mounting the stairs, he had an idea and ran out to the yard to cut some fresh roses from their garden. Derrick placed them in a vase on the tray. It felt strange for him to knock on his bedroom door, and then have to wait until he was given permission to enter.

"What do you want?" Staci asked when she opened the door, then stepped back when she saw the tray in his hand.

"I figured you weren't coming back down, so I brought dinner to you." He smiled although she scowled at him.

"Derrick, what's going on? You're never home this early, and you certainly don't make dinner anymore. What is it you want?"

He lifted the tray. "Do you mind if I set this down?" She wanted to say no, get away from me, but he had made his chicken tacos. She loved his tacos, and he knew that. Besides, she was hungry. She stepped aside and waited for him to station the tray on the nightstand.

"Now, tell me what you want," she ordered.

He stood as close to her as possible, considering she had her arms folded.

"It's not what I want, Staci; it's who I want. I want you."

"Certainly you don't think you can get me by coming home early and feeding me tacos?"

"That's not what I think. I'm trying to show you that I'm willing to do whatever I have to do to restore our marriage."

"Dr. Garrison, we don't have a marriage; we have an arrangement. Nothing more." She then sat down on the bed and took a bite of her taco. "Close the door on your way out." She hit the remote for the plasma screen TV, and then proceeded to surf the channels as if he wasn't in the room.

Staci waited until she heard the door close before she examined the tray more closely. The roses were beautiful, and although he'd made a simple meal, Derrick used the china they'd received as a wedding present from Grandma Ana. He made the tacos just the way she liked them with salsa, Colby and Monterey cheese, baby spinach, and just a drop of sour cream. It wasn't until Staci bit into the second taco that she noticed the papers tucked underneath the plate.

Tears welled in Staci's eyes as she read the handwritten words on the lined paper. The words "I love you" were written 540 times. One for each day they'd been married. "You're too late," she said, then ripped the papers up and threw them into the trash.

As soon as she finished her second taco, she called Malcolm.

"I knew you would be calling me," were the first words out of his mouth. "I knew you wouldn't last too long with your boring husband."

"Whatever, Malcolm."

"Tell the truth, Staci; you know you miss me."

Staci was not going to lie to him; she really didn't miss him. At the moment, she was angry with her husband. That's why she'd called him; to vent. She was about to tell him that when the thought occurred to her that she was using Malcolm for companionship, just like Derrick used her to hide his guilt.

"I have to go; I'll talk to you later," she barked and hung up the phone.

The brief phone call last night wasn't enough to suffice his need. The following morning, Malcolm showed up at Staci's office with flowers.

"Thank you, but you really shouldn't have come here," Staci said after closing her office door.

"Why, sweet Staci, if I didn't know any better, I'd think you weren't happy to see me." His voice was meant to be seductive, but it yielded more irritation to Staci than seduction, he guessed by the distortion on her face.

"Malcolm, Derrick's back home."

Malcolm's face further contorted. "What do you mean he's back home?"

"He moved back into the house."

"Are you trying to tell me that you're going to allow that sorry man back into your life?"

Staci had called Derrick sorry on numerous occasions, but that was all right because she was his wife. She didn't like it one bit hearing those words come from Malcolm's mouth.

"Malcolm, you don't have a right to say anything negative about my husband. Besides, we're not back together. He's staying in the guest room."

"Make sure he stays there," Malcolm ordered.

"What exactly do you mean by that?"

Malcolm walked around the desk and towered directly over her. "You better not allow him back into your bed." His voice was so cold a shiver ran down her arm.

Malcolm didn't know Staci as well as he thought. Her next statement revealed to him how much she hated being ordered around.

"Malcolm, you don't own me, and you certainly don't run my house. If I want to allow *my husband* back into *my* bed, that's a decision for me to make, *not* you!" She picked up the floral bunch and shoved it at him. "Now get out of my office!"

Staci's position surprised him. Malcolm was sure he had more control over her. He had to think fast before he messed up completely. He stepped back and softened his stance.

"Staci, I'm sorry. I'm just concerned about your feelings. I remember how hurt you were when he left you the first time. I don't want you to be hurt when he leaves you again."

"Malcolm, let me worry about my feelings when it comes to my husband."

Marcus's knock and sudden entrance prevented Malcolm from saying anything else stupid.

"Staci, we're ready to start," Marcus said in reference to the scheduled management meeting, then waited for his sister to introduce him to the man who was standing just a little too close to her.

"As soon as Mr. Leblanc leaves, I'll be right out," Staci answered, still looking Malcolm dead in the eyes.

When Malcolm realized Marcus wasn't going to leave until he did, he said to Staci, "Keep the flowers," then left.

Marcus stood as if waiting for an explanation from Staci, but she didn't give him one. She simply grabbed her portfolio and headed for the conference room.

Chapter 32

Sunday morning Staci started to sleep in and skip church, but a knock on her bedroom door by the home intruder ruined her plans. It had been almost two weeks, and no matter how much she ignored Derrick, he wouldn't go away.

Every morning before he left for work, Derrick wrote her a note telling her how much he loved and appreciated her. By midmorning she would get a follow-up phone call. Of course, she wouldn't answer it, choosing to let the voice mail get it instead. Every night, Derrick was home by 6:30, and if he didn't fix dinner, he would help her prepare the meal, and then help with the dishes.

During those moments, he attempted to hold conversations with her, but Staci wouldn't respond. She did, however, pause from chopping onions when he announced he'd been living in the studio above the dental office during his hiatus instead of with his mother. He explained that he didn't want to burden Miss Cora with his marital problems. Staci was relieved to know that he hadn't been living with another woman, particularly Rhonda, but she didn't tell him that.

Friday afternoon he showed up at her office with flowers and offered to take her to lunch, but she refused. Saturday, he stayed around the house all day, working in the garden. Derrick even went grocery shopping and picked up her clothing from the dry cleaners. When he hung the clothes in her closet, she didn't bother to acknowledge his presence. When asked if she wanted to watch a DVD with him, her response was a hard slam of her bedroom door. Now he was pestering her again.

"Sweetheart, it doesn't make sense for us to take two cars to church. I'll be ready to go at 10:30 if you would like to ride with me," he offered.

"Oh no, he's not going to church without me," Staci fussed and sat up in bed. She was aware of Derrick's counseling sessions with Reggie, but was he ready to attend church services on a regular basis again? At any rate, there was no way she was going to let him go to church and not be with him. Not after all of the prayers she'd sent up for him. Not after all the encouraging words she'd received from the seasoned saints. Staci was not going to let the church know that now *she* was the one acting crazy.

"I'll be ready," she yelled back.

At 10:25, Staci walked down the staircase to find Derrick seated at the kitchen table with his Bible open. *When did he start reading the Bible again?* She thought she'd heard him praying in the guest room a few times, but had no idea he was studying the Word again too. Maybe he *was* serious.

"Good morning, sweetheart. You look nice today." He looked up from his Bible and admired the turquoise suit with black square buttons Staci was wearing.

Staci rolled her eyes. "Good morning, Dr. Garrison." That's how she addressed him now. "I'm ready to leave when you are." Before Derrick could respond, she walked out the door.

During service, Staci watched in amazement as Derrick praised and worshipped the Lord. He stood and sang along with the praise leaders, then had the audacity to take notes during the sermon. He was like the old

Derrick she fell in love with. Today, she got the same joy from watching him dance in the spirit that she did when she first met him. But when Pastor Reggie asked the congregation to hug your neighbor, she still couldn't bring herself to touch him. She turned to Lashay and hugged her instead. Derrick nodded his understanding.

After service, Derrick cornered his boys, Marcus, Craig, and Brian. It was time he started mending fences and friendships.

"What's up?" Brian asked guardedly. Marcus didn't address him, just stared at him with his arms folded. Craig's lips moved, but he didn't speak. Derrick assumed he was praying for the Lord to hold his tongue from spitting out the four-letter words he had for his estranged brother-in-law in church.

"I owe you guys an apology for my behavior toward you since the announcement of your impending fatherhood," Derrick apologized.

Craig smirked. "Dude, I know that's not all."

"And for the way I've openly mistreated Staci," Derrick continued.

"What happened, man?" Brian wanted to know.

"I'm ashamed to admit this, but I was jealous because you're having children and I'm not."

Marcus finally addressed him. "And you thought walking out on my sister would help you have a baby?"

"No." Derrick sighed. "The jealousy was just a smoke screen for the deeper and real issue I refused to deal with. I was mixed up about a lot of things, and I made a lot of bad decisions, but leaving your sister was the biggest mistake I've ever made, and I'll spend the rest of my life making amends for it."

"Are the two of you back together or what?" Craig questioned.

"I'm working on it." Derrick's peripheral vision caught a glimpse of Staci laughing across the sanctuary with Shannon and Lashay. "Anyway, I just wanted you to know that I am sorry, and I hope we can be boys again. I really miss you guys."

The boys looked at each other, then back at Derrick.

"We all make mistakes, man, but next time, don't isolate yourself like that. We're helpers to one another, but we can't help if you shut us out," Brian said, and then gave Derrick a brotherly hug. "Welcome back, man."

Her brothers weren't so easy.

"I know the Bible says we are to forgive seventy times seven, but, man, if you ever hurt my sister like that again, I'm going to lay hands *and* a two by four on you," Craig declared before embracing him.

Marcus shook his head. "I'm still mad at you, man. I never treated you like an in-law. Since day one, I considered you a brother. You didn't just walk out on Staci. You walked out on our friendship. I thought we were closer than that."

"Marcus, he's human, and humans make mistakes. That's why every day God extends His grace and mercy upon us. As long as God continues to be merciful toward us, we are required to be merciful toward our brother, no matter how jacked up he is. Jesus is our perfect example, and until He runs out of mercy, we don't have a right to." When Craig finished talking, the three men were looking at him with astonishment. "What?" he asked when they were still staring at him a full minute later.

Marcus laughed. "Mama's prayers are really working."

"Preach on, Preacher," Brian chided.

Derrick pulled a twenty-dollar bill from his wallet and held it out to Craig. "We need to raise this preacher a love offering."

"Forget, y'all," Craig said after snatching the bill from Derrick.

The boys finished poking fun at Craig; then Derrick extended his hand out to Marcus. "How about extending some mercy to a jacked-up brother?"

"Will you look at that," Shannon said, as the ladies walked over and joined the men. The guys commenced to doing their ridiculous chest butt and handshake and signal ritual.

"I'm glad that's over," Lashay said, rubbing her belly. "Now, can we go out to eat?"

Staci watched too, but didn't comment. It was a good thing Derrick had mended fences with his boys. He was going to need some friends after the divorce.

"Shannon cooked. You guys want to come over for dinner?" Marcus asked the group.

Lashay and Brian readily agreed.

Staci ignored the invitation. "Are you ready, Dr. Garrison?" she asked in an even tone.

"Marcus invited us over for dinner and I thought—" Derrick started.

"Whatever you say, Dr. Garrison. It's all about you, remember?" Staci cut him off, and then walked away.

"Dr. Garrison, you've got your work cut out for you," Shannon said, and the group agreed.

Chapter 33

Derrick stared out of his living-room window and watched Staci as she sat in her car and talked on the phone. He knew without a doubt she was speaking with Malcolm. Just like he'd known three weeks ago at Marcus's house when she had to step outside to answer her cell phone and every time she had to suddenly get off the phone whenever he entered her presence. He fought hard to control his anger at the thought of his wife talking to another man and appearing to be happy about it without ever acknowledging his presence. No matter how hard he tried, Staci refused to pay him any attention. Last night at his counseling session, Pastor Reggie suggested it was time for Staci to join them, but how could Derrick get her to agree to that when she wouldn't even talk to him?

The only time she spoke more than two words to him was when she had a question about the house. She still wasn't taking his phone calls during the day, and when she came home in the evenings, she ate, and then hibernated in the master bedroom. She never commented on the notes or the flowers he left for her every day, or even said thank you for the meals he served her. She never said one word about him changing his schedule to hours that would give them time together. But hadn't he done the same thing to her? he often wondered.

"Be not deceived, God is not mocked. Whatsoever a man soweth, that shall he also reap." *Reaping sure is hard,* Derrick thought after quoting the scripture.

"What time shall I expect you?" Malcolm asked Staci for the third time.

"Malcolm, I never agreed to see you tonight," Staci answered while trying to look through the windows of her house; wishing she had x-ray vision. Derrick was in there, somewhere, watching. He was always around lately.

"Come on, Staci, we haven't had any time together in a long time. I miss you, baby."

Staci pulled the phone from her ear and rubbed her stomach. The sound of Malcolm's voice referring to her by an endearing term nauseated her.

"Staci, how can you just shut me out like this?" he asked when she didn't immediately respond.

"Malcolm, it's not good for me to spend time with you now that Derrick is back home. These phone conversations are bad enough."

"Was it good when he left you and hurt you? I don't mean to sound cruel, but Derrick doesn't want you. The only reason he's there is because he's grieving over his mother."

Malcolm's words stung. Staci had been thinking the exact same thing, but hearing Malcolm voice her fear only rekindled her resentment toward Derrick.

"What time is dinner?" she asked, then turned her head away from the house.

Five minutes later, Staci rushed into the house. As usual, she didn't acknowledge Derrick's presence. She just ran up the stairs to her bedroom. Half an hour later, she had changed from her business suit into a blue knee-length dress and four-inch heels. Just as she opened the front door to leave, Derrick's voice stopped her.

"Tell Malcolm your husband said hello." He arose from the couch and solemnly went upstairs to the guest room.

Those six words penetrated Staci's resistance and paralyzed her. It wasn't until that moment did the realization that she was about to leave her husband at home and go out on a date with another man penetrate her brain. Suddenly, she was ashamed and couldn't move. Staci remained frozen for what appeared to be an eternity in the same spot until she was able to walk back to the couch.

Forty-five minutes later, she was still sitting on the couch trying to sort through her emotions. Why was she still communicating with Malcolm? He wasn't in her future. She wasn't attracted to him. In the beginning, he was a good distraction, but lately, he'd started to annoy her. It used to be exciting to have someone to talk to; now, most of their conversations bored her. Yet, if she met him at his loft tonight, there was a good chance they would sleep together.

Why, after all the praying and hoping she'd done for Derrick to come home, did she now refuse to allow him back into her life? Yet, she tolerated Malcolm, knowing full well he only wanted to get her into his bed.

There was no doubt in Staci's mind that she loved Derrick. But Derrick had wounded her, and now she was inflicting him with the same wounds. She complained that Derrick didn't pay her any attention, and now that he was trying, she wasn't paying him any. She refused to forgive him and give him another chance. It was just too hard for her to do on her own right now. She knelt in front of the couch.

"God, please help me. I want to forgive him. Please show me how to forgive him. Take this anger and bitterness away from me. I love him so much; but show me how to love him unconditionally like you love me. Help me to open up so I can trust him again. Give me the patience I need to wait while you mend us back together."

After she finished praying and was seated back on the couch, Staci heard the still small voice.

"That's what I was waiting for. Now I can work."

This time, Staci allowed the still small voice to comfort her.

"Back so soon?" Derrick's voice startled her.

Too engrossed in her thoughts, she hadn't heard him come down the stairs. "I never left," she answered softly. Staci didn't bother hiding the evidence that she'd spent nearly an hour crying. Her tears had left a trail down her cheeks.

"Are you hungry?"

"Yeah." The timid voice sounded strange coming from her.

"Give me a few minutes." Derrick left for the kitchen. Minutes later, Staci reveled in the garlic aroma floating through the house.

Derrick returned shortly thereafter and offered to escort Staci into the formal dining room. For the first time since he'd returned home, Staci touched him. She quietly accepted his arm and followed his lead.

Once inside the dining room, she gasped. Derrick had beautifully set the table, complete with candlelight and china.

He pulled out her chair. "Have a seat."

"Thank you." She made eye contact with him for the first time in days. Staci wanted to kiss him, but was afraid to after pushing him away for so long.

Her eyes watered again as Derrick served her seafood Alfredo and Caesar salad with garlic bread. It was one of her favorite meals. They ate in silence, occasionally one glancing up at the other. Then Derrick asked her if she knew what special day it was.

"No, I don't know," she answered, while cutting fettuccine.

He took a sip of nonalcoholic wine, then leaned back in his chair before he responded. "Today is our anniversary."

"No, it's not." She shook her head and tried to block images of their disastrous first anniversary from creating a collage in her mind.

"Not our wedding anniversary. It's the anniversary of when we officially started dating," Derrick clarified.

Staci looked perplexed as she thought for a long hard moment. Derrick was right. They had their first official date exactly eight years ago on this very day. She gasped again, looking down at her plate. Derrick had prepared the exact same meal for her that night in his dorm kitchen. Staci then looked up at him in amazement. Derrick never remembered any of their special days, and now when he did remember, she was about to go out with another man! And he was going to freely let her go, knowing he had prepared a special celebration for them.

Too overwhelmed with emotions, Staci couldn't eat anymore. She pushed her plate away and lay her head on the table. "Oh, Derrick, I'm sorry," she cried. "I'm so sorry."

"Sweetheart, stop crying. This is our eighth year. It's a new beginning for us." He had walked around the table and squatted next to her and cautiously placed his arm around her. Staci, in a surprise move, placed her arms around his neck and pressed her head against him.

Derrick stopped talking and enjoyed the closeness of her, stroking her head and squeezing her. It had been way too long, and he didn't know how soon this chance would come again.

"Derrick, I'm so sorry," she continued to say between sniffles.

"For what?"

"For my relationship with Malcolm."

"It's all right. I understand your reasons." He brushed her curls back and gently kissed her on the forehead.

"No, it's not all right," she said, shaking her head. "I was wrong for getting involved with him while we're still married. Being hurt is not a reason for getting involved with another man, even if I felt justified. I'm sorry for not being willing to allow you the time you needed to work on yourself. I'm sorry for not being willing to give you another chance."

Derrick tilted her chin upward. "Sweetheart, I promise you won't have that problem again. I will never neglect you like that again. I'll never walk away from you again. Only death can take me away from you."

"I believe you," she responded from someplace deep inside her heart.

Before he could kiss her lips, she lay her head against his chest. Derrick held her tightly, as if he were trying to mold her into him.

Staci moaned as she enjoyed the solid muscular feel of her husband. She had almost forgotten what it felt like to be so close to him. To have his big arms covering and warming her. Basking in the feel of her teddy bear, Staci felt something she hadn't felt in a long time: secure. And she felt loved, and she loved it. She loved him.

She broke their embrace. "I can't eat anymore. I'll help you clear the dishes and put the food away."

Derrick watched her stand and walk around the table, then blow out the candles. "Why don't you let me take care of this and you can relax," he offered.

"All right, but don't take too long. I don't want to relax," she said with desire she hadn't felt in far too long.

The knowing smile that creased his face made Staci's heart and the rest of her body warm. She wanted to jump into his arms, but forced her feet to stay planted.

"Sweetheart, what do you want to do?" He took slow strides toward her. "Baby, I'll do whatever you want."

"I want to make love to my husband," she answered right before her lips touched his.

When their lips finally parted, Derrick had lifted her off the floor and her legs were wrapped around him with the back of her dress unzipped. Both were nearly breathless.

"Why wait? We can always buy more food," Derrick said, trying to regain control of his breathing. He then headed for the stairs with Staci still glued to him. Derrick never appreciated being physically fit more than he did climbing the staircase that led to their bedroom carrying his wife.

"I missed you." He laid her on their bed, then removed his shirt, popping the buttons in the process.

"Derrick, that's your favorite shirt!"

"You can buy me another one."

"I love you, teddy bear. I've always loved only you. You're all I ever wanted," she confessed and reached for him.

"I love you too my beautiful Stacelyn."

On this night, her husband made perfect love to her. Derrick gave himself to Staci completely, and she felt the pure love he had for her in every microscopic cell running through her body. She felt love in his touch. She heard love in his voice every time he whispered her name, which was almost constantly.

Derrick cherished her, even worshipped her, being deliberate and methodical in the way he loved his wife; recapturing his place in her heart. He wanted to make sure Staci knew without a doubt that she would never be loved by anyone but him.

During intermission, Derrick allowed her to see his raw emotions toward her for the first time. Staci held him and kissed his tears away, then proceeded to love him back in a way that let him know that she didn't want anyone but him for the rest of her life. When she finished loving him, he wouldn't let her get up; he was too vulnerable; too open; too happy; too afraid to let the moment end. Derrick held her against his body. They fell asleep that way.

Chapter 34

Derrick forced himself out of bed and into the guest room to take a shower. After he dressed, he returned to find Staci still asleep. He smiled appreciatively as his eyes roamed up the curvature of her limp body. She looked so peaceful with her curly hair dangling in her face. As long as he lived, he would never forget how beautiful she was at that moment or how wonderful she had been to him last night. If he didn't know any better, he would think that was the first time they'd ever made love. In a sense, for him, it was. That was the first time he'd freely opened himself up to her without reservation. He literally lost himself in her last night.

He briefly bowed his head and prayed. "God, I thank you for my gift. Thank you for helping me to realize how precious she is to me. Thank you for showing me how to love myself so I can love her the way she deserves to be loved. Help me to always love her the way you love me. Help me to always be open and receptive to her."

Returning from the garden, Derrick found Staci still asleep. It took every ounce of his willpower to keep from climbing back into bed beside her. If they were physically able, he wanted to spend the day making love to her for each day they'd been married. He wanted to hold her for each time he pushed her away. But he couldn't undo the past. But he vowed from that day forward, every day Staci opened her eyes, she would know how important she was to him.

***

When Staci finally awakened, her husband was gone. She nearly panicked until she saw the red roses in the vase on her nightstand and the note in the shape of a heart. Silently, she read the note.

It was the first Saturday of the month; the one Derrick had chosen to work every month until noon for his patients whose schedules wouldn't allow them to come on weekdays. In his note, Derrick promised to return straight home and do whatever she wanted.

What Staci wanted was more of what she got last night. It had been the most powerful, intimate experience of her life. Derrick was the only man she'd been intimate with, so she didn't have any comparison, but after last night, she was positive Derrick Garrison was the best lover in the world! Even the time when they were intimate before they married didn't compare to last night. Just thinking about how Derrick made love to her last night brought tears to her eyes. Her mother was right. Her marriage was worth fighting for, and the bigger the fight, the better the making up! She had to call her parents and tell them the good news.

Staci could barely contain her excitement as she listened to the phone ring. Alaina could barely get the word "hello" out before Staci screamed into the phone, "Derrick and I are back together!"

It was Alaina's turn to scream. "Thank you, Jesus!"

Carey came on the line, and Staci just knew her mother had dropped the phone and was dancing in the spirit around their Napa Valley home.

"Baby girl, I'm so happy for you," Carey said.

"You were right, Daddy. Everything is working out."

Carey asked to speak to Derrick. "Daddy, he's at work. He'll be back in a few hours, but we'll probably be busy," Staci giggled.

Carey joined in her laughter. "How long were you separated?"

"Four months."

"You're going to be busy for a while. I'll call him next month," her father joked.

"Thank you, Daddy," Staci said once she stopped laughing. "Thank you for encouraging me to hang in there. I love you. Give Mom a kiss for me."

"Love you too, baby girl. When your mother gets back inside, I'll give her a kiss. Right now, she's outside on the front lawn dancing."

Staci shared another laugh with her father before she ended her call. She totally understood her mother's joy. Staci felt like dancing across Highway 24.

She showered and dressed in shorts and a tank top and filled the house with sounds of New Direction. She then went into the guest room and started moving her husband's belongings back into their bedroom. It amazed her how little he had accumulated in there. Derrick unpacked only the bare necessities; everything else remained boxed. He had literally been living out of boxes. It also surprised her that he kept a picture of her on the nightstand next to his Bible.

"He never stopped loving you."

"Then why did he leave?" she audibly asked the still small voice.

"Just wait; my servant will tell you."

While collecting his toiletries from the guest bathroom, she remembered her wedding ring. It was time she put it back on. She walked into her bedroom and was just about to place the ring on her finger when her cell phone rang. She already knew who it was without checking the caller ID.

"Hello, Malcolm."

"Staci, what happened to you last night? I called you at least four times and you didn't pick up. I even texted you twice." Somehow his voice didn't sound appealing or soothing anymore.

"Nothing happened. I decided to stay home with my husband."

There was a long pause. "The old man wouldn't let you out, huh?"

She took a deep breath. "Malcolm, Derrick and I are back together—really together."

"That's a big change." Malcolm let out a snort. "Yesterday you were ready to divorce him. What will it be tomorrow?"

"Malcolm, I know I sound flaky, but I know for a fact that I love my husband and I want our marriage to work."

"I guess that means you slept with him, and for once, the sex was good."

Staci wanted to kick herself for discussing her intimate frustrations with Malcolm. She started to tell him the sex was better than good, but that wasn't his business. "Malcolm, I'm not going to discuss my sex life with you anymore. It's best if we stop communicating with each other completely. For real this time."

She could imagine the sneer on his face when he said, "Why, Staci? You don't think you can handle talking to me? Am I that powerful?"

"No, Malcolm, you're not. But the love I have for my husband is, and I don't want to do anything to jeopardize our relationship."

"Funny, you didn't say that when you were over here at my loft."

Staci accepted responsibility. "You're right, Malcolm, I didn't, and I shouldn't have been at your loft in the first place. But I was hurt, and I made a bad decision. The fact remains, I love my husband, and we're going to work things out."

Just then, she felt Derrick's arms from behind reach around her waist. She hadn't heard or seen him come in. Malcolm was saying something, but Staci couldn't decipher what it was because she was distracted by the warm kisses her husband planted along the back of her neck.

Without any protest from his wife, Derrick removed the phone from her ear and set it on the mahogany chest, but not before speaking into the phone and saying, "Good-bye, Malcolm," then disconnected the call.

Still kissing her from behind, Derrick removed the wedding ring from inside her right palm and replaced it back on her left ring finger.

"Sweetheart, you belong to me forever," he said after bringing her hand to his lips. "And I'm yours, completely."

Staci moaned, but she really felt like screaming. "Did you work hard today?" She leaned against him and enjoyed the feel of his arms and lips. It felt so good to have her teddy bear back.

"Not as hard as I am about to."

Dr. and Mrs. Garrison spent the afternoon and part of the evening getting reacquainted with each other. During breaks, they talked, laughed, and played with each other like the newlyweds they were. She'd almost forgotten what it sounded like to hear Derrick's laughter fill a room. Staci had just finished a round of giggles from Derrick's tickling when she noticed a sudden change in his demeanor. His laughter ceased, and his eyes glossed.

"Honey, what's wrong?" She wrapped her arms around his neck. To her delight, Derrick was completely transparent with her.

"Stacelyn, I love you so much, it hurts me when I think about how close I came to losing you. Thank you for letting me back into your heart," he answered and nuzzled against her neck.

"I love you too, teddy bear." She squeezed him. "And you never left my heart." She rested her head against his.

In one swift motion, Derrick stood straight up. "Come on. Let's take a bath." He lifted her from their bed and carried her into the bathroom where he prepared a hot bubble bath for them in the black oversized oval-shaped bathtub. Afterward, Derrick carried Staci back to their bed and treated her to a body massage.

The feel of his hands gliding over her body was just as delectable as the chocolate-dipped strawberries he fed her. Staci moaned from the pleasure. "You have the most magnificent hands."

"Turn over," Derrick whispered in her ear after he finished ministrations to her back.

Watching him stroke her body with such care, Staci had to ask him the question that had been troubling her since the day he left.

"Derrick, I need to ask you something, and I need you to be completely honest with me."

Derrick recognized the seriousness in her tone and stopped massaging her and gave her his full attention. "What is it, beautiful?"

Staci sat up with her back against the pillows and covered herself with the satin sheet. "Derrick, what was so wrong with me that you had to leave? What did I do to make you grow tired of me? I mean, what did I do to make you leave our home?" She hesitated long enough to summon the courage to ask the questions, the answers, of which, could crush her. "Did you fulfill your needs with someone else, like Rhonda?"

With his thumb, Derrick wiped the lone tear that slowly glided down Staci's cheek. Then he held her face and kissed her gently, but passionately. The kiss was meant to reassure her that there was nothing wrong with her; that she was perfect for him. Staci accepted his kiss, but he sensed she needed to hear his words.

"Staci, my leaving had absolutely nothing to do with you." He positioned himself against the pillows alongside her and took her hand in his. "As I told you before, outside of conversation and a few lunch dates, I wasn't involved with Rhonda. I'd be lying if I said I never thought about it, or that she's not interested."

"Then why did you leave?" She had to know.

Derrick took a deep breath. "The day I left was the same day I met my father for the first time."

"What?" Staci was shocked. "Why didn't you tell me you were going to see your father?" She thought back to that morning. "Was that the 'important meeting' you were talking about?"

Derrick nodded. "I didn't tell anyone, not even my mother, but that morning, I walked into Dr. John Archer's office and introduced myself to him."

"What happened?"

Derrick inhaled deeply, and Staci saw that his eyes glossed over. She knew the outcome was not good.

"Nothing happened, at least not what I had expected. Dr. John Archer knew exactly who I was; even told me I looked like him." Derrick smirked. "My mother always said I look just like my father, and she was right."

Observing the strain on Derrick's face, Staci waited quietly and patiently for him to continue.

"First, he started by saying how happy he was the money he spent on my education didn't go to waste. He then congratulated me on graduating from dental school and opening up a practice and wished me well in my career."

Derrick stopped talking, but Staci knew there was more to the story. "What else did he say?" she asked softly, while turning Derrick's head toward her so she could read his eyes. This time she wiped the tear that trickled down his cheek. "Baby, tell me what your father said."

Derrick held her gaze. It was time for him to trust her with his whole heart. He wanted to trust her, but it was still hard. As soon as he answered her question, chances were he would break down. The love in Staci's eyes, however, assured him it was all right for him, a thirty-two-year-old man, to cry and show his insecurities. His wife wouldn't think any less of him.

He cleared his throat. "Then he told me that my identity as his son would have to remain a secret because of his career." Derrick paused. "Neither the board of directors nor his wife of thirty-five years would take the news of the medical director's illegitimate black child too well. Because of that, he didn't think it was a good idea for us to communicate with each other outside of a professional relationship." Derrick's jaw flexed beneath Staci's fingertips.

"Then he said to limit my communication with him to the telephone. He figured once we're seen together, it would be easy to see that I'm his son because of the strong resemblance, and he couldn't risk that. However, he assured me I'd be named as one of his heirs in his will." Derrick used the back of his hand to wipe his face before asking Staci a question she probably didn't know the answer to, but at least he could safely vent. "What good is it to have a father if the only time he's willing to acknowledge you is when he's dead?"

As suspected, Staci didn't have a verbal answer for him. Instead, she wrapped her arms around him and placed his head in her bosom and stroked his curls to comfort him.

"He had birthday and graduation pictures of his other children—his white children—sitting on his desk. There I was, his firstborn, standing right in his face, and he talked to me like I was a stranger. It didn't matter to him that I wasn't a criminal, that I obey the law and don't do drugs. It didn't matter to him that I graduated at the top of my class or that I initially pursued medicine because I wanted to be accepted by him." Derrick's voice broke, and so did Staci's heart. She held him tighter. "No matter what I do, I'll never be accepted by him. He views me as nothing more than his big mistake. That's all I'll ever be to him—a mistake."

Staci felt the satin sheet next to her skin moisten with Derrick's tears and cried tears of her own for him. She'd known he was wounded by the lack of his father's presence, but didn't know just how deep those wounds ran until she heard the horrific sobs coming from deep within his wounded soul. She could not have known; she had a wonderful father. Staci held her husband and rocked him back and forth, while praying fervently for him to find peace and for him to heal.

"Staci," Derrick said after awhile. He sat up and reached for the box of tissue on the nightstand. "That day, all of my insecurities took over, and I couldn't handle my father's rejection. I hated him, and I hated the world, but most of all, I hated myself because I had become him. I realized I was just like him when I chickened out the day you had the abortion."

"That's not true," Staci disagreed with him.

"Yes, it is. I wanted our baby, but I didn't want it to get in the way of my future. I had plans. I was scared and confused, but the bottom line is, I viewed the baby as an obstacle to achieving what I wanted. I wanted to finish dental school, and I didn't see how I could do that with a child to support." Derrick sniffled and regained Staci's hand.

"The day I left, I didn't like my life anymore. I was so depressed I was going to commit suicide."

Staci gasped. "No!"

"When I came home that afternoon, I had planned on overdosing on valium, but you came home early, and I couldn't do it. That's why I fought with you. I was mad because you stopped me from ending my life." He kissed her forehead. "Baby, you saved my life."

When Derrick's fingers stroked her cheek, Staci closed her eyes and tried to recall that day. She remembered her reason for coming home early. Her secretary was out sick that day, which left Staci responsible for making her own copies. Unfortunately for her, the machine was out of toner. Staci removed the empty cartridge and attempted to insert a new one. In a freak accident, the toner cartridge from the office copier had spilled on her clothing, and she had come home to change.

"Derrick, you should have told me what you were going through," she said, after opening her eyes.

"I wanted to, but I'd pushed you away for so long, I thought you wouldn't listen. Subconsciously, I was afraid that one day you would reject me too, like my father had done. I really wanted to open up to you, but I didn't have the courage. That's why I could never share my deep feelings with you, that and the truth about the abortion."

"But you were gone for four months. After all that we've been through over the years, in four months you couldn't find a way to talk to me?"

He didn't argue or deny the truth. "I knew how much I had hurt you, and I couldn't deal with that. I couldn't risk another rejection. I actually thought you had stopped loving me until my mother's death."

Staci didn't understand the connection. "What happened then?"

"You happened. After the way I treated you, you were still right there supporting me. Staci, physically, I'm stronger than you, but emotionally, you have always been my rock. Now, we can be each other's rock," he said before kissing the back of her hand.

"Derrick, honestly, I wanted to stop loving you," she admitted. "I tried hard to will myself not to love you. But when you really love someone, you can't make it go away, no matter how much they hurt you. It's like the unconditional love God has for us. No matter how much wrong we do, He's still waiting to welcome us back home."

"Thank you, baby."

"For what?"

"For loving me when I didn't know how to love myself." Derrick was about to kiss his wife, but she held up her hand to stop him.

"Derrick, I thought you weren't attracted to me anymore and that you had stopped loving me. That's why it was so easy for me to spend time with Malcolm. He filled the void left by you." She paused to outline his lips with her fingertips. "Promise me that you'll tell me when you're hurting. Promise me you'll share your feelings with me and not shut me out anymore. That's what I'm here for."

"From this day forward, I promise never to leave you out. My heart's an open book to you, and, sweetheart, you'll always be beautiful to me."

After a long conciliatory kiss, Derrick nibbled her neck and ear. "Do you want to know what I'm feeling right now?"

"Probably the same thing I'm feeling," she answered, and pushed the satin sheet back.

Chapter 35

"Thank you, Dr. Garrison." Staci smiled and sniffed the red roses Derrick had sent to her office on Monday morning.

"Anything for you, Mrs. Garrison."

Staci giggled, unable to remember the last time hearing her husband's voice over the telephone made her feel giddy.

"I miss you."

"How can you miss me? You just left me three hours ago." She leaned back and swiveled her chair to face her office window that overlooked the Bay Bridge and San Francisco skyline.

"Three minutes is too long to be away from your soft, beautiful body."

Staci shifted in her chair as her body began to respond to her husband's flirtations. "Keep talking like that and I might come to your office and take advantage of you," she flirted back.

"Any time you want, baby. The office is half yours, and you can use your half however you wish."

Staci enjoyed a few more minutes of flirting with Derrick. The entire time she kept pinching herself to make sure she wasn't dreaming. After disconnecting the call, she bowed her head and silently prayed. *God, thank you so much for restoring my marriage. Thank you for helping me to forgive my husband. Thank you for helping Derrick to open up to me and for help-*

ing me to be receptive to him. God, please continue to show us how to love and communicate with each other.

The peace that enveloped Staci brought a smile to her face. However, her smile vanished the second she swiveled around to face her desk.

"Malcolm, what are you doing here?" she asked with disdain. Hadn't her husband given him the benediction?

"I'm here to see you."

"How did you get past my secretary?"

"She's not at her desk." Without an invitation, Malcolm seated himself in one of the guest chairs.

"Malcolm, you really shouldn't have come here." Staci ignored the flowers in his hand.

"Then you should have answered my telephone calls," he snapped.

He had called so much Saturday evening that she eventually turned her phone off.

"Malcolm, I told you on Saturday, Derrick and I are back together." Staci used her left hand to push back the curls that had fallen into her face.

Malcolm flinched when he saw the glistening shine of her wedding ring. As he placed the flowers on her desk, he noticed the red bouquet on Staci's left.

"Are those from him?" he asked, gesturing toward the red roses.

"Yes, they are." Staci started to smile, but stopped when she saw the fire in his eyes. "Malcolm, I want to thank you for being there for me when I needed someone to talk to, but it's not a good idea for us to continue communicating with each other."

"Is that you or your sorry husband talking?" he smirked.

Staci rose to her feet and pointed a finger at Malcolm. "You don't know enough about my husband to call him sorry."

Malcolm rose to meet her glare. "I know what you've told me, and based on that, he's worse than sorry. And you're stupid for letting him back into your life."

Staci closed her eyes and counted to ten. This was her doing. She'd known better than to bad-mouth her husband to another man, but at that time she didn't care. She had been so angry with Derrick, she didn't care who knew how bad of a husband he was.

"Malcolm, I realize you don't respect my husband, and that's my fault. But I love him, and we're going to make our marriage work," she said without blinking.

"What about me?" Malcolm's voice softened.

"What do you mean?" Staci thought she read hurt in Malcolm's eyes.

"I love you, Staci."

Staci's shock instantly showed in her burning cheeks, and she mechanically sat back down. "Malcolm, you can't be serious," she said after a long silence.

"Yes, I am. I've loved you almost from the beginning."

Staci leaned back in her executive chair, then leaned forward, placing her elbows on her mahogany desk.

"Malcolm, I'm sorry. You've been a good friend to me, and you've helped me through one of the most difficult times of my life, but I don't love you. I love Derrick. I'll always love him." Although she spoke the words gently, Staci knew the words she'd just spoken hurt Malcolm by the change in his facial expression. She expected a reaction from him, but his response threw her off balance.

"What am I supposed to do now that you've finished using me? Do you think that I'm going to just walk away after all the time I've invested in us? I don't think so!" Malcolm yelled and backhandedly knocked the red roses from Derrick off Staci's desk, causing water and splinters of glass to stain the carpet. Then he walked around her desk and stood over her. "I don't care what you or your sorry husband think. Staci, you belong to me, and it's time you started acting like it!" Malcolm bent down and tried to kiss her, but she pushed him off.

"Malcolm, get out before I call security!" she screamed.

"I love you, and you *will* love me back!" he growled just as Marcus and Chloe burst through her office door.

"Staci, what's going on?" Marcus demanded.

Staci assumed her older brother sensed her fear when he didn't wait for an answer. He started for Malcolm and directed Chloe to call security.

"You better walk out of here before I throw you out," Marcus ordered and pushed Malcolm away from Staci, causing the angry man to fall back against the wall.

Malcolm sneered at Marcus as if he wanted to throw him out of the tenth-floor window. Maybe he would have attempted the task if Marcus wasn't taller and broader than he was.

"You heard me—get out!" Marcus said, again ready to make good on his threat to physically throw him out.

"Malcolm, leave and don't ever come back!" Staci ordered, standing next to her brother.

"You won't get rid of me that easy." Malcolm's words sounded more like a threat than a mere statement.

"Whatever, Malcolm," Staci said just as two armed security guards entered her office.

"It doesn't have to end like this." Malcolm tried one last time to get through to Staci.

"Whatever business you had with my sister is over. Now will you prefer these officers escort you out of my place of business, or would you like for me to throw you out of the window?" Marcus threatened, stepping closer to him.

Malcolm turned to Marcus, then retreated with his hands raised. "I'm leaving." He then glared at Staci. "But this is *not* over."

His stare sent chills through her, and she knew this was long from being over.

"What's going on, Staci?" Security had barely closed the door before Marcus began his interrogation. "Who is that? How do you know him?" Marcus ended his questioning only after he saw tears in Staci's eyes. "Come here, baby girl," he said, and gently took his sister into his arms where her tears stained his shirt. When she finished crying, he handed her the box of tissues from her desk and waited for her to explain what had just transpired.

"I met Malcolm after Derrick left," she began. "We've been spending time together, a lot of time together. The other day I told him that Derrick and I are back together. He's not too happy about that. In fact, he just told me he's in love with me."

"Are you serious?" Her disclosure surprised Marcus. "Staci, are you trying to tell me you've been having an affair with this man?"

"No. Not exactly." Staci looked up at Marcus briefly, then lowered her head. "We didn't sleep together, but . . . I spent time with him and shared things that I shouldn't have. I'm certainly not in love with him."

"Does Derrick know about him?"

Staci nodded her answer.

"How does he feel about it?"

"He's not happy about it, but he understands why I started seeing Malcolm."

Marcus listened carefully to Staci as she shared the details of her immoral relationship.

"Now that you've ended the relationship, this Malcolm is in love with you?" he questioned again.

"That's what he said." Staci's voice broke once more. "But his actions today scared me. I've never known him to act the way he just did."

Marcus placed his arm around her. "I can contact security and have him blocked from entering this building, but you need to tell Derrick what happened here today." Staci looked up at her big brother with dread and fear. "Derrick is your husband, and he has a right to know when you've been threatened."

"But Marcus, we just got back together," she whined.

"If you want to stay together, you can't keep secrets like this from him."

"But—"

"Malcolm is the other man, and you can't expect your reconciliation to work if you're going to keep secrets about seeing him and his alleged feelings for you."

Staci knew he was right, but she was afraid of how Derrick would react to hearing Malcolm's profession of love. She didn't know what Derrick would do to Malcolm once he found out he'd threatened her. "Marcus, I know you're right, but—"

Marcus interrupted again. "No buts, Stacelyn. If you don't tell Derrick by tomorrow, I will."

Staci knew Marcus was serious; he never called her by her given name. She conceded because she really didn't want to keep any secrets from Derrick, but she also knew Marcus wasn't going to wait until tomorrow. Within an hour, Marcus would contact her uncle, Lieutenant André Simone, and learn everything there is to know about Malcolm Leblanc and would pass that information on to her brother Craig and possibly Derrick.

"You're right. I have to tell him. I just hope this isn't a setback for us."

"I wish I could tell you this thing will just blow over, but I have a bad feeling about this Malcolm guy."

By late afternoon, Staci had completed outlining the quarter's goals for the store managers and was ready to go home and take a nap before Derrick arrived. Fatigue weighed on her from lack of sleep over the weekend and the stress of Malcolm's unexpected visit. She logged off her computer and buzzed Marcus's office and told him of her plans.

Just as she buttoned her suit jacket, Chloe's voice sounded on the intercom. "Miss Staci, you have a call on line three." Staci took the call without bothering to ask who was calling.

"This is Staci. How may I help you?" She automatically smiled when answering every business call.

"Why won't you answer my calls?" Malcolm's voice was cold and brassy. He had called her cell phone almost constantly since being escorted out earlier that morning.

Staci was taken aback. "Because I don't want to talk to you."

"I told you before; you aren't getting rid of me that easy."

"Malcolm, let it go. Our friendship is over."

"Staci, you don't understand. I love you, and I'm not going to let you go."

Malcolm's declaration made Staci nervous. He had said it with too much finality. She swallowed hard. "Malcolm, I'm sorry you feel the way you do, but—"

"Don't be sorry, Staci; at least, not yet."

Staci's hands shook when the line went dead. "Has he always been this crazy?" she asked audibly just as Craig appeared in her doorway.

"Are you ready?" he asked.

She shook her head. "I knew Marcus was going to tell you. How did you get here so fast?"

"Of course, that's what brothers are for. And husbands," he added. "I was in Marcus's office when you buzzed."

"I'm going to tell Derrick tonight, okay? Now, are you just going to escort me home, or do you have to accompany me to the ladies' room also?" Staci rolled her eyes, but she really loved being the only girl in the family and relished all the concern her brothers showered on her.

"If you knew Malcolm Leblanc's history, you would take this more seriously." Craig's face told her there was a lot more to Malcolm than she knew.

She stopped packing her briefcase. "What are you talking about?"

Craig walked over to her desk. "His mother walked off and left him with his father at the age of ten to be with her lover. A short time later, his father died in a mysterious house fire in which Malcolm miraculously survived." Craig used his fingers to emphasize the word *miraculously*. "After that, he was placed in foster care until age eighteen. He was removed from three foster homes because of sexual abuse from his foster parents. One foster home alleged that he raped their twelve-year-old daughter.

"Staci, two weeks after aging out of foster care, his mother was struck and killed in a hit-and-run accident. The driver of the car was never found, but it was registered to Malcolm's last foster parent. He'd reported it stolen two days prior."

Staci's face flushed. "Are you sure?" The Malcolm Craig described was nothing like the man she'd been sharing her time with the last three months. Malcolm had never talked about his childhood with her. He had, however, told her his mother and father had been killed in an automobile accident.

"Malcolm is a dangerous man, and my guess is he's also a little crazy."

"What have I gotten myself into?" Staci's eyes watered again, and for the second time that day, she found comfort in the arms of one of her brothers.

Staci waved good-bye to Craig after her garage door opened and she saw Derrick's SUV inside. She waited and prayed before getting out of the car. "God, please don't let this be a setback for us."

She found Derrick out on the patio lighting the grill. He was a beautiful sight to behold in shorts and a tank top. For as tall and as big as he was, Derrick was solid all around, like he'd never stopped playing football. The developed muscles in his arms appeared to be as big as Staci's thighs. And his thighs—they looked like tree trunks. Looking at his massive torso, she let out a soft moan of appreciation.

Noting her dreamy look, Derrick walked over to her. A grin spread across his face. "You like what you see, don't you?" Without waiting for the answer he already knew, he leaned down and kissed her.

"Oh yeah." She returned his kiss with a bit of desperation, and she realized Derrick must have sensed something was wrong when his smile vanished.

"Go change while I put the steaks on." His statement wasn't a mere suggestion; it was more like a command. Staci wondered if Marcus had told him already.

"Okay." Staci slowly walked into the house wondering how the evening would end.

***

Derrick watched his wife cautiously. Something was bothering her, and it had something to do with Malcolm. When he called Marcus earlier that day to make plans to watch the fight this upcoming weekend, Marcus had told him that Malcolm had come by the office, but didn't go into any details. "Staci should be the one to tell you details," Marcus had told him. Derrick prayed she hadn't changed her mind about their marriage.

Staci returned wearing the new sundress Derrick had bought and placed on their bed. "Do you like it?" he asked. "I saw it in a window on Bay Street two weeks ago and thought of you."

"I love it." She twirled for him. "What's amazing to me is that you will select the perfect clothes for me, but can't coordinate your own wardrobe to save your life."

"That's because I get lots of help from the salespeople." Derrick pulled her closer to him and held her for a moment before taking her hand and leading her over to the iron bench in the far left corner of the backyard next to the fountain.

Instead of sitting next to him on the bench, Staci sat on his lap and kissed him deeply, like she was trying to make him understand how much she loved him.

"Baby, what's wrong?" he asked after he returned her kiss. "You can tell me. I won't run away. I promise."

Staci lowered her head, but her arms remained around his neck. "Malcolm came to see me today," she whispered.

Derrick used his fingertips to raise her chin, and their eyes met. "I know. What I don't know is what happened in your office." Derrick's gaze never left hers.

"He was angry because I wouldn't take his calls." Staci recapped how Malcolm reacted to Derrick's roses and her ending their relationship and how Marcus had him thrown out.

Remarkably, Derrick remained calm. "What else did he say?"

"He says he's in love with me."

His arms tightened around her. "How do you feel about that?" Derrick asked guardedly.

Staci focused her eyes on his and stroked his cheek. "I don't love him. I never have. I was only substituting his company for yours," she answered honestly. "I was missing you and used him to fill the void."

He needed more. "You said you almost slept with him. What happened?"

Derrick listened as she told him about the night she went to his loft and ended up running out.

"Honey, I never really wanted him. I'm not attracted to him, and I don't have any emotional attachment to him." He loosened his grip. "I know I handled our problems wrong by getting involved with him, and for that I am so sorry."

Derrick wiped the tear from her cheek. "That's in the past, but now I need to know that we're still on the same side and we want the same thing."

"I want you," she answered quickly. "But there is something else you should know."

When Staci finished telling him about the information Marcus and Craig had come up with and Malcolm's threats, Derrick's face had turned a deep shade of red, and his grip on her had tightened again; like he was trying to protect her.

"Has he been here at the house?"

"No, he doesn't know where I live. He doesn't even know my last name. He thinks it's still Simone."

"Baby, I'll take care of Malcolm," he said after awhile.

"But, Derrick, he sounds dangerous," she protested.

"Sweetheart, I know I've let you down in the past, but if we're going to rebuild our marriage, it's important for you to trust me. You have to allow me to be a husband to you, all right?" He brushed a curl from her face.

Staci both nodded and voiced her consent. "Just be careful. I don't want anything to happen to my teddy bear. I love you too much."

"I'll be fine. Let me worry about you for a change."

This time the kiss she gave him was sweet and passionate, inviting him for more. An invitation he gladly accepted.

Chapter 36

With an assured swagger, Derrick walked up to the information desk at Smith & Lowe. "Can you tell me where I can find Malcolm Leblanc's office?" he asked the receptionist.

"Third floor and to the right," the receptionist answered, giving him a flirtatious smile.

Derrick ignored the intent and headed straight to the elevator. "I'd like to see Malcolm Leblanc," he told the secretary on the third floor.

"Do you have an appointment, Mr. . . .?"

He read Malcolm's name on the gold plate affixed to the door behind the secretary's desk. "Derrick. Just tell him Derrick is here. I'm sure he'll want to see me."

"Just a moment, please." When the secretary picked up the phone to call Malcolm, Derrick hurriedly walked past her desk and into Malcolm's office. He startled Malcolm when the door slammed against the wall.

"Mr. Leblanc, I'm so sorry," the middle-aged secretary stuttered. "Should I call security?" she asked hesitantly.

"That won't be necessary," Derrick answered for Malcolm. "I won't be staying long."

Malcolm looked nervously from Derrick to his secretary, then nodded for the woman to leave.

Derrick visually assessed the man who'd been spending time with his wife. Malcolm was a cross mix between Martin Lawrence and David Chappelle. Not what he would consider good-looking competition at all. *Staci was lonelier than I thought*, he mused.

Derrick didn't allow Malcolm a chance to speak. He planted his fists on Malcolm's desk, leaned forward, and stared Malcolm down.

"I'm only going to say this once. Stay away from my wife. Don't call her. Don't stop by her office. Don't write her a letter or even send a telegram. If you happen to see her on the street, act like you don't know her. Anything you need to say to my wife, you can say to me. Any more threats you have for her, you can give them to me, now. But, you better not speak one word to her. Is that understood?" Derrick said all that without blinking.

Malcolm's fear was evident in his shifty eyes and shaky hands. Derrick was eight inches taller than he and more than twice as broad, but Malcolm didn't let that stop him.

"If you had of spent more time talking with your wife and pleasing her in bed, she would not have come looking for me in the first place. Don't get mad at me because I did for your wife what you couldn't," Malcolm sneered.

Derrick expected as much. "What goes on between me and my wife is none of your business."

Malcolm smirked and leaned back in his chair and appeared relaxed. "Who do you think was there comforting her at night while you were gone? Who do you think rocked her to sleep?" Derrick remained silent, and Malcolm took that as Derrick weakening. "Who do you think gave her body the pleasure you can't?"

Derrick swallowed hard, and his temporal veins flared. The thought of this man in his house, in his bed, with his wife made Derrick see red—as he visualized Malcolm's blood slowing draining from his body as Derrick squeezed

Malcolm's carotid arteries until no life remained. *God, please help me not to knock that silly grin off his face,* he prayed fervently.

Derrick stood straight up, ignoring the sinister look. "I don't know what fantasy world you live in, but if you touch my wife, I'll see to it that you check out of the real world." He turned and started for the door.

"How does Staci feel about this? How do you know she's willing to give up everything between us and go back to being unfulfilled? I mean, I've given her so much." Malcolm's tone didn't leave doubts he meant sexually.

Derrick let his ego get the best of him. "Apparently you didn't give her enough; she's back with me. You were just a stand-in for the real thing. The only man who has and will ever pleasure my wife is me. You are just an unpleasant memory. Now stay away from her."

After Derrick slammed his door, Malcolm cursed him, calling him everything but a child of God. "An unpleasant memory," he snarled.

His mind went back to the day he confronted his mother for leaving him and the harsh words she'd told him. "I never wanted kids . . . You're slowing me down . . . Having you was a mistake."

"You sound like my mother," he grunted. "Maybe you should ask her what happens to unpleasant memories. They come back to haunt you."

Chapter 37

Watching Derrick bent over, setting the table for Sunday dinner, Staci couldn't resist. Without warning, she jumped on his back and wrapped her legs and arms around him.

"Woman, what are you doing?" he chuckled.

"Going for a ride. Would you like to join me?" Staci replied and nibbled his ear.

Derrick moaned at the soft feel of her lips moving from his ears to his neck and her hands massaging his chest. "Baby, I'd love to, but if the family hears you screaming, they'll think I'm trying to kill you," he teased.

Carey and Alaina were already in the living room with Craig. Marcus and Shannon were on their way.

"Whatever." Staci jumped down and pinched his arm. She hadn't taken three steps when Derrick's strong arms pulled her back to him and squeezed her.

"I'll take you for a long, slow ride later," he assured in a voice that stimulated her.

"Promise?"

"Promise." Derrick's deep passionate kiss gave her a preview of what was to come. Then he released her.

Staci loved her family, but she couldn't wait for them to leave. She went back into the kitchen, but her mind never left Derrick. Six weeks ago, Staci didn't think the happiness she now felt was possible. Her marriage wasn't perfect, but it was certainly on the right track.

The weekly counseling sessions with Pastor Reggie were the catalyst to the changes. It was during those counseling sessions she was able to finally fully understand how Derrick was able to do the things he had done to her and still claim he loved her. He was acting out of the fear of rejection and his insecurities brought on by his father's rejection. He was afraid that eventually Staci would reject him like his father had. That explained why he withheld his feelings for her until she expressed hers first. He needed to make sure that she really cared before he opened up. When Staci realized how deep his scars ran, she felt like walking up to Dr. John Archer and slapping some sense into him.

Two weeks ago, they ended the counseling session by spontaneously repeating their marriage vows to each other. Staci enjoyed the impromptu ceremony over her lavish wedding because this time, she knew she had Derrick's heart completely, without reservation.

She and Derrick communicated now more than ever about everything. They were finally able to openly discuss how the abortion affected them emotionally. Neither of them realized they hadn't completely mourned the loss until Reggie pointed it out. Although permanent scars from the incident remained, Staci and Derrick had gained closure and were now closer than they'd ever been.

They resumed praying and studying the Bible together and attended Bible Study and Sunday service together. The times when Derrick would become too overwhelmed with grief over the loss of his mother, he would turn to Staci for comfort instead of isolating himself, like he had done in the past.

The new Derrick was everything Staci needed. He gave her more than enough attention and affection. Not one day went by that he didn't tell her and show her how much he loved her in word or deed, and sometimes both. Whenever she entered his presence, he paused and gave her his full attention. He constantly kept physical contact whenever the situation allowed.

Derrick also planned new and exciting ways to please his wife. Like last week when he invited her for lunch at his office. Staci ordered takeout from his favorite spot, only to learn Derrick had a "working" lunch in mind. Afterward, Staci noticed Rhonda watching them poised in his doorway sharing a lingering kiss.

"Good-bye, Rhonda," Staci smiled when she walked past the clean utility room. The next day, Rhonda put in her two week's notice of resignation.

But what really took the cake was when Staci arrived home two nights ago. Attached to the front door was a note that read, *Take off your shoes and follow the path.* Staci stepped inside, took off her shoes, and walked softly on the rose-petal path that led to the living room where Derrick had moved the dining table to. The table was set elegantly with candlelight. The fireplace was glowing, and soft vanilla fragrance filled the air. What nearly made her hyperventilate was the image of Derrick positioned next to the table wearing black silk, waiting to serve her.

Now, almost seventy-two hours later, the rest of the evening was still foggy. She remembered him escorting her to her seat and pulling out her chair. She vaguely recalled tasting shrimp scampi. She remembered him leading her to the fireplace and telling her to sit down on the marble. She vividly recollected him modeling and dancing for her. The rest was a blur. Oh, how she loved being a newlywed.

Miss Cora was right. Derrick was turning out to be a very good husband. His light was shining real bright. If the illumination shined any brighter, Staci would have to wear sunglasses just to stand in his presence. There were times, though, when Staci pinched herself to make sure she wasn't dreaming.

Everyone noticed the change in her, and she didn't mind sharing who was responsible for the change. In fact, today, she welcomed her mother's teasing.

"Did he make you scream yet?" her mother pestered. The three women were out on the lanai enjoying appetizers and beverages.

"So much that I'm hoarse," Staci laughed.

"We'll be sure to leave right after dinner, so y'all can continue and make me some grandbabies," Alaina laughed.

Shannon laughed at her too.

Alaina turned to Shannon. "I don't know what you're laughing at. My son made you scream so loud, you got pregnant with twins."

"Sure did. And as soon as I have these," Shannon patted her stomach, "I'm going to scream some more." Staci and Shannon exchanged high fives.

Alaina smiled deeply. "I'm so happy for you. Aren't you glad you didn't give up?" she asked her daughter.

"More than you know, Mama." Staci turned to Shannon. "I used to be jealous of your and Marcus's relationship."

"What?" Shannon asked incredulously.

"It wasn't due to the pregnancy," Staci explained. "It was the way the two of you expressed your love for each other. I would catch Marcus making goo-goo eyes at you or I'd see him whisper something in your ear, and girl, you would just fall apart. I would wonder what that felt like. Whenever your name leaves his lips, he always wears a smile and a look in his eyes that says, 'God, I love this woman.' I wanted Derrick to look at me like that. It's the same way my father looks at my mother."

"And the same way Derrick's looking at you right now," Alaina observed.

Staci turned to see Derrick's eyes fixed on her from across the lanai. She blushed when he lifted his glass to her in a private toast. She did the same for him with her glass. Just as she was about to take a drink from her glass, he mouthed the words, "I love you." The simple romantic gesture had an unnerving effect on Staci. She missed her mouth and ended up pouring her drink on her top.

Alaina and Shannon laughed, but Staci didn't care. She had the love of her husband, and that's all that mattered to her. She could buy another blouse.

"Man, why'd you mess my sister up like that?" Craig, who had been watching the exchange, teased.

"What are you talking about?" Derrick's innocent role wasn't even convincing to him.

"It's so good to see the two of you together again," Carey smiled and patted Derrick on the back.

Derrick braced himself to contain his emotions, but then decided, what's the point? This was his family, the people who loved him. "It's good to be together, not just with Staci, but with the family. I really missed you all."

"We've missed you too, son," Carey said, giving him the ritual handshake.

Derrick looked at his father-in-law. It was then he realized that the only man in his life who referred to him as son was Carey. He was also the only man to treat him like a son. His gaze then switched to Marcus and Craig. Derrick couldn't recall one time when they added "in-law" to his name. It was always simply "brother" or "my boy."

Derrick's shoulders slumped, and Staci started to him from across the lanai, but Alaina's voice stopped her. "Whatever is going on over there is good for him. He could use some male bonding."

The women watched in silence as the men exchanged words that could only be heard amongst each other. After that, the men shared hugs and that ridiculous handshake ritual again. Finally, the men beckoned for the women to join them in their circle of prayer. Marcus stood behind Shannon with his hands resting on her extended belly. Staci took Derrick's hand, bowed her head, and listened to her father pray.

"Heavenly Father, we thank you for reuniting our family. We thank you for the unconditional love that flows through our family. We thank you for a love that is both generous and longsuffering. We thank you for restoring my son and daughter's marriage. We thank you for the new lives my daughter Shannon shall bring forth in just a few days. We thank you for Marcus's success as a father and a provider. We thank you for Craig's success in his business and pray that soon he'll make a solid commitment to you. We pray that as this family grows, our love and devotion to you will also grow. In your son Jesus' name we pray, amen."

Derrick and Staci lingered, holding each other long after the rest of the family went inside for dinner.

Sunday dinner was interrupted when Brian called to say Lashay was in labor. Staci grabbed her digital camera as the family rushed out the door for the birth of the first Simone great-grandchild.

By the time they arrived at St. John's Hospital, the waiting room was already packed with Simones. Nearly all of the first-generation siblings were present, including patriarchs, Carey Sr. and Ana Simone. No one wanted to miss the birth of the first Simone great-grandchild.

Staci was enjoying a hug from her grandfather when Julia came out and informed her that Lashay had requested her presence in the delivery room.

Inside the delivery room, Lashay was surrounded by her mother and Brian's mother. And, of course, Brian was right there, looking like a helpless puppy, Staci thought.

When the force of her contraction subsided, Lashay called Staci over to the bed. The intense look in her eyes implied that what Lashay had to say would make sense and was very important.

"What is it, Lashay?" The look in Lashay's eyes scared Staci. Brian wiped his wife's forehead, and the soon-to-be grandparents remained quiet so they could hear Lashay.

"Go and get Uncle André's gun and please shoot me. Please put me out of my misery," Lashay panted. Everyone in the room but Brain laughed at the request. "I can't take it anymore," she moaned and braced herself for yet another contraction.

"Yes, you can," Staci said, taking Lashay's hand in hers. Thirty seconds later, Staci wished she'd kept her hand to herself.

An hour later, Staci and the rest of the Simone clan celebrated the birth of the first great-grandchild. Briana Alysse Pennington made her debut at eight pounds and twenty-one inches.

Out in the waiting room, tears welled in Staci's eyes as she watched her family enjoy the pictures from her digital camera. Her arms instinctively covered her abdomen, and she bent over as her desire to have a baby overwhelmed her.

Derrick sensed her longing, placed his arm around her shoulder, and pulled her to him. "Come on, let's go home and take that ride I promised you."

Chapter 38

Staci quickly packed her briefcase and grabbed her jacket. She was in a hurry to get home to see Derrick's face when the new wardrobe she'd picked out for him arrived. The elevator arrived just as she said bye to Chloe. As she walked to her Mercedes, Staci fished her keys from her purse. She was just about to deactivate the alarm when her knees buckled.

"Oh my God!" she gasped.

"I've already phoned security." One of the other building merchants came running to keep her from falling.

Once she was steady, Staci looked at her car in disbelief. She knew Malcolm was behind this. Who else would smash out all of the windows and spray paint *U b long 2 me* in red letters all around her car?

Staci leaned against the cement pillar and closed her eyes. Since Derrick bought her a new cell phone, Malcolm hadn't been able to call her. He had tried to reach her several times at work, but couldn't get past security and Chloe. Staci wondered how he was able to sneak into the reserved parking garage and deface her car without being noticed. In her head, she could hear Malcolm telling her he wasn't going to just go away, but she didn't know that meant he'd resort to vandalism.

"Staci, what's going on?" Marcus asked, stepping from the garage elevator.

Staci gestured toward her car and tears trickled down her cheeks.

"Do you have any idea who could have done this?" the security officer asked, looking back at the vehicle.

"I know exactly who's behind this," Marcus answered, pulling out his cell phone.

While Marcus talked on the phone, Staci answered questions from security, and then waited for the police to arrive and take her statement. She held her emotions intact until Derrick arrived fifteen minutes later. No sooner had he touched her, she fell apart in the comfort of his arms. The depth of her fears poured out in deep sobs and spilled over on Derrick's shirt.

On the ride home, Staci didn't say a word. She couldn't; she was too scared. She wasn't afraid for herself. She was more afraid for Derrick. She didn't know what he was going to do to Malcolm, but she knew her husband was not going to let this deed go unchecked. Neither were Marcus and Craig. She just prayed that none of them would have to suffer consequences because of her wrong relationship. She didn't want her husband or brothers to do anything to jeopardize their lifestyle by beating the life out of Malcolm.

Slowly, she climbed the stairs and dragged into her bedroom. She looked around her empty room, then collapsed onto her bed, and between sobs, she prayed for a simple resolution.

Derrick lingered downstairs. He needed time to sort through his emotions. Malcolm had gone too far for Derrick not to respond. Verbal threats were one thing, but Malcolm proved tonight that he was capable of physically harming Staci. Derrick couldn't allow that. And what about Staci? He saw the raw fear in her eyes and figured she blamed herself for what Malcolm had done. He also knew Staci was afraid of how he would handle the situation.

Derrick knelt down in front of the fireplace and prayed. He needed to get the vision he had of him strangling Malcolm with his bare hands out of his head before he acted on it.

Staci was still lying on top of the covers when Derrick entered their bedroom. When she felt him lie beside her and take her into his arms, the dam broke again.

"Derrick, please."

"Shush." He held her tighter. "Let's take a shower," he whispered in her ear after the tremors subsided.

Derrick took his time and literally washed away Staci's fears—for a while anyway. The lovemaking that followed was powerful, each sending the other a message.

For Staci, she needed Derrick to know that she loved him and needed him around; that her world didn't exist without him. That she didn't want him to do anything that would have an adverse effect on their marriage.

For Derrick, he wanted her to fully understand that it was his job to protect her and that he would give his life to protect her and keep her safe.

Snuggled on top of him with his hands and arms still cuddling her body, Staci looked into her teddy bear's eyes. "Just be careful," she whispered, then buried her head in his chest.

Derrick held her tighter. He didn't know what he was going to do when he confronted Malcolm, but he knew it wasn't going to be good.

The next morning, after instructing Phyllis to cancel his morning patients, Derrick dropped Staci off at her office building. He walked around the SUV and opened the passenger door for her, but she hesitated before climbing out. She didn't say a word, but he read the plea in her eyes.

"When I pick you up this afternoon, we'll go and select your new car." Derrick knew that wasn't what she wanted to hear, but that was the best he could give her. Staci gave a slight nod and grabbed her briefcase, then stepped onto the curb. She looked over Derrick's shoulder to see Marcus and Craig appear through the revolving glass doors. Her brothers' faces bore the same hard look as Derrick's. Chances of convincing them not to confront Malcolm were slim to none.

She turned her attention back to her husband. After dropping her briefcase on the seat, Staci took him in her arms and kissed him like it was her last time. "I love you," she whispered, then grabbed her briefcase and rushed past Marcus and Craig and into the building.

Derrick's eyes followed her.

"She'll be okay," Craig said, and Marcus quickly agreed.

Derrick quietly walked around and jumped in the SUV.

"Isn't that lovely?" Malcolm sneered from the confines of his vehicle. Watching Staci kiss the big coward was sickening to him. And Malcolm was tired of being sick. He was tired of Staci refusing his phone calls at work after she changed her cell number. He was tired of not sleeping at night because of the nightmares he had of Staci being intimate with Derrick. Malcolm was tired of trying to find Staci.

He'd searched the public records for her address, but couldn't find Staci Simone or Dr. Derrick Simone listed anywhere. He'd tried the DMV, even called MS Computers and pretended to be a repairman calling to verify her home address, but didn't get anywhere. It wasn't until last week when he went online and pulled up an old article about MS Computers did he find out her name is Stacelyn and not Staci and that the man who'd thrown him out of her office was Marcus Simone, the gospel artist and her brother. He found out her last name after following her to Derrick's dental office one afternoon. She stayed there for over an hour. He could only guess what she was doing with him.

At first he tried to forget about her, but he couldn't. He tried to turn his attention to other women, but it didn't work. He wanted Staci. She reminded him too much of his mother, and that made him need her more. He thought she would come to her senses or that the coward would leave again. In six weeks that hadn't happened, and now he was tired of waiting. That's the reason he defaced her car; to remind Staci that she was his. He'd expected a call from her last night, apologizing for neglecting him, for leaving him, but that didn't happen. Now it was time to put a stop to this. Staci didn't understand that she was his woman. Today, he would open up her understanding.

He drove across Bay Street and parked in the parking garage. From his position he had an unobstructed view of the Mexican Restaurant where he and Staci met. He'd known the moment he saw her that they were destined to be together. The date he had planned to meet there that night had called and cancelled just as he'd pulled into the parking stall. Instead of going straight to the club, he decided to stay and eat dinner. When he saw Staci sitting alone, sipping a drink, and the epitome of loneliness, he knew it was fate showing him favor.

Malcolm fantasized about their future until his cell phone vibrated from the alarm he'd set. It was time. He turned off the ignition and hastily got out of the vehicle. He donned his sunglasses and adjusted the empty package under his arm. Stealing the delivery uniform made things easier than he'd thought. When he entered the office building, no one gave him a second glance. He nodded to the security guard at the information desk and headed straight for the elevator.

Chapter 39

"Are you praying yet?" Shannon asked as soon as Staci answered the line.

"Harder than ever. I have a real bad feeling about this," Staci answered, rubbing her forehead.

"I kept Marcus up half the night talking—well, arguing—about this. I told him to let the police handle it, but you know them stubborn Simone men better than I do," Shannon sighed. "When it comes to protecting their women, ego and testosterone are a deadly combination."

"I also know my husband, and teamed with my brothers, Malcolm's in for a triple beat down."

"Staci, all we can do is pray that everything works out without anyone, including Malcolm, getting hurt."

"You lead, I'm too nervous." Staci closed her eyes and listened to Shannon pray God's protection over their husbands and Craig.

". . . and, God, help Malcolm to see his wrong and turn to you for help. In your son Jesus' name, amen."

"Amen," Staci echoed.

"Try to relax. I know everything is going to work out. I'll even bring you lunch to celebrate after my visit with Lashay."

The gesture got a smile from Staci. "Thanks, I love you, girl."

"Love you too. Bye."

Staci hung up the phone feeling a little better in her spirit, but her stomach still felt uneasy. That would remain until she heard from Derrick.

"What do you mean he's not here?" Derrick barked at the secretary.

"I'm sorry, but Mr. Leblanc quit this job two weeks ago."

Derrick made the secretary so nervous, her hands were shaking. "Miss, I don't mean to scare you, but I *need* to find Mr. Leblanc."

She nervously eyed Marcus and Craig, then looked at Derrick. "I could tell when you were here the last time he'd done something scandalous. Try his loft on Embarcadero," she suggested. "I'll give you the address. Mr. Leblanc treated me so badly; I want him to get everything due him, especially since he skipped my Christmas bonus for two years."

Derrick's patience wore thin during the minute it took for her to look up the address. "Thank you," he said, after retrieving the Post-it note. "I know exactly where this is."

"You're welcome," the secretary replied, although they didn't hear her. Derrick, Marcus, and Craig were halfway to the elevator by then.

What should have been a ten-minute drive Derrick made in half the time. After knocking on Malcolm's door for the third time, Derrick broke the door open. The three men stepped inside without hesitation. A disgusting sight greeted their eyes. The 1,800 sq foot loft was littered with filthy clothing and half-eaten food, some of which was covered with green fuzz and crawling maggots.

"Man!" Craig said when the stench reached his nose causing him to gag. "This place smells like something or someone died in here."

Marcus searched for a window to open, and that's when he saw it. On the one clean side of the room was an overblown picture of Staci. The hardwood floor beneath it was covered with a sticky white substance. To the left of Staci's photo, a picture of a closed casket with Derrick's name written on it. To the right, a picture of a bride with Staci's face.

"He's planning for both a wedding and a funeral," Marcus stated the obvious.

Derrick's cheeks burned as rage, and fear raced through his body. He had to keep this insane man away from his wife. Malcolm was more mentally unstable than previously thought. And for the first time in his life, Derrick acknowledged that although he was trained to preserve life, he'd kill in an instant to protect his wife.

Chapter 40

Staci leaned back in her chair and massaged her temples. It seemed as though she'd been working for hours; in actuality, it had been less than an hour. She decided to take a much-needed restroom break. This morning she just couldn't shake the queasiness in her stomach. The same queasiness visited her the day before, but by noon she was fine. What she experienced today was almost unbearable. She decided to purge herself in an effort to make the feeling go away.

Her plan didn't work, and now she felt worse than she did before. She stood over the sink holding her hair back with one hand and used the other one to rinse out her mouth. As she gazed in the mirror, she used her fingers to put her curls back into place. Her eyes caught a glimpse of her ring, and she stopped and stroked the shiny baguettes. "I know this is my fault, but, God, please show me mercy and keep my husband safe."

When she finished praying, she felt the urge to regurgitate again. She barely made it inside the stall before the bitter yellow bile erupted from her.

"Ms. Simone needs to sign for this one," the delivery man said to Chloe. Before Chloe could tell the young man that Staci wasn't in her office and that it was Chloe he needed to see if he wanted a signature, the man headed for Staci's door.

Just as Staci rounded the corner from the staff break room where she filled a mug with hot water for some tea, the screams started.

"Where is she?" Malcolm shouted, waving the gun in the air, sending the office staff running for cover. Everyone was too busy trying to hide to give him an answer. That only angered him more. He held the gun in the air and fired two shots.

"Malcolm, what are you doing?" Staci screamed from behind him.

He lowered his weapon and turned to face Staci. For a split second, Staci thought she saw a smile on his face.

"Hello, sweet Staci. Or shall I say, Mrs. Stacelyn Garrison?"

Staci remained silent.

"You're just the person I want to see. Did you like your car?" he asked, taking steps toward her.

She was right. That was a smile on his face; a sinister smile; a deadly smile; a twisted smile. With his unshaven and uneven bearded face, Malcolm looked like a madman; and what was he doing in that brown delivery uniform?

The desperate prayers and cries of her employees caught Staci's attention. As crazy as Malcolm was, he could start shooting people at any moment. She had to clear the office before someone innocent got hurt.

"Everyone out!" she ordered.

A couple of her employees attempted to come out of their place of refuge, but Malcolm held his gun in the air and fired another shot.

"Malcolm, if you want me, you can have me. But you have to let these people go first."

"You're in no position to tell me what to do! This is *my* show!" he yelled, waving the gun in her face. "I let you call the shots before. Now it's my turn."

Staci sucked her breath and swallowed her fear. "If you don't let them go, then shoot me now, because I'm walking out of here."

Malcolm must have thought she was bluffing until Staci started for the glass door. He didn't want to give in to her, but he needed her there if his plan was going to work.

"It's me or them," she said and placed her hand on the knob.

After the revealing visit to Malcolm's loft, Derrick's SUV pulled up in front of the office building just as a flood of people ran out. He instantly panicked and jumped out, barely putting the gearshift into park. By the time Craig climbed over the front seat to take over the wheel, Derrick and Marcus had entered the building.

Derrick's eyes frantically scanned the chaotic lobby. People were screaming and running toward the exit.

"What's going on?" he yelled at the information desk.

"Evacuating the building; reported gunfire!" the security officer hollered over the noise.

"Stairs!" Marcus yelled, then led Derrick to the stairwell, but there were too many people running down the stairs for them to climb up. Marcus stopped dead in his tracks when he recognized the faces of his employees among the throngs of people.

"Chloe!" he yelled. "What's going on?" The fear in her eyes answered his question.

"That man came back, and he has a gun!"

Chloe barely got the words out before Derrick shouted, "Where's my wife?"

Chloe, breathing heavily, but steadily moving toward the exit, yelled, "She's in the office with him."

"No!" Derrick groaned. In an instant, his anger toward Malcolm turned on to himself. He was supposed to protect Staci, and now she was being held by a psychopath. He would never forgive himself if anything happened to her.

"Let's go." Marcus was about push his way up the stairs when Derrick stopped him.

"No, man, I'll handle this alone."

"What? That's my sister in there!"

"I know." Derrick's face held a blank stare, like he'd just made a life-altering decision. "But she's my wife and my responsibility. All I have is Staci. Any day now, your wife will give birth to two babies. They will need their father." The intense gaze on Derrick's face told Marcus more than the words he used. Derrick continued up the stairwell. Marcus followed the crowd back outside.

Now alone with Malcolm, Staci feared for her life. If the grimace on Malcolm's face was any indication, today would be her last day on this side of heaven. Her entire life flashed in front of her. She did the only thing she knew to do. She lowered her head and prayed, repenting for every wrong thing she'd ever done.

"God, please forgive me for every sin and every evil thought I've ever had. Forgive me for not always being obedient to your Word. Forgive me for allowing myself to get in this situation."

"Why did you leave me?" Malcolm demanded.

"Forgive me for not loving everyone like I should have. Forgive me for the times I was disobedient to my parents, for all the times Marcus and I snuck off to parties and did things we knew were wrong. Forgive me for not listening to the sound advice my mother and my girls gave me."

"Answer me!" Malcolm shouted.

"Forgive me for every lie I ever told. For procrastinating and using my circumstances as an excuse for not doing what you told me to do, please forgive me. Forgive me for every day I didn't make time to read your Word. Forgive—"

The force of Malcolm's fist slamming against her face knocked Staci from the chair. "See what you made me do!" Malcolm roared when he saw the blood trickle from her nose and down her lip. "Why didn't you answer me?" He tried to lift her, but she pushed him away.

"Get away from me!" she screamed, using the chair for support. Trembling, she used the back of her hand to wipe away the blood.

Malcolm leaned against the receptionist's desk. "Why did you leave me? Didn't you know I needed you? You know I love you. Why did you choose him over us?"

The faraway look in his eyes told Staci he wasn't talking to her. He held conversation with someone not visible to the naked eye.

Chapter 41

Julia parked her Jaguar on the side street and ran to the front of the building in search of her brother, André. Carey and Alaina, who were with Julia at the hospital visiting Lashay when she received the call from the building manager, followed close behind.

"What's the latest?" Julia immediately questioned upon approaching her youngest brother, Lieutenant André Simone.

"Julia, this is Lieutenant Clark. He's in charge," André answered, then introduced Julia. "This is my sister, Julia. She owns this building. These are Staci's parents and her brothers." He pointed in their direction.

Lieutenant Clark didn't waste any time. "Is there another way to access the tenth floor, other than the stairwell and elevator?" he asked Julia.

"There's a crawl vent on each floor with an outlet in the executive office, which would be Marcus's office. You can access it from the floor above."

Lieutenant Clark spotted the hostage negotiator and excused himself.

André explained to Carey that with the help of the hostage negotiator and after getting a visual on Malcolm, they hoped to coax him out without having to use deadly force.

"My baby girl had better walk out of there alive," Carey stated plainly.

André patted Carey on the back. "Don't worry, big brother. If Staci doesn't come out alive, neither will Malcolm." Of that, André was certain, speaking as an uncle and not an officer sworn to uphold the law.

"What are you doing here?" Marcus asked when Shannon waddled toward him.

She ignored his question. "Any news?"

"You shouldn't be out here this close to giving birth," Marcus warned.

Shannon smirked. "And you shouldn't be out here this close to becoming a father."

Marcus started to argue the point, then remembered Derrick's words and decided against it. Standing behind his wife, Marcus rested his arms round her extended abdomen and kissed the top of her head. "Stay close to me."

Shannon placed her hands on top of Marcus's and looked around. "Where's Derrick?"

"I don't love you," Staci said for the third time. "I'm sorry, but it's the truth."

"How can you not love me, after all we've shared?"

"Malcolm, the only thing we've shared was friendship; at least, what I thought was friendship." Staci tried to ignore the piece of metal that was now pointed at her chest.

"Are you scared, Staci?" Malcolm leaned closer to her and planted his free hand on her knee, then slowly moved up her thigh. He tuned out the ringing telephone.

Staci stared stone-faced at him, refusing to give him the satisfaction of knowing she was terrified.

"I know you want me, and I'll let you have me later." He was just about to place his hand under her skirt when she slapped his hand away.

"I don't want you! Now answer the phone!" she barked.

Malcolm stepped away from her and looked out the window at the ground below. The streets were covered with police cars, news vans, and throngs of people. This was turning out just the way he'd planned.

"Call him," Malcolm ordered when he faced her again.

Perplexed, Staci asked, "Call who?"

"Why, the great Dr. Garrison, of course. Tell him to get his sorry behind over here, now. We have some unfinished business."

Oh my God, she thought. Her mind instantly went back to the dream she had two months ago. Malcolm was going to kill Derrick! That's why she didn't see Derrick in the dream. It's was Derrick's body Pastor Reggie was leaning over. Miss Cora was happy because her son was coming to join her. Staci hurriedly pushed that thought out of her mind. Malcolm was not taking her husband from her.

"You leave Derrick out of this. You wanted me; now you have me." For the first time, Staci's voice trembled with emotion.

Malcolm laughed. "If I didn't know any better, I'd think you really love the coward."

"I do love him. And that's something you'll never hear me say about you!"

Malcolm's hand raised, but he resisted the urge to punch her again. Instead, he unclipped his cell phone and thrust it in her face. "Call him!"

"That won't be necessary," Derrick said as he stepped into the reception area.

Chapter 42

"Any updates?" Pastor Reggie asked when he and Staci's grandparents joined the family gathered across the street from the building's entrance.

"He won't answer the phone. The hostage negotiator has been calling every minute. The air conditioner has been turned off in hopes he'll get too hot and decide to come out," Julia answered after embracing her husband.

"Are you in charge, son?" Grandma Ana asked her youngest child, André.

"No, Mom. I can't lead an operation I have a personal interest in," André answered. "But Lieutenant Clark is doing everything by the book."

"Humph, I'm going to do everything by the book too—my book," Grandma Ana replied. "*My* book tells me that the effectual fervent prayers of a righteous man, or woman, avails much. And that no weapon that is formed against me, or my family, shall prosper."

"Amen, Mama," Carey Jr. said. He, along with the rest of the family, knew what was coming next. In the midst of all the chaos and confusion, the Simones assembled in a circle with hands held and prayed out loud. What did surprise everyone was Craig's offer to lead the prayer.

"Thank you, son, but we need this prayer to get through," Carey Jr. said.

"It will, Dad. I've stopped running and turned my life over to Christ. He's now the Lord of my life."

Alaina gasped. "Since when?"

Craig looked thoughtful. "Mama, I guess since the day you dedicated me to Him. As far as I can remember, I've heard God calling me. I've felt Him tugging at my heart, but I wanted to do my own thing. Today's events have helped me to fully understand that life is too short and holds no promises." He pointed to the ground. "I knelt right here and repented, then surrendered my life to His will."

Marcus embraced his brother. Carey wrapped his arms around both of his sons. No words were exchanged.

"If my baby wasn't being held by a madman, I'd dance in the spirit right here on the sidewalk in front of these news cameras." Instead, Alaina leaped a few times.

The prayer and praises sent up by the family caught the attention of onlookers. Craig prayed with such fervor and power, some of the spectators joined in. No sooner had Pastor Reggie echoed Craig's amen, Shannon's water broke.

Staci temporarily forgot Malcolm was pointing a loaded gun at her and instantly jumped up and ran to Derrick. She reached up and draped her arms around his neck and buried her face in his chest.

"Are you all right?" he asked. He returned her embrace, but kept his eyes fixed on the gun-toting madman.

Staci nodded her answer, too overwhelmed with emotion to speak. Feeling safe in her husband's arms, she released the tears she'd been holding. "Honey, I'm so sorry. This is my fault."

"Shush." Derrick brushed the curls from her face. He flinched when he saw the dried bloodstain trailing from her nose to her lower lip. He glared at Malcolm. It took every ounce of restraint in him to keep from grabbing him by the throat. He couldn't do that until he was sure Staci was safe.

"Take your hands off my woman!" Malcolm roared, then yanked Staci away from him.

Derrick started for him, but stopped when Malcolm aimed the weapon at Staci's head. Avoiding Staci's face, Derrick focused his eyes on Malcolm. The horror on her face almost made him lose it.

"Let her go; then you and I can handle this, man to man."

Malcolm smirked. "What man is going to stand in for you?"

"You should answer the phone. It's probably the police wanting to know what your demands are," Derrick suggested.

"I don't have any demands, other than seeing you beg for your life like a dog." Malcolm then reached back with his free hand and yanked the telephone cord out of the socket.

Outside on the sidewalk, Shannon moaned, "Oh, God," while rubbing her stomach.

"Baby, we need to get to the hospital." Marcus massaged her lower back.

"I know, but I don't want to leave until I know Derrick and Staci are safe." Shannon looked over her shoulder at Marcus. "And neither do you."

"Listen to your husband. You need to go."

Shannon knew Grandma Ana's suggestion was really a command, but she decided to challenge her anyway. "St. John's is only ten minutes away, and my contractions aren't real hard yet."

Grandma Ana was about to give Shannon one of those Oh-no-you-didn't-challenge-me looks, but she didn't have to. Shannon's next contraction almost knocked her to her knees. After that, she didn't protest. She gladly let her husband carry her to the car.

"Lieutenant Clark, the phone line went dead," the hostage negotiator called over her shoulder.

Lieutenant Clark looked up to see André staring at him, waiting for him to make the call. The lieutenant gave the signal, and immediately, the SWAT team rushed into the building.

"Why did you have to come back?" Malcolm asked while waving the gun in Derrick's face like a toy. "Why didn't you just stay away? My family and I were doing fine until you showed up." Malcolm was standing in front of Derrick, taunting him, but Derrick knew mentally Malcolm had left the building. "Now you're going to pay for it, but not before you beg for my forgiveness." Malcolm aimed the gun at Derrick's chest. "Beg! Say you're sorry!" he ordered. His head dripped with sweat.

"Jesus, Jesus, Jesus," Staci said repeatedly. There was no way her husband would beg Malcolm for anything.

Derrick's only response was a hard stare that made Malcolm flinch, even though he was the one holding the loaded gun. He then pointed the barrel at Derrick's head. "Beg!" Malcolm screamed.

Staci slowly moved over to Derrick and interlocked her arm with his.

"I will not beg you for anything," Derrick said calmly and stepped in front of Staci.

Malcolm was confused. This was not turning out like he'd planned. Derrick was supposed to beg for his life.

Malcolm would enjoy that more than he would enjoy blowing his head off. He needed him to beg so Staci could see for herself what a coward he is. Malcolm glared at Staci standing behind Derrick. She was supposed to be on his side. How else would Staci let him make love to her after he killed Derrick? That was his plan: make Derrick beg for his life, and then blow his head off. Then after he and Staci made love, use the remaining two bullets to make sure she would die his woman.

When Derrick didn't budge, Malcolm rubbed his head and stepped back.

"Why can't you do what you're supposed to do?" he yelled, waving the gun in the air. "You're supposed to beg!" Malcolm was near tears. "Now you'll pay double!" He cocked the gun, but before he squeezed the trigger, they heard a thud coming from Marcus's office.

The last thing Staci saw was Marcus's office door open abruptly. Derrick threw her down on the floor and covered her with his body just before the sound of gunfire erupted.

Chapter 43

Lieutenant André Simone waited with Lieutenant Clark for word from the SWAT team. He breathed a sigh of relief when he heard through the two-way radio that the suspect was no longer a threat, but stiffened again when he heard one of the hostages had been wounded. He motioned for the paramedics.

Inside the office, Derrick slowly moved off Staci with eyes glued on the officer checking for Malcolm's pulse. Derrick wondered if the relief he felt in knowing Malcolm was dead was good or bad, but didn't dwell on it. The man was no longer a threat to him or his wife. That mattered the most. Staci's shaking and whimpering redirected his attention.

"Everything is all right, sweetheart," he said and stroked her back.

Staci turned over and lifted her head, then shrieked when she saw Malcolm's brains splattered over the carpet. Derrick used his arms to turn his body so she wouldn't be able to see the bloody corpse. Staci gripped him like he was her last lifeline. Derrick grimaced, but held on to her trembling body.

"Dr. Garrison, the paramedics are on the way up," the young officer said.

"Thank you," Derrick answered, but continued to focus on Staci.

When she processed the officer's words, Staci turned and looked into Derrick's face. "Why are the paramedics coming?" She pointed in Malcolm's direction. "He's dead, and I wasn't hit."

"The paramedics are for me."

Staci followed his eyes to his left thigh. "Oh my God, you've been shot!" She jumped to her feet and began running frantic around the room. She was so hysterical, two officers tried unsuccessfully to calm her down. "He needs to get to a hospital!" she screamed.

"Mrs. Garrison, the paramedics are already outside. They will be up here any second."

"Baby, it's not as bad as you think. I don't think the wound is that deep," Derrick tried to assure her, but he wasn't so sure himself.

"Yes, it is!" she screamed. His blood-soaked leg told her another story. "There's blood everywhere!"

André came up with the paramedics. Relieved to find his niece all right, he talked with the SWAT team. He learned that Malcolm fired two shots. The first shot, intended for Staci, was lodged in Derrick's leg. Malcolm then pointed the firearm at his temple and literally blew his own brains out.

"Come on, let them work." André ordered Staci to let go of Derrick so the paramedics could tend to him.

"But look at all this blood!"

"Stacelyn," her uncle's voice remained firm, "let the paramedics take care of him."

"Okay." She nodded and moved out of the way. She never relinquished Derrick's hand, and she never stopped praying.

Once outside, Staci waved to her family as she walked alongside the gurney transporting Derrick, but didn't stop to talk.

"What hospital are they taking him to?" she heard someone ask.

"St. John's," she called over her shoulder, just before climbing into the ambulance.

Chapter 44

Finished with the Business section of the local newspaper, Dr. John Archer refolded the paper and laid it on the round table in the physician sleep room. "Four more hours," he mumbled after checking his Movado. Serving as attending physician in the emergency room was not one of his favorite activities, but as medical director of St. John's Hospital, it was his job to make sure every service had adequate coverage. The Emergency Department was currently short staffed by three physicians. That meant Dr. Archer had to work a twenty-four-hour shift in ER.

So far, the day had been quiet, but he knew that was about to change. He'd been following the local news coverage of a hostage situation in Emery Bay all morning. Before Dr. Archer turned off the television, the reporter announced the standoff was over, but one of the hostages had been shot. There wasn't any doubt that the victim would be sent to St. John's, with it being the closest trauma center. No sooner had he taken his last sip of strong black coffee, his pager went off.

The ER resident, with chart in hand, met Dr. Archer as he rounded the corridor. As usual, he took the chart and quickly read the history and physical report as he continued walking toward room twenty-seven.

Thirty-two-year-old black male; six foot five, 250 lbs, GSW to the upper thigh . . .

When he finished, Dr. Archer agreed with the resident's assessment; the patient needed surgery immediately to remove the bullet and repair the tissue. "Let's get his consent," Dr. Archer said and pushed open the door to room twenty-seven.

"Mr.—" Dr. Archer started, then looked in the top right corner of the chart for the patient's name. At that moment, his face turned beet red.

"Oh my," Staci whispered. She had never met Derrick's father, but she knew without a doubt the tall red man in the green scrubs and white lab coat was her father-in-law. The resemblance was uncanny. The only difference between Derrick and his father was Derrick had a permanent tan. They were even the same height and shared the same curly black hair. Derrick's was just a little coarser, and Dr. Archer had a few gray strands.

Somehow the resident didn't notice the resemblance or that Dr. Archer looked like he would keel over and die at any moment. When Dr. Archer continued to stare, the resident took over.

"Dr. Garrison, Mrs. Garrison," he started. "This is Dr. Archer, the attending physician. He's also the medical director for the hospital."

Staci nodded. This is not the way she imagined meeting her father-in-law for the first time. "Hello, Dr. Archer. My name is Stacelyn."

Dr. Archer finally found enough air to breathe and extended his hand to Staci. "Hello." He shook her hand, then gestured toward her face. "Have you been seen yet?" he asked in reference to the dried blood.

His concern for her was unexpected. "No. I wanted to make sure my husband is taken care of first."

"I'll send someone in here right away." Dr. Archer finally turned his attention to his son, who he hadn't seen since that day, about six months ago in his office. He didn't know what to say to him then, and he didn't know what to say to him now.

"How are you, Derrick?" After Derrick looked at him like he was crazy, he added, "Outside of being held hostage, and then shot."

"Life is good. I have a beautiful wife and wonderful family."

That reminded Staci she should call Keisha.

"Sorry to hear about your mother's death." Dr. Archer sounded sincere.

"Losing your one good parent is part of life."

When Derrick said those words, Staci knew it was time to fast-forward. "My husband is in a lot of pain. Can we hurry this along, please?"

"Sure."

Staci felt the grip Derrick had on her hand tighten as he listened to Dr. Archer explain the surgery to him like Derrick was a stranger off the street and not his own flesh and blood. Staci looked down at Derrick's face. The water in the corner of his eyes told her seeing his father hurt more than the gunshot. Their eyes locked, and she kissed his tears.

After obtaining the signed consent, Dr. Archer left the room with the resident on his heels, and placed the chart directly in the charge nurse's hand and barked out his orders. "Mrs. Garrison needs a complete physical right away. Page Dr. Price and have him meet me in operating room five."

The last order took the resident by surprise. "Dr. Price? He's the chief of surgery. Any surgeon can perform this surgery."

"I know he's the chief of surgery. I hired him." The tone and Dr. Archer's facial expression was enough to keep the resident from asking more questions.

***

Back inside the room, Staci soothed her husband's heart. "Honey, I know that was hard for you." She wiped his eyes and kissed his cheek.

With his eyes still closed, Staci examined her husband. Her teddy bear was wounded, but he was her hero. The bullet in his leg was meant for her, but he lay there taking the pain without complaining one time. She didn't think it was possible, but somehow, the love she had for him had grown immensely.

"Thank you for coming for me," she whispered and stroked his curly hair.

Derrick finally opened his eyes. "Anything for you, love."

Chapter 45

Staci entered the emergency waiting room and was instantly greeted by a group hug from her parents and Craig. Alaina's tears of joy unleashed both Staci's and Carey's. Staci wanted to hold on to the security her family gave her and clung to them with everything she had. Today had shown her that life is precious and shouldn't be taken for granted.

Still holding on to her father, Staci hugged and kissed her other relatives who flooded the waiting room. She gave them an account of how Derrick ended up being shot. She could tell her father wasn't happy about Derrick being shot by a deranged man, but he respected him more for putting Staci's life before his own. Carey voiced as much, wearing the smile of a proud father.

"Where's Marcus?" Staci asked, looking around.

"He's upstairs with Shannon—she's in labor," Alaina beamed. "I'm going to check in on her soon."

"Wow, this is really something! Lashay is in postpartum, Shannon's in labor & delivery, and Derrick's in surgery."

"And you need to get in some water," Alaina said. "I stopped by the house and got you some clean clothes. Have you been checked out by a doctor?" she asked, brushing her daughter's hair from her face.

"Yes, Mama." Staci leaned her head on her father's shoulders, knowing Alaina was about to treat her like she was a little girl. She didn't mind either.

"Come on." Alaina pulled her away from Carey by the arm. "There's a restroom over there, and I have a fresh pack of wipes in my purse."

"And if that's not enough, you can use some of mine," Grandma Ana said and followed them to the restroom.

"Hey, guys," Staci whispered, while slowly opening the door.

Marcus perked up at the sound of his sister's voice. Sensitive to his dilemma—wanting to support Shannon and also wanting to touch his sister—Staci walked behind him and gave him a big hug. Staci thought the tears in Marcus's eyes were because he was glad to see her. During Shannon's next contraction, however, Staci learned those tears had nothing to do with her ordeal.

She hugged Shannon between contractions. "How's my girl?" Staci took her hand, and Marcus took a break to ice his hand.

"How's Derrick?" Shannon panted.

No sooner had Staci finished with the update, including Derrick's unexpected sighting of his father, Alaina and Julia came prepared to work until the end. Staci relinquished her seat to her mother and stood against the door watching and cheering.

Forty-five minutes later, her nephew was born, followed six minutes later by her niece. Being able to watch the vaginal birth was an honor for her. Just hours ago, Staci didn't think she would get the chance to see the babies at all. They were the cutest little babies. Staci used Marcus's digital camera and took pictures for the family. As she focused the lens on Marcus holding his son and daughter, one in each hand, tears rolled down Staci's face. This time, she cried because for the first time she didn't feel the emptiness she usually felt at the birth of a baby and she no longer felt jealous.

She inconspicuously left the delivery room and headed down to the surgery waiting room.

"Mrs. Garrison," Dr. Archer's voice startled Staci and she suddenly spun around. "I'm sorry. I didn't mean to scare you."

"How's my husband?"

"Better than expected," Dr. Archer said proudly. "The bullet missed the two main arteries in his leg and the bone. Basically, all we had to do was to remove the metal, then clean and repair the tissue. With good physical therapy, the only reminder he'll have of this incident is a small scar."

The look on Dr. Archer's face was that of a relieved father, not that of an emergency room physician, Staci observed. She stared at him, debating if she should say what was on her mind or just keep it to herself. Today had proven that life is short, with no guarantees, no second chances. Staci took advantage of the opportunity.

"Dr. Archer, let me tell you something about my husband and your son." She waited for him to walk away, but he didn't. Dr. Archer didn't show any emotion. "I've known Derrick for eight years, and I wouldn't trade anything for the times we've shared, not even the bad times. Despite your rejection and the lack of a father figure, Derrick has grown into a great man, whom I love with all my heart. He's a great dentist and now a great husband.

"Do you want to know how great he is?" Dr. Archer didn't answer, and she pressed on. "Derrick is here because he took the bullet that was meant for me. He lay on top of me and left himself at the mercy of a crazed maniac. Derrick was willing to give his life to keep me safe." She stepped closer to him and asked. "Why can't you accept him? From where I stand, he's a better man than you are."

Dr. Archer swallowed hard at Staci's statement. "That's very noble of him, protecting his wife and child."

Staci expected him to give her an explanation for rejecting Derrick, but what he said confused her. "Derrick and I don't have any children," she replied, shaking her head. "And what does that have to do with you not accepting him?"

Dr. Archer motioned his hand toward her stomach. "I was referring to the child you're carrying."

Staci shook her head once again. "I'm not pregnant."

"According to the lab test from your exam, you are."

"What are you talking about?"

Dr. Archer realized his daughter-in-law really didn't know. "For some strange reason, I feel honored to be the one to announce the pending birth of your first child. We routinely check urine for pregnancy, and your urine tested positive."

"Oh my God." Staci instinctively covered her stomach, trying not to get too excited. "Are you sure?"

"If you want, I'll have the lab draw your blood for a stat BHCG," he offered. He explained the test checked for pregnancy hormones in the blood.

Staci tried to remember the last time she'd had a visit from Mother Nature. She hadn't had a period since two weeks prior to her and Derrick's reconciliation. That was eight weeks ago. She'd been so caught up in the euphoria of their reunion, she'd lost track of her cycle. Then her mind went back to the nausea that had awakened her for the past two days. *Could I really be pregnant?*

"Where's the lab?"

Chapter 46

"Father, thank you for your never-ending grace and mercy. Thank you for your protection and love. Thank you for your forgiveness and restoration. Thank you for being true to your Word. You are a very present help in trouble. Thank you for helping me out of trouble today. Thank you for the life you've given us. Amen."

"Amen," Derrick joined in Staci's prayer.

"I didn't know you were awake." Staci stood from kneeling in front of the guest chair and walked over to the bed. "Hey, you."

She would never tire of looking into his eyes and playing with those curls.

Derrick received the gentle kiss on his lips, but was concerned. "The surgery must have gone well. You look pleased."

She happily gave him his prognosis and filled him in on current events. "Guess what?" she asked, placing her hand on his. "You're an uncle."

"When?"

"A few hours ago. Shannon went into labor during the standoff."

His smile disappeared, replaced by as sullen glaze. "I'm glad I made Marcus turn back."

Staci assumed his change in demeanor was due to their inability to conceive and attempted to soothe him. "Honey, it's all right."

Derrick corrected her. "No, baby, everything is better than all right." His smiled returned. "Tell me, what are the names of my niece and nephew?"

"First of all, you have the order wrong. Your nephew was born first, and, of course, his name is Marcus Jr. Your niece, Mariah, came into the world six minutes later."

"Marcus and Mariah." Derrick pronounced the names while shaking his head.

"Or, as my brother refers to them, Prince Marcus and Princess Mariah."

"I should've guessed. Your girls are too much. Brian got Briana, and now Marcus has his two." Derrick always made fun of how Lashay and Shannon wanted all of their children to be named after their husbands.

"I wouldn't laugh at my girls if I were you. I love my man, just as much as they love theirs, if not more. When I have our baby, I'm going to name her after my man too." Staci laughed, but Derrick knew she was serious. "Something like . . . Derrika or Derisha."

"Lord, please help me." Derrick chuckled. "I pray by that time, your crazy self would have come to your senses."

"I don't know." Staci shrugged her shoulders. "I'm pretty crazy about you and nine months is not a long time."

Derrick's eyes were focused on the curve of her lips; it took a moment for him to digest her words. His face twisted with confusion. "What did you just say?"

"I said, we're going to have a baby. Our baby," she beamed.

Derrick was stunned. "You're pregnant? How?"

"Dr. Garrison, if you don't know how . . ." She raised an eyebrow.

"Well, not how, when?" Derrick couldn't believe his ears.

"My guess is the night we got back together." They both smiled and reminisced on how wonderfully magnificent and powerful that night had been. "It's early, but both the urine and blood test show I'm definitely pregnant. And the vaginal ultrasound your father—I'm sorry—Dr. Archer had radiology perform, shows a seven-week-sized embryo. That would put us right at that night or that weekend."

Derrick was elated and didn't ask why his absent father knew about his wife's pregnancy before he did. All he wanted to do was hold her in his arms, but the IV line was in the way.

Once again, Staci read his mind and walked to the opposite side of the bed and leaned against him. He squeezed her as hard as he could with his free arm. "Baby, you've made me the happiest man in the world. I love you so much."

"I love you too, teddy bear."

First she heard him sniffle; then she felt his teardrop on her forehead. She knew those were happy tears, just like hers.

"Since we're sharing good news, I have some of my own," Derrick stated.

"What's up?" She lifted her head so she could see his face.

"How do you feel about being a minister's wife?"

Staci's eyes bulged. "Derrick, when did the Lord call you into the ministry?"

"Years ago, but I've had Him on hold, and He refuses to hang up. That was a big part of my struggle. I have been running from the call since before I met you."

What he said just made perfect sense to her. From the first day they met, Staci thought he should be on a platform of some kind, witnessing and telling others about Jesus. Derrick, an astute student of the Bible, could expound on the Word better than most preachers she knew. And now since his rededication, his revelation of the Word was deeper than ever. He'd even brought Staci to her knees a few times during their Bible study time together. Derrick definitely had what it takes to become a great minister. He loved God, and he loved God's people.

"I'd be honored," she answered, then added, "as long as I get my own ministry time."

Her grin made him grin. "You and our children will always come first."

"Just how many children do you want?"

"As many as you're willing to give me."

"Dr. Garrison, you keep being as good to me as you are now and I'll have as many of your babies as you want." Staci kissed him, and it happened again. She didn't think it possible, but the love she had in her heart for her husband expanded once more.

"In that case, Mrs. Garrison, we're going to need a bigger house."

"You are so bad." Staci removed Derrick's hands for the umpteenth time. She'd been trying to dress him for discharge, but now with the IV gone, he couldn't keep his hands off her. She'd been there an hour, and he *still* didn't have his shirt on. But he had allowed her to carefully slip his shorts on over his bandages.

"I can't help myself. Besides, it's all I can do for the next two months," he pouted.

"If you're a good boy, one day we can go for a ride, and *I'll* drive," Staci winked.

"I promise to be a very good boy." His facial impression of a little boy was so cute, Staci couldn't help but to lean over and kiss him.

Derrick wrapped his arms around her waist and pulled her close to him, laying his head against her abdomen. "My baby," he moaned and squeezed her. "My baby is growing in there."

She stroked his curls and pressed him even closer to her body. That's how Dr. Archer found them.

"I'm sorry. I didn't mean to interrupt," he said entering the room.

"Then why didn't you knock?" Derrick snapped.

Dr. Archer's eyes bounced from his son to his daughter-in-law. He didn't know if he should leave or not.

Finally, Derrick asked, "What brings you here? Are you filling in for the discharge nurse today?"

"I wanted to speak to you before you left."

Derrick didn't say another word, but waited for John Archer to say whatever it was he had come to say.

Staci used the distraction to finish getting Derrick dressed. Now he allowed her to slip on his shirt without any resistance.

"Let me help you with that," Dr. Archer said when Staci moved the wheelchair next to the bed. Without hesitation, he helped Derrick maneuver into the wheelchair.

His heart pounded, and his eyelids blinked violently, but miraculously, Derrick's breathing maintained an even rhythm. As a child, he'd imagined his father's first touch would be a warm embrace or a pat on the back, not the vice grip John Archer used to lift him from the bed into the wheelchair. "Thank you," Derrick mumbled, suppressing his emotions.

"Ready to go home, Dr. Garrison?" The discharge nurse walked into the room carrying the discharge medication and instructions. "Hello, Dr. Archer." The curly redheaded nurse paused. Her eyes studied her patient, and then the medical director. "Wow, Dr. Archer, a couple of hours in a tanning salon and a little black hair dye and the two of you could pass for twins. Are you related?"

Derrick mentally prepared himself for his father's denial. Staci stood behind the wheelchair with her hands resting on his shoulders. Nothing could have prepared them for what they heard next.

"Derrick is my eldest son," Dr. Archer smiled at the nurse.

Derrick swallowed hard—real hard.

"That explains the strong resemblance. Dr. Archer, you sure have some strong genes," the nurse commented before going over the instructions with Derrick and Staci.

Derrick was grateful for his wife because he couldn't comprehend anything the nurse said. "What did you say?" he asked Dr. Archer the second the nurse made her exit.

"Honey, I'm going to get the car." Staci paused in front of Dr. Archer. "It's way past time for you to have a talk with your son."

Father and son stared at each other, both with a look of fear. Dr. Archer nervously rocked back and forth on his heels, as if the motion increased his courage.

"I've arranged for a physical therapist to come to your home three days a week. That way, Staci won't have to drag you down the hill." Dr. Archer talked as if he hadn't just dropped a bombshell. "I know you and Staci are financially stable, but if you need anything, give me a call. Here's my home number."

"How do you know I live on a hill?" Derrick asked, reluctantly accepting the card from his father.

"Derrick, from the day you were born, I've always known where you were. I knew every house you lived in and every school and graduation you attended. I was there the day you graduated from both Humboldt and UCSF."

"You knew all that, yet you didn't want me?"

Dr. Archer placed his hands inside his pockets. "Derrick, I'm a selfish person. I've been that way all my life. Every decision I've made in my life has been to please me and to further my agenda. I married my wife because marrying into a prestigious family would help further my career. You were conceived because I wanted to know what it felt like to have sex with a black woman. Once I found out, I was hooked so I continued. When Cora announced her pregnancy, I paid her to remain quiet because I didn't want an illegitimate child to interfere with my professional goals. Back then, moral reputation was important."

Derrick lowered his head and massaged his forehead. He didn't want to hear any more, but he had to know the reason why his father rejected him.

"I've treated my two other children the same way I've treated you. Sure, I lived in the same house with them when I was home, but I didn't make myself available to them. Outside of graduations, I never made one recital or one performance where my kids were involved. There's not much I can tell you about my children other than their sex and birthdates. I provided a good life for them financially, but they wanted me. They wanted my time, and I wasn't willing to give them that. Now that they're adults, we're more like strangers. I haven't spoken to either of them in almost a year. My wife and I have a living arrangement, not a marriage."

Derrick exhaled long and hard as his heart pounded in his chest. Every day of his life he'd carried the burden of rejection—all because of selfishness? This was unbelievable.

"So you don't hate me because I'm black; you're just a self-centered jerk."

Dr. Archer hung his head. "I didn't think my life was so bad, until you came into my office that day. I didn't know how to respond to you, so I babbled a bunch of nonsense. I wanted to call you and explain, but I didn't have the courage. Then the other day, I had a talk with Staci." Dr. Archer sighed. "She said that you're a better man than I. And I agree."

Derrick swallowed the lump that threatened to explode in his throat and saturate his being with raw emotion.

"I've achieved every professional goal I'd set for myself, but now that I've reached the top, I have realized that's not enough. I realize that success is nothing if there's no one to share it with."

Dr. Archer appeared afraid to make his next statement. He wrung his hands, then ran a hand through his hair. "I'm not saying I want to hang out with you every day, but, Derrick, I would like to get to know you. I would also like to see the baby after it's born, if that's all right with you and Staci."

Derrick remained quiet and still. He wanted him to leave. He needed the seed donor to vacate. His father sounded sincere, and the look in his eyes said he was sincere, but Derrick wasn't ready for his father to see him cry.

"I'll give you a call." Derrick's voice was so faint, he wasn't sure he'd said the words out loud.

"I'll call and check on you in a few days," Dr. Archer offered, seemingly understanding Derrick's need to be alone right now. Derrick nodded, and Dr. Archer left the room.

Epilogue

Fifteen months later . . .

Staci was on her third pack of tissues, and the service wasn't halfway over yet. No matter how she tried, she just couldn't stop crying. She was too happy and too grateful.

"Would you like for me to ask the usher for a bucket for all of your trash?" Keisha asked, referring to the mountain of soiled white tissue on Staci's lap.

"That won't be necessary. I came prepared."

Keisha could do nothing but shake her head when her sister-in-law pulled out her own personal garbage bag.

Staci scanned the center section of True Worship and almost started crying again. Everyone in her immediate family was present, and a good number of extended family as well. She smiled down the row at her younger brother, Craig, who was still "holding on," as he put it, and who was scheduled to enroll in seminary in the fall. Sometimes she wondered if Craig would be saved today had the incident with Malcolm never happened. Only God knows, she decided.

She smiled proudly at her big brother, Marcus, and her girl Shannon. Nothing had changed between them. At that very moment, Marcus whispered something in Shannon's ear, and she giggled. She really admired how well they worked together with the twins. Once again, her big brother set the example for her to aspire to. Little Marcus and Mariah were adorable in their coordinating outfits, looking more like Shannon than Marcus.

Lashay must have forgotten about wanting to kill herself during Briana's delivery, because now, she was five months pregnant once more, and Brian couldn't be happier knowing Brian Jr. was on the way.

Staci nearly laughed out loud when she noticed her mother's leg shaking. It was just a matter of time before she went forth in dance. Today, Staci believed the entire center section would join in with her.

Mingled in were Derrick's aunts, uncles, and cousins. Miss Cora had been gone for nearly two years, but Staci could feel her presence as if she were standing right in front of her. *Miss Cora would be so happy,* she thought.

Seated next to Staci on the left was John Archer, and next to him, Derrick's half brother and sister. John turned out to be sincere about wanting to be a part of his son's life. Over the last year, the two spent time together at least once a month. John even came over for dinner a couple of times. In the beginning, it was hard for John's other two offspring to accept Derrick, but after learning Derrick wasn't trying to hurt their mother or run a con game, they adjusted, actually finding Derrick a fun guy to be around. John, as well as his children, still had a hard time adjusting to the excitement of a Pentecostal worship service, though. Derrick's stepmother still refused to meet him, and he was okay with that. The only person's acceptance he sought after now was God's.

John Archer sure does have some strong genes, Staci thought, looking into the big brown eyes of Derrick Garrison Jr. who snuggled comfortably in his grandfather's arms. Her six-month-old son was the spitting image of his father and grandfather, except for his mocha color. She didn't mind, though, believing this time around she was carrying a girl, and Coriana Garrison would look just like her. She'd have to wait seven months to see if her prediction was right.

She turned her attention back to the front of the sanctuary just in time to hear Pastor Reggie instruct Derrick to lie down. Staci's heart bubbled with pride as she watched her giant of a husband humbly lie prostrate on the floor in his ministerial cassock in front of all those people. In no time, the tears were back. It wasn't until Pastor Reggie raised both arms and began praying did she realize the scene was what she saw in her dream almost two years ago. It was Derrick's ordination, not his funeral. When Derrick stood upright again, she could have sworn he was glowing. Her mind went back to what Miss Cora told her: "His light is going to shine bright."

Pastor Reggie beckoned for her to come, and with pride, she stood by her teddy bear. The smile Derrick gave her almost made her come out of the spirit. Without trying, the man could turn her into mush. She was relieved when Pastor Reggie asked them to kneel. With her head bowed and her hand laced together with her husband's, she listened to the praise and worship ministry sing "Alpha and Omega." Tears rolled down both their cheeks. At the end of the song, they were still on their knees, holding each other.

That's all Alaina and the rest of the Simone and Garrison families needed. In no time the sanctuary erupted with praise and dancing. It seemed as though everybody felt the spirit that afternoon.

After assisting his wife to her feet, Derrick noticed his father's wet cheeks. Staci freed John of his grandson. John stood to his feet and with both hands raised, surrendered his life to God.

"Thank you, Father. It was worth it all," Staci whispered, watching father and son embrace. "Yes, indeed, it was worth it all."

Discussion Questions

1. Derrick and Staci participated in premarital sex that resulted in an unplanned pregnancy and subsequent abortion. Yet, they were able to restore their relationship and eventually marry. Do you think it's possible for a relationship to survive this type of stress?

2. Staci acknowledged that although Derrick was her soul mate, she married him before the right time. Is this a common practice among Christians today? How do you think this practice affects the high divorce rate in the church?

3. Staci and Derrick came from opposite family backgrounds. Do you think Derrick's family dynamics are what attracted him to her?

4. When contemplating marriage, should a suitor's family history be taken into consideration?

5. Do you agree with Miss Cora's decision to tell Derrick he was the product of an interracial, extramarital fling? How do you think this affected his self-image?

6. Casual sex is a common and acceptable practice in this day and age. Before partaking in that life-

style, should we consider the long-term emotional effects on the children produced from this activity?

7. Although Staci had a strong family support system, she found comfort with a stranger. Why do you think it was so easy for her to ignore the morals she'd been taught?

8. Why do you think it took Staci so long to end contact with Malcolm?

9. Do you agree with Derrick's decision to leave Staci in order to work on his issues?

10. Although absent, John Archer cared for his son. Why do you think it was so hard for him to interact with Derrick?

11. Did Derrick's call to the ministry surprise you?

About the Author

A romantic at heart, Wanda Campbell uses relationships to demonstrate how the power of forgiveness and reconciliation can restore us back to God and to one another. Wanda is a graduate of Western Career College. In addition to building a career in health care, she is currently pursuing her bachelor's degree in biblical studies. She currently resides in the San Francisco Bay Area with her husband of twenty-three years and two sons, and she enjoys spending time with her grandson.

She is an award-winning author of four Christian fiction novels.

Visit the author's Web site:
www.wandabcampbell.com

Or contact her at:
wbcampbell@prodigy.net

Wanda loves hearing from readers.

UC HIS GLORY BOOK CLUB!

www.uchisglorybookclub.net

UC His Glory Book Club is the spirit-inspired brainchild of Joylynn Jossel, Author and Acquisitions Editor of Urban Christian, and Kendra Norman-Bellamy, Author for Urban Christian. This is an online book club that hosts authors of Urban Christian. We welcome as members all men and women who have a passion for reading Christian-based fiction.

UC His Glory Book Club pledges our commitment to provide support, positive feedback, encouragement, and a forum whereby members can openly discuss and review the literary works of Urban Christian authors.

There is no membership fee associated with UC His Glory Book Club; however, we do ask that you support the authors through purchasing, encouraging, providing book reviews, and of course, your prayers. We also ask that you respect our beliefs and follow the guidelines of the book club. We hope to receive your valuable input, opinions, and reviews that build up, rather than tear down our authors.

What We Believe:

—We believe that Jesus is the Christ, Son of the Living God.

—We believe the Bible is the true, living Word of God.

—We believe all Urban Christian authors should use their God-given writing abilities to honor God and share the message of the written word God has given to each of them uniquely.

—We believe in supporting Urban Christian authors in their literary endeavors by reading, purchasing and sharing their titles with our online community.

—We believe that in everything we do in our literary arena should be done in a manner that will lead to God being glorified and honored.

—We look forward to the online fellowship with you. Please visit us often at *www.uchisglorybookclub.net*.

Many Blessing to You!

Shelia E. Lipsey,
President, UC His Glory Book Club